Hiding Behind The Couch Series

Alumni: Reverberations

by
Debbie McGowan

Beaten Track
www.beatentrackpublishing.com

Alumni: Reverberations

First published 2023 by Beaten Track Publishing
Copyright © 2023 Debbie McGowan

Paperback: 978 1 78645 574 1
eBook: 978 1 78645 575 8

Beaten Track Publishing,
Burscough, Lancashire.
www.beatentrackpublishing.com

Dedicated to…

…my alumni, without whom I would undoubtedly
have failed social psychology and statistics but also
would not have been barred from the Buck i'th' Vine.

Contents

1: L'Alouette 1

2: Lovely Girls 12

3: Building In-spectres 25

4: Most Haunted 37

5: Uneventful Vigil 47

6: Another Morning 57

7: The Only Way is… 67

8: Clocking Out 78

9: Best Behaviour 89

10: To-Do 101

11: Privilege Is as Privilege Does 109

12: In Front of Every Good Man… 120

13: One Man's Treasure 131

14: Into the Light 141

15: Too Much 154

16: The Wrong Side 166

17: Lonely Women 177

18: To Love and Friendship 189

19: Unsettling Symmetry 198

20: By One's Teeth 208

21: Abstinence 219

22: Party 232

23: Spa Partners 245

I count myself in nothing else so happy
As in a soul rememb'ring my good friends

William Shakespeare
King Richard the Second,
Act II, Scene III

1: L'Alouette

Rowan Mews
Present Day
Monday, 15ᵗʰ April

PINK DUVET, BLACK headboard, two beanbags—one blue, one yellow—chocolate-brown desk, orange wall units. To Genie Rowan's eye, her daughter's room was reminiscent of an upended box of giant-size Liquorice Allsorts. Phee had chosen the design herself and gabbled for weeks about how excited she was to come home for spring break—all those lie-ins in her plush, comfy, boldly striped pink and black bed.

Two nights, she'd stayed. That was all. In normal circumstances, Genie would've been furious. But these were *far* from normal circumstances. Nor in Phee's absence was the room vacant, for dead centre of the colourful chaos stood the monochrome, slight form of Lord Xander Etherington-Bowes, flapping his hand— palm up, palm down, palm up, palm down—and humming a monotone melody.

"What's he doing?" Genie whispered, consigned to watching from the doorway, her entrance barred by Jonathan's arm. He seemed nice—Jonathan, that is. Xander was the same as ever. But neither man need worry. With all the strange goings-on, Genie had no intention of setting foot in that room.

"Checking for air disturbance." Jonathan inclined his head to return Genie's attention to Xander, still humming and flip-flapping his hand, though he was on the move, his regimented steps spiralling out from his starting point.

"Does it work, whatever it is he's doing?" Genie asked.

"If there's anything here."

"There is." Xander stopped both walking and flapping to stare at the air above the queen-size bed. "Where is she?"

Genie shook her head and made a guess. "The poltergeist? That's why I called—"

"No."

"I believe His Lordship means your daughter," Jonathan explained.

"Oh! She's at a friend's for a few days. Why?"

"We will stay here tonight," Xander said.

"Yes, that's…fine." Genie doubted her agreement was required. If she told them to leave, they would, but the entire situation was utter insanity to begin with and certainly couldn't be made more so by having Xander Etherington-Bowes and his personal assistant sleep over. "You will keep it to yourselves, won't you?"

Xander marched across the room and stopped a few feet from her location. No eye contact. She remembered now. He'd been the same when they were children.

"His Lordship speaks to no-one," Jonathan assured her on Xander's behalf.

Or no-one living, Genie thought but refrained from saying lest Xander interpret it as anything other than flippant humour born of ill ease. "But *you* do, Jonathan."

Xander smiled grimly and took another step towards them. "He won't tell anyone about your…poltergeist. Excuse me. Please."

"Sorry." Genie moved aside, and Xander marched past, out of the room and along the hallway to the top of the stairs. Jonathan raised his eyebrows at Genie and strode after Xander; she had to jog to catch up. "Where are you going?"

"To fetch the equipment."

"Equipment?"

"Meters, cameras…"

Xander reached the front door and halted, waiting for someone to open it.

"Hang on!" Breathless from the chase, Genie slid past and stood between him and the door with her arms outstretched. Xander startled and stepped back. "Take the car around to the side of the house," she instructed Jonathan.

He bowed his head. "As you wish, Your Ladyship."

"Margaret?" Genie called. Her assistant appeared a mere second later. "Can you direct Jonathan to the side entrance, please?"

**

Campus Restaurant

MID-AFTERNOON AT THE start of the exam period, the university restaurant was dotted with procrastinating revisers eking out their 'just a quick one before I make a start' coffees. From the dregs of the lunchtime menu, Doctor Sean Tierney selected a chicken salad bowl for himself and a plate of wrinkled chips and mushy baked beans for his surprise guest, paid for both meals and carried them over to the table at which she sat scrolling morosely through social media on her phone. Sean set the plate down next to it. "Here you go, young Phee."

"Thanks."

Scroll. Pause.

Sean slid onto the seat opposite and picked up his fork.

Scroll. Pause.

"Shall we talk while we eat, or wait till we're finished?"

Phee shrugged and switched off her phone screen. "We can eat first."

"All right." Sean speared a tomato slice and put it in his mouth. Being told to reduce his fat intake had transformed his previous indifference towards salad to loathing, and it tasted of nothing, not that it mattered when the stress had done for his appetite. Phee's call had come three hours ago as he was leaving his office for his final lecture of the academic year, so he'd had no time to speculate on why she was on her way to see him, and she seemed in no hurry to explain.

"How's school?" he asked.

"All right. It's school."

"And your A' Levels? Are they going OK?"

"I suppose."

Sean chanced his luck with the cucumber. He couldn't taste that either. He put down his fork and rubbed his eyes, dragging his hands over his cheeks. "Look, Phee, I think you'd be better just telling me why you're here."

She ate the chip on her fork and took her time chewing and swallowing. Sean was sure the heavy-headed sensation was his blood pressure notching upwards.

At last, Phee said, "I need your help."

"OK?"

"I wouldn't ask if I didn't have to."

He was guessing the kind of help she meant was financial, which could be anything from a loan of a few grand to buy a car to a lifetime in maintenance payments. A car he could stretch to without having to rethink his plans. Anything more and he'd be having some difficult conversations later, not that this one was a walk in the park.

Phee was waiting for him to agree to help. It was a trick people generally left behind with their adolescence, attempting to secure someone's agreement without them knowing what it was they were agreeing to. Had he known Phee better, emotional attachment would have made Sean fall for it. As it was, he held his tongue and gestured for her to explain.

"You've met Paul—Mum's boyfriend—haven't you?"

"Only the once." On first impression, he'd seemed a decent guy, but there was more to that question, so Sean kept his opinion to himself and waited for Phee to gather the words or courage or whatever she needed to spit out what she'd travelled 100 miles by train to say.

"He…I mean, I…um…" She cleared her throat. "Me and him are…" She left it there, but she need say no more. The statement completed itself, ticker-tape style, in the airless expanse between them.

Sean's world lost focus while the scenario played out in his head of Phee as the victim of some dirty old man, but Paul was fifteen years younger than her mother, putting him closer to Phee's age. Even so, she wasn't yet eighteen.

"How long's it been going on?" he asked.

"A month. Maybe a bit longer."

"How much longer?"

Phee grimaced and dropped a grainy black-and-white image onto the table. "Twelve weeks."

***

Rowan Mews

XANDER PIVOTED AWKWARDLY on the spot, neither watching Jonathan's departure nor looking Genie's way.

"Would you like a drink, Xander?"

"May I have a Scotch with no ice, please?"

"Of course. Come through to the drawing room." Genie moved off, glancing back to check he was following. "I haven't seen you in such a long time. It would be lovely to catch up."

"Lovely," Xander repeated. "Yes, it would, but you asked me here to look into your…"

Genie couldn't tell if he'd intentionally left off or become distracted mid-sentence. "Poltergeist?" she suggested and opened the drinks cabinet, eyeing the three bottles of whisky, one of which had been her grandmother's; Genie rarely drank the stuff. "Do you have a preferred brand?"

"Ardbeg. You won't have any."

"No, you're quite right. I'm a wine drinker myself."

"I drink wine."

"If you'd rather have whisky—"

"I'd rather you chose for me."

"As you wish." Genie picked up the bottle of red she'd opened at lunchtime and retrieved two clean glasses, watching Xander out of the corner of her eye. He was soundlessly clicking his fingers and circling, inspecting the room.

"When did you move into this house?" he asked.

"Thirteen years ago. It belonged to my grandmother. I needed somewhere to live, and the house was standing empty, so I bought it from my father."

"You didn't inherit it from your grandmother?"

"No, I—"

"Did she die here?"

"No. On the way to the hospital. Why? Do you think—"

"She's not your...poltergeist. How old is your daughter? Seventeen."

Genie had already answered the question but confirmed it again. "Yes. Eighteen next month." She held out one of the glasses to Xander. When he didn't take it, she put it on top of the cabinet and slid it towards him.

"Thank you." He picked it up, took a small sip, and put it down again. "Your daughter wasn't here when it happened, you said."

"That's correct, yes. She slammed the front door—you know how teenagers are, or perhaps you don't—"

"My second cousin is thirteen years old."

"Right." Genie gave herself a mental ticking off. "As I told you, I heard the front door slam, then Phee's bedroom door, and I went up to investigate."

"That was when you saw the bed levitate."

"I may be mistaken about the bed."

"And the lamp flew into the mirror."

"Yes." She'd almost convinced herself it was an acid flashback triggered by Phee's tantrum, but the mirror was crazed, and the lamp was in two pieces. She hadn't been mistaken about that. Hence she'd called Xander, whose attention had drifted again, this time to the grand piano in the bay window.

He pointed at it. "Who plays?"

"Phee sometimes. And Paul. Is *poltergeist* the wrong term?"

"Paul?"

"My partner. I notice you always hesitate—"

"He's not your daughter's father." Xander stalked over to the piano.

"No." Whether he'd missed her question or deliberately ignored it, Genie was growing tired of the constant interruptions. "Do you still play?"

"A little." He tapped one of the keys near the top of the keyboard. "It's out of tune."

"It was tuned less than a month ago."

Xander pressed another key and held it. "I hear perfect pitch. Heat, humidity." He tilted his head back and blinked up at the ceiling. "Reverberation. No piano is ever perfectly in tune." He released the key and hummed the same note, or that was how it sounded to Genie's non-musical ear. Still, she nodded her understanding.

"May I play?" Xander asked.

"Knock yourself out." Genie pursed her lips, tried again. "I mean…yes, by all means, do."

"I'm familiar with figurative speech." Xander moved behind the piano and perched on the stool. "Do you have any music?"

"In the stool."

He rose and opened the lid, transferring all the music to the top of the piano. He closed the lid and sat again, plucking the topmost score from the pile.

Taking her wine with her, Genie sat on the sofa and kept her eyes on the rug as she prepared for Xander's performance, recalling his recitals from their youth. He could play almost any piece put in front of him, but it was always in the same dry, mechanical style, and she didn't wish to insult him. However, as he began, it was apparent he had at some point learned to interpret dynamics: there was surprising musicality to his playing, although still no sense of him *feeling* the music, and he remained starchly upright through to the very end of the piece. By then, Jonathan had returned, and both he and Genie applauded Xander's efforts.

"Bravo! That was marvellous, wasn't it, Jonathan?"

"Yes, Your Ladyship."

"Please, do call me Genie."

"As you wish. Now, if you will excuse me, my lord, Genie, I will set up for tonight."

"Of course. Thank you."

With another head bow, Jonathan retreated.

"What shall I play next?" Xander asked.

Before Genie could reply—and it would only have been to give him free choice—the entire stack of scores flew from the top of the piano, scattering and sliding across the parquet floor.

Genie stared at the mess in astonishment. "Xander! Really!"

He shot from the piano stool as if it were a headstrong horse that had thrown him and backed right up against the bay window, his eyes fixed on where the scores had been. "Who are you?" he demanded. Aside from his rapid blinks, his gaze remained fixed on the same spot. "I asked you a question!"

Fighting to not further voice her annoyance at Xander's outburst, Genie slowly rose to her feet and bent to retrieve the score closest to her, but Jonathan must have opened a door, as a draught wafted the papers out of reach. She tried again; the papers slid another few inches across the floor.

"Xander, what the hell's going on?"

"There's a boy."

"A...*what?*"

"A young boy. Sitting at the piano."

Genie turned, keeping her eyes averted until she was facing the stool. There was nothing for her to see. "Who is he?"

"He won't say. What is the music he has chosen?"

"What do you mean?" When Xander didn't answer, Genie followed his gaze to the score on the music rest. She edged closer. "Can't you read it from there?"

"I dropped my glasses. What is it?"

Genie moved closer still, taking care not to step on Xander's glasses. "L'Alouette."

"'Alouette' or 'The Lark' from *A Farewell to Saint Petersburg*?"

Genie squinted at the subtitle. "'The Lark'."

"What's the significance?"

"None I can think of." Genie couldn't recall ever having heard it played. "But—"

"I wasn't asking you." Xander's voice rose to a shout. "He can't hear me over the music."

Genie eyed the unmoving piano keys, her panic mounting until she thought she might vomit.

"It is not he who is playing, it's…" Xander gasped. "We must leave. Now." Without further warning, he bolted past Genie and the piano and out of the room.

"Xander—wait!" Genie dashed after him, in her haste treading on one of the music scores. She skidded and waved her arms in an attempt to catch herself. The piano lid crashed shut as her back and then her head collided with the hard floor.

***

A Hotel Room

PHEE RETURNED THE ultrasound image to her bag and flipped her phone face down on the duvet. It was easier to lie and say she'd missed the call if she couldn't see it, but it wouldn't stop him calling back. Her gaze drifted up and around the bare cream walls, almost as basic as the dorms though infinitely smaller… cleaner…nobody asking questions.

What's wrong?

Nothing. Just being quiet.

You're lying.

However much she'd wanted to confide in her school friends, she couldn't. One or two had been through terminations, but they'd known they were pregnant almost as soon as it had happened, and they'd been certain they didn't want to stay that way. They'd never understand how she felt. How could they when she didn't understand herself?

Shuffling back on the hard mattress, she crossed her legs and sat, pixie-like, absently tracing the grey stripes on her school socks until she remembered in disgust that she hadn't changed them in three days—since she'd arrived home on Friday claiming she'd caught the sickness bug going around school. Other than bringing her a new bottle of water every couple of hours, her mum had left her 'to sleep it off'—better she thought Phee was hungover than this horrible reality.

Another wave of nausea lapped at her throat, although not enough to send her running to the bathroom, which was an improvement on lunchtime. Still, she should shower; she hadn't had one of those in three days either.

She shouldn't have come, but she couldn't stay at home, staring guiltily at her newly decorated room—exactly how she'd wanted it, and after all those awful things she'd screamed at her mum on Christmas Day. It hadn't even been important—just an ungrateful brat mouthing off because she didn't get what she'd asked for, which somehow got twisted into *no wonder Grandma and Grampy disowned you—as long as you're happy, what do you care?* And now this. Her mum was…*had been* her best friend, but what kind of person slept with their best friend's boyfriend?

So really, three-day-old socks were the least disgusting thing about her. She was the worst, and she shouldn't have come here looking for sympathy she didn't deserve, but she didn't know what else to do. She'd told him, then watched through her eyelashes, waiting for him to react while he'd stared at the salt and pepper pots and pinched his chin.

He'd sighed, laughed bleakly and shaken his head—"God, what a mess"—looked up at the ceiling, at the table next to theirs, anywhere but her face. She'd willed him—*look at me!*—and at last, he had.

"Sorry. You took me by surprise."

She'd broken down then, in a university café, in front of a man she hardly knew; the same man who kept calling, leaving voicemails and text messages to ask if she was doing all right, was the hotel up to scratch, how was the sickness, and had she spoken to her mum yet? No pressure, but she felt it even so, over their uneaten lunch when he'd squeezed her hand, called her sweetheart, said, "We'll go somewhere a bit quieter and talk, OK? Don't you worry, we'll figure it out," and brought her to this hotel, not his home, and why would he? He had no responsibility or obligation to her. He was not much more than a sperm donor, Mum said. But he hadn't sent her away. Not yet.

2: Lovely Girls

Off Campus
Nineteen years ago
May

R IGHT, LET'S SEE what this one's got to say." Moving the papers back and forth in front of his face, Sean found a distance at which he could mostly read the words. Nothing to do with bad eye sight: too much studying, nowhere near enough sleep, and he was hammering the whiskey, but it was the only way he could drag himself through to bedtime each day. The words swam out of focus, though it made little difference when not a single one of them was sinking in.

He needed a break, some time away from the house to recuperate, and he'd have taken it if he'd anywhere close by he could go. Maybe he'd walk up to the uni, dodge into his old halls for a shower, pop into the off-licence on the walk back. It would fill the couple of hours until visiting time and ensure he was in a reasonable state to face it.

"That's what I'll do." Decision made, he shoved the papers back into the folder and pushed it across the desk, his eyes drawn to a coffee ring, like the sun against the horizon of the ocean-blue folder.

Nudging the folder with his finger, he emulated the sunrise, noticing another ring intersecting the first, and another. And another. His eyes roamed to the desktop clutter beyond— dirty mugs and plates, days-old toast crusts, a pizza box, chip wrappers, three empty bottles—and beyond those the mess of the room—his filthy quilt curled on the sofa, a crumpled pair of jeans on the floor and a singular shoe. Books littered the carpet, hardback stepping stones to nowhere, terminating a few feet from where he sat.

"Jesus, what a pit." At some point, before Josh was discharged, he'd give the place a damn good clean. But not today. Today, he couldn't look at it a moment longer. In the absence of a second shoe, he ran up to his room, stepped into the worn-out trainers he should've binned months ago, and left.

**

Post-exams, Lloyd George halls of residence were next to dead, and the few residents Sean saw didn't recognise him, nor he them, though he doubted even the powers-that-be would care that one of their postgrad students was availing himself of the facilities. In the event he was caught, he had a story ready—problem with the boiler, waiting on the landlord. It happened often enough to be plausible. But no-one did ask, today or any other day, as if he were invisible to those he passed by. He wasn't sure if that was better or worse than the alternative.

He was lonely. Lonely and bored. Lonely and tired. Lonely and hungry. Lonely and drunk. Sick of the sound of his own moaning drone, of reading papers so pointless he could no longer remember why he'd wanted to study this shitty subject in the first place. And mad.

Mad as hell.

Who was to blame? Was anyone to blame? What did it matter? It wouldn't change anything. Couldn't rewind.

"Sean!"

He'd almost made it to the gate out onto the road and at first didn't recognise the voice. Lonely as he might be, he was in no mood for socialising, but he was also too polite to pretend he hadn't heard. Imagining some terrible ailment that would offer an excuse to dash off, he turned around, and his heart sank right down into his holey footwear.

"Hello, Hillie." Their research and ethics lecturer. "How are you doing?" Of course it would be someone who knew what had gone on.

"Sean," she said again, quieter this time, accompanied by a warm, caring smile as she came to a stop in front of him. "I'm OK, thanks. How are you?"

She was asking for real, and it whipped every possible response from Sean's head. Every one but the truth, which leapt from his mouth in desperation. "Falling to pieces."

"Oh...Sean."

Christ, if she starts crying, I'm done for.

A group of students neared their location, and Hillie moved to block their line of sight. Her palm landed on his bare, still-damp arm, steadying, comforting. Lonely, yes, but he didn't deserve the company, the sympathy.

Once the students had passed them by, she squeezed gently and said, "My car's just behind those trees. Come and sit with me awhile."

He hadn't the strength to argue. Besides, what would he be arguing for? Another hour of silence in the psych unit followed by more hours of silence in an empty house, followed by whiskey coma and a new day when he'd do it all over again? If he could break the cycle...

"Let me get this junk out of your way." Hillie dodged around him and opened the passenger door, scooping armfuls of folders and papers over the back rest and leaving them wherever they fell before gesturing for Sean to get in. "Sorry it's such a mess. There's rarely anyone in it but me."

"It's plenty tidy enough." He was living in a hovel of his own making; the local tip would have been a step up. He got in and stared out the windscreen, not sure what to say, afraid to talk lest she'd tire of his company too soon. Like a starving man offered a benevolent feast, he wanted to gorge on her kindness.

"Pull that door shut, will you, Sean? The wind's cold."

"Sorry." He was impervious but did as she asked and sat back, letting his eyes close. The lids ached, and his eyeballs felt like they were on fire. The image swam into view, and he opened them again, turning towards her, offering the best smile he could dredge up.

She'd changed, no longer the newly badged PhD who'd prattled for two hours, fuelled by nerves and only vaguely aware of the disdain rising from the undergrads before her. Empathy had arrived with her self-confidence, and it reached over the centre console, tethering him to her.

"Are you receiving any support, Sean?"

"From the hospital?"

"The hospital, university...any at all."

"I didn't request it."

"You shouldn't need to."

"It's not really about me, is it? Josh—"

"Is getting the help he needs," she said. "But I'm not asking about Josh. How can I support *you*, Sean?"

That was an interesting question. How should he answer? *Rewind time, stop me coming home from the conference...* "I'll have to work through it." It was how he'd survived the past month. His thesis crowded out all other thoughts; only when he stopped did they seep into his relaxed mind, infiltrate his dreams. Study, whiskey: the royal road to lost consciousness.

"Do you want to talk about it?"

"I don't know. D'you think it'll help?"

"It might, it might not. But I'm listening if you want to try."

Unsure where to look, his gaze fell to her hands resting on the steering wheel as if the car were waiting at traffic lights. Red, amber...

"I wish I'd remembered my notes. For the conference. I'd have come home to the same bloody mess, but it would've been done and dusted and saved us all a lot of unnecessary grief." The next sentence stalled somewhere between his brain and his mouth. *He hates me.* "I'm sorry, I can't...no, it's not helping, but thank you." He reached for the door handle, pushed the door open with his knee. "I'm grateful."

She watched without argument, said only, "If I can do anything, anything at all…"

"Thanks, Hillie. You're very kind." He closed the door and walked away.

***

"Sean!"

Jesus wept. Can I just get off this fecking campus?

"Evening, ladies. You're looking fine. Are you off celebrating?"

Jess looped his left arm—"Last exam"—Imogen his right.

"Is that you now? All done?"

"Yep." Jess skipped a step or two, light-hearted and joyous. "Graduation, here we come!" The two women high-fived in front of his face and laughed, exhilarated by their achievement.

"Congratulations!" The switch flipped in his head to *Sean the cheeky, chirpy Irish lad*. He had no right to rain on their parade.

"Thanks." Imogen—or Genie, as she preferred—kissed his cheek, lingering to murmur, "Love the beard."

He hadn't grown one intentionally, simply hadn't got around to shaving, since it required going into the bathroom.

"You should come with us," Jess said, glancing past him to check Genie was OK with it. Genie nodded, her heavily made-up eyes transforming from sultry to wide and sparkly.

"Yes, you should."

"You're all dressed up," he protested, painfully conscious of his crumpled T-shirt and jeans that were passable but far from clean, not to mention he felt the gravel underfoot with every step.

"We could go back to your place and—" Jess began, but he cut in.

"No, it's all right. You go on and enjoy yourselves."

"If you're sure…" Genie said.

"I'm sure." Sure he wanted to go with them so desperately it was giving him belly ache.

"We'll walk with you," Jess suggested. It was non-negotiable. He shrugged within their clutches and then listened to their chatter. Like being gently splashed with warm water. He drifted along in a pleasant daze, imagining their perfumy smell, trying not to imagine them drinking and dancing into the night with the dashing young men of this town.

His and Josh's place was down a little side road off the high street, and as they approached the corner, Sean attempted to ease out of their huddle. Simultaneously, they squeezed, tightening their grip on his arms.

"*Please* come with us." Genie pouted and blinked, all heavy lids and lashes.

"But Josh—"

"He can come too," Jess said.

"Oh…he won't want to," Sean blustered. *Tell them what the hell you like*, Josh had said in the spew of awful things, hate, lies, denial, before the pills kicked in and Josh checked out. *They can't know, Sean. Please don't tell them.*

Jess cupped her hand around her ear. "Do I hear the whirr of cogs?"

Genie mimicked, staring into the distance, listened, nodded. "I do believe he's reconsidering."

Sean laughed and sighed. "All right, all right. I'll pop home and change. You go on ahead. Where will you be?"

"The wine bar by the roundabout," Jess said as they finally released him. "If you don't show within half an hour, we'll be back." She flashed a seductive smile over her shoulder, linked arms with Genie, and the two of them sauntered away.

***

Pop anthems blasted from the wine bar's many speakers— background music, allegedly, but Sean could hardly hear himself think, which suited him perfectly. Jess and Genie danced a few feet from the table, sucking on the straws in their drinks, miraculously without spilling a drop. Such beautiful young women, and great company; he'd miss them tremendously. Both were heading home at the weekend, their law degrees completed, jobs already lined up.

An empty glass thumped down on the table, drawing Sean out of his mope-lust stupor.

"Did we get you drunk?" Jess's open-lipped smile had its usual effect.

"Aye, you did," he said, though it was more to do with the swift glug of whiskey he'd taken on his way out of the house, finishing off the last inch in the bottle. He checked the time: almost ten. He'd need to leave now if he was to make the off-licence.

Genie grabbed his hand. "Come on," she said, tugging. "Dance with us."

"I'm a shocking dancer."

Now Jess had his other hand, and he probably could've fended them off, but concerned sideways glances had punctuated their revelry all evening; they wouldn't care how terrible he was as long as he appeared to be having fun.

As it turned out, being pressed between two writhing warm feminine bodies meant 'appearing to have fun' was no longer a problem. His troubles temporarily forgotten, even the guilty nag of missing visiting hour subsided to a grumble. They danced until they were breathless, bought another round, popped to the Ladies' to freshen up, on their return sandwiching him where he sat intoxicated less by the alcohol than their presence.

"We should continue this at home." Genie's thigh slid over Sean's as she intentionally leaned across him for her glass. The flash of flesh caught his eye, and he peered down into her cleavage mere inches beneath his chin. A slight dip of his head and he could have pressed his lips to her soft, plump breast.

The thought that it would be safer—less likely to result in arrest—barely registered when Jess reached over and tugged Genie's shirt shut, her fingers lingering on the edge of the fabric as she met Genie's gaze. "Your nipple's showing."

Genie looked down, as did Sean, at the bumps of nipples pushed against the silky fabric, teased to erectness by Jess's fingertips.

"You're killing me here," Sean mumbled, pulling back on the seat, arousal taking over.

"So what do you think?" Genie asked, watching his face as she poked her thumb in between his shirt buttons and stroked his chest. "Want to come home with us?"

"What do *you* think?" Sean grinned, gladly casting himself upon the whims of the two women who had both—singly—shared his bed on more than a few occasions over the past three and a half years. Whether this was a regular indulgence of theirs or a one-off fuelled by alcohol and celebration? Well, he wouldn't be wasting his efforts on analysis, that was for sure, but he took his time with his drink, not wanting to appear too eager, particularly when he was so turned on he'd shoot in seconds.

And that was precisely what happened. They took a taxi back to Jess and Genie's place. No airs and graces, the three of them were naked and sharing three-way kisses on the sofa almost before the taxi drove away. Genie left the lip foray, licking a trail down Sean's chest and abdomen while Jess's tongue thrust into his mouth, her breasts filling his hands. He muttered a desperate warning as Genie's lips closed around him, sucking his orgasm from him, grunting as she swallowed, smiling as they kissed, moaning as she ground her pelvis against his thigh. They were all one in his climax, no beginning or ending, an all-consuming bliss.

The orgasm never quite relinquished its grasp on his senses; Jess and Genie didn't give it a chance. For the time being, they were done with him, and he assumed a spectator's seat in the middle of the sofa while they cavorted on a sheepskin rug. It was a glorious privilege to witness Genie's enjoyment of oral sex at a near distance and the effect her expert actions had on Jess, who lay back, leaning on her elbows, knees raised, hips lifting to meet the bob of Genie's head between her thighs. She arched and cried out, beauty distorted by the contortions of pleasure until she fell, panting, onto her back.

"Ready for more yet, Sean?" Genie asked, slowly withdrawing. Jess laughed and pulled Genie close again to kiss her.

"Whenever you are," Sean replied. He could have gone again right away, but watching them was easily as much fun.

Genie rose and scooted to where she'd dumped her bag and her clothes, rifled through the pile and pulled out a condom, unwrapping it as she came over to the sofa.

"I want you inside me," she said, already rolling the condom onto him. He nodded his consent and awaited further instruction, but her actions spoke for her. Straddling his thighs, she slid down onto him, pausing as their bodies joined and then slowly tilting her pelvis back and forth, maximising contact. The rhythm steady, she bent to kiss him, the taste of Jess transferring from her mouth to his. His hands found their way to her breasts, cupping, squeezing, weighing them in his palms. She straightened, briefly denying him contact before pushing a nipple against his lips and holding on to the back of the sofa as she lifted and plunged, lifted and plunged.

"Going to bed. See you in a bit," Jess said and stumbled away.

Sean watched out of the corner of his eye, asking in the next brief pause, "Is she all right?"

"Gone to play with her toys. We'll join her when we're done here—if you can handle it."

He was heading rapidly into his second climax and doubted he had any more in him, but if this was his one and only chance to spend the night with the two most beautiful women he knew, he'd do his level best to make the most of it. It occurred to him it wouldn't have been a possibility at all if Josh weren't in the hospital, and the resultant guilt brought a few moments' staying power, along with the realisation that Genie had done all the giving so far. With that thought, he lowered his hand and sought out that spot he'd been told men could never find. More like they'd never tried.

"Oh, God, yes. Keep doing…that…" Genie's up-and-down became jerky and erratic, and then ceased completely as she bore down on him, breath held, eyes closed, her entire body tensed. It was a good twenty seconds before she came out of it, panting and smiling. "Did you come?" she asked. The word always sounded so much dirtier in her plummy accent.

"No, but it's OK." More than OK. He kept hold of the condom as she lifted and climbed off, collapsing beside him.

***

"Morning!" Genie squeezed his hips from behind as she stepped past him to reach the coffee he'd made. "Sleep well?"

"Grand, thanks." Better than he had in months—since Josh's first attempt. No dreams, no recollection of anything after Jess draped a heavy arm over him, until half an hour ago. "Is Jessie still asleep?"

Genie nodded and swallowed down the coffee to answer. "Yes. I don't think we'll see her for a few hours yet. While we're alone, I need to talk to you."

"Oh, right?"

"Actually, I want to ask you a massive favour."

Sean was intrigued but made himself another coffee while he waited for Genie to find her voice. She was unusually nervous and nursing an empty mug before she spoke again. "Would you let me have some of your sperm?"

Sean swayed backwards in his surprise. "I… Could you repeat that?"

"Your sperm. I'm willing to pay for it."

"You want to get pregnant?"

"I do."

"Since when?"

"Since always. I even went to the sperm bank, but it dawned on me. I don't know who any of those men are. However, I do know you."

"What about your career?"

"I can do both." Her eyes beseeched his agreement at the same time registering something else. "Ah. Maybe it would help if I explained."

"No, Genie, there's no need. How you live your life is entirely your own business, but can I think about it for a while?"

"Of course. I just thought, with me leaving at the weekend, well...yes. Sorry. I was worried I wouldn't get the chance to ask you."

"You didn't orchestrate last night for this reason, did you?"

She laughed and edged closer. "Not at all. Last night was very much spur of the moment." Her index finger trailed down his chest and came to a rest in his belly button. She leaned in and left a soft, lingering kiss on his lips. "Did you have fun?"

"That I did." He was rising to the possibility of more. "So if we do this thing, are you wanting to go with the whole turkey baster delivery method, or..."

"Natural is good." Her breath was hot on his neck. "You went for the screening, didn't you?"

"Yeah." There had been an outbreak of chlamydia on campus a couple of months earlier, and most of the student body had taken up the offer of the sexual health check. Since then, Sean had been too preoccupied to do anything that might change the clean bill he'd been given.

"Me too. But really, there's no rush, Sean. You take your time. As I say, I will pay you."

"You don't have to do that."

"Will you at least let me clear your student debt?"

"Have you any idea how much—"

"Shhhhh." She kissed him again, more forcefully, and took his hand, leading him out of the kitchen and up to her room. "We can discuss the details later."

***

"I didn't realise you were still here." Jess flopped onto the sofa with a pained moan. "God, I'm so hungover."

"Are you?" Sean asked. It was almost three in the afternoon—several hours since he and Genie had decided to let Nature do with it as she would and had unprotected sex. Genie had left to meet up with friends, and Sean, in no hurry to go home, had hung around waiting for Jess to get out of bed.

"Aren't you?" She studied him dubiously and sniffed. "Still drunk?"

"Maybe." He quickly changed the subject because the alcohol she could smell on him was recent. "What are your plans for the rest of the day?" Only a mouthful. "Anything?" Not even a double.

"I thought I'd spend it with you and Josh. We've hardly seen each other lately. I know, I know. It's my fault."

"You had your exams. It's understandable."

"It's not. I've been neglecting you both. Is that all right?"

Sean floundered, lost for words. "I...I've still got a fair bit of research to do. And I need to do some washing. Plus the house is a mess, and—"

"Ha! I don't believe it for a second."

"Which bit? The research?"

"You're telling me Mr. Neat Freak has finally abandoned his lifelong habits to become a slovenly student?"

"No... Well, see, he's...gone away."

"Really? He didn't say anything. Where?"

"Newcastle? I'm not too sure." It was the only place Sean could think of that Josh had ever been, other than back home.

"Oh, he's gone to see Ellie? When's he due back?"

"Couldn't say for sure."

"You don't sound sure of anything today, Sean."

"Aye, well, you and your girl Genie kind of blew my mind."

Jess laughed and patted his knee. "You're lying—by which I mean I'm sure we did blow your mind, but there's something you're not telling me." She walked her fingers up the inside of his thigh. "I wonder if you could be persuaded..."

"Jessie." He covered her hand with his, stopping her. "Will you let it go? Please? For me?"

For a moment, she watched him, frowning and trying to gauge if she could push him, but—to his relief—relented. "OK. For you."

"Thanks."

"So…what shall we do with our day? How about I give you a hand with the cleaning?"

"You don't know what you're letting yourself in for."

She patted his knee again, no ulterior motive this time. "I know enough to understand you need your friends right now. Come on." She grabbed his hand and pulled as she got up. "Let's get the place in order for when Josh comes home. It'll make you feel better."

He let her haul him upright. "Do you think so?" he asked.

She shrugged and smiled sadly. "It can't possibly make you feel any worse."

3: Building In-spectres

"DID YOU HAVE a couch?" Libby spun on a spot almost dead-centre of what was, in the not-so-distant past—although long enough ago to precede Libby's entrance into their lives—Josh's consultation room. She was enthralled by the place and the glimpse of Josh's history that came with it, while he lingered in the doorway with ghosts clutching at his limbs and refusing to release him. Libby drifted out of his hazy field of vision. At least it had taken her mind off 'Sean's secret love child' for the time being.

"This looks couch-sized," she said.

He blinked and refocused on where she was crouched, examining the lighter rectangle of carpet where once his couch had been.

"Yes," he confirmed and finally stepped into the room. "My desk was over there—" he pointed at the near-right corner "—and the bookshelf was against the back wall."

"Has nobody been in here since you left?"

"A few people came to look around, and one rented it but didn't use it, the landlord said." Or former landlord, seeing as Josh now owned the building.

"It's an amazing space." Libby sprang to her feet and dashed past him. He followed her out and watched on in silence as she circled the expansive hallway at the top of the staircase—what used to be his reception/waiting room—peering in through

25

doorways to inspect, in turn, the kitchenette, bathroom, broom cupboard and storeroom. "*Loads* of space," she said, returning to his location. "You know what I think?"

"What do you think?"

"You've been haunting it."

He folded his arms, made vulnerable by her observation. His adopted daughter shared his knack for people-reading and could hack through his defences in seconds. Even so, he attempted to downplay how astutely she'd given form to his feelings. "Is that right, *Shaunna*?"

Libby gave him a disapproving look. "I'm gonna tell her you took her name in vain. Can't you feel it?" She held up her hands as if she were carrying a beachball. "Shaunna says it's residual energy—"

"That's physical, not *psychic*."

"Why can't it be both? I mean, all that concentrated thinking and talking must leave something behind."

Josh partly drew a breath but thought better of arguing that hard science said she was wrong. He was sceptical himself when the simple act of being there was affecting him more than he'd anticipated, largely in a positive way. For the first time in his life, he felt content, at peace, as if this were the mislaid final piece in the flatpack from which Joshua Sandison-Morley had been constructed.

"You *know* I'm right," Libby said. He didn't appreciate her victorious tone, but she scooted away before he had a chance to tick her off for being cheeky. "It'll need brightening up a bit," she called back, once again in Josh's ex-consultation room.

"It *is* bright," Josh grumbled. It was cream; the only colour brighter than that was white.

"But it's so…boring."

Josh sighed and went to join her, wishing she'd either stay in one place or stop calling for his attention. "It needs to be neutral, not too much colour or clutter."

"Why? Because *you* don't like colour and clutter?"

This time, his response was interrupted by a bang—not loud, but sudden—and it echoed around the empty rooms. They both jumped, clasped hands to chests and stared at each other.

"What was that?" Libby asked, edging closer until she and Josh bumped arms.

"I don't know. Maybe one of the vents is open."

Libby nodded. "Yeah." Neither of them moved. "Are you g—"

Another bang: same kind, but it sounded like it came from a different location. Josh didn't recognise the noise.

"Let's go and investigate," he said, heart in mouth, and stepped off, only then realising he had hold of Libby's hand. She stumbled along behind him, back out to the hallway, where they both paused. The doors to the other three rooms were ajar, as Libby had left them, and there was no discernible draught.

"We should check the windows," Libby suggested.

"Good idea."

They'd barely taken one step when there was a third bang directly behind them.

"Shit!"

"Libby, language!" Josh snapped, but if she hadn't said it, he would have because he recognised that sound all right. He'd caused it often enough himself. It was the slam of his consultation room door. That explanation stretched only as far as knowing the source of the noise but not the cause. There was no draught; the windows were double-glazed. There was no subsidence—he had a surveyor's report to prove it—and the doorframes were square to the floor.

And *there was nobody there.*

"Somebody's playing a joke on us," Libby said.

"Who?"

"I dunno. Sean?"

"No." More than twenty years had passed since the strange goings-on in their uni halls of residence and they still couldn't explain what had happened. But where Josh flat-out refused to believe in the paranormal, then and now, Sean had merely suspended his disbelief until he saw conclusive proof to the contrary. Still, he had as much invested in this new venture as Josh and wouldn't risk it all on a prank that neither would find amusing.

Before Josh could impart his reasoning, there was another noise, not a bang this time, but the rustle of paper, followed by a dull thud.

"That came from the toilet," Libby said. Her expression hardened. "I'm going in. Cover me."

Stunned, he watched her march over to the toilet door and assertively push it open.

"There's nothing in here that—"

"Libby."

She turned to look at him. He pointed downwards. Libby slowly lowered her chin. A roll of toilet paper unfurled at her feet.

"Oh my… Run!" She took flight, grabbing his hand on the way past and pulling him—unnecessarily, he was going as fast as he could—across the hallway and down the stairs. They flew out onto the forecourt, not even thinking to check for moving vehicles. Luckily, there were none.

"I think it's time for a coffee," Josh panted once they'd put a few more feet between them and the building.

"Yeah," Libby agreed, equally breathless. No doubt their expressions matched too, as hers was one of sheer fright. "Where are we gonna go? George has got the car."

"There's a place down the street. We can walk there."

"OK."

It wasn't a long walk, less than five minutes at the speed they were doing, but it was enough for them to calm down and reinstate some sense of rationality. Josh ordered their drinks— cappuccino for him, caramel latte for Libby, no chitchat as the barista was unfamiliar—and they found a table near the front windows.

"This is nice," Libby said, taking in her surroundings. Josh did the same, in his case to refresh his memory. He used to visit this coffee shop thrice daily but had only been in once since he gave up his surgery. His haunted surgery, filled with things that went bump in the middle of the day. He was having flashbacks to his uni halls again.

"Did you notice if the window was open?" he asked. He was desperate for a logical explanation.

Libby shook her head. "It looked like it was shut, but…it had to be open. It just had to be."

"Or the loo roll might've been balanced on the holder and was disturbed when you opened the door the first time."

"Maybe." She sounded far from convinced, and in any case, it only explained the unravelling toilet roll, not the two loud bangs before it or the door that slammed all by itself.

"We'll get Sean to investigate later," Josh said.

"Oh, yeah! I'd forgotten about that!" In an instant, Libby brightened. "Is she really his secret love child?"

Josh laughed. "No. She *is* his daughter, but it's not a secret."

"But nobody knows about her."

"I do."

"Does Sophie?"

"I think…y…I don't know."

"George?"

"We haven't discussed her, so no."

"Shaunna?"

Josh sighed. He genuinely took no issue with Sean confiding in Shaunna, particularly as it meant Sean wasn't bending Josh's ear all the time. However, Shaunna had been Josh's friend first— by some thirty years, seeing as they'd done the entirety of their schooling together—and he envisaged she would have said something if she'd known. "OK. Maybe you have a point, but it's not as if Sean's hidden Phee's existence. He was a sperm donor— he might still be a sperm donor for all I know."

"Was it through a clinic?"

"Not on this occasion. It was someone we knew at university— when we were students." He felt it best to clarify, seeing as they were still 'at university', albeit a different institution. "She wanted a baby but didn't want a partner."

"Jess went to your university, didn't she?"

"She's not Phee's mum."

"I bet Sean told her, though."

"He might've done. Actually, Phee's mum probably told Jess. They were very close, or they were at uni." For all the hours they'd spent talking, Josh had known next to nothing about Jess's social life beyond their mutual circle of friends. It was sad but likely intentional on Jess's part to obscure her less savoury endeavours.

"I wish I'd got to meet her," Libby said.

Josh nodded and said, "Me too," but he was secretly glad Jess would never have an influence over his daughter.

"Shaunna showed me photos of her. She was beautiful."

"She was." *On the outside.*

"And successf—oh! I've got it! Jess used to come to your surgery, didn't she?"

Josh groaned. "All the time, and no, I don't think she's haunting it. Ghosts aren't real."

"You can't disprove their existence."

"On balance—"

"And if it is Jess, then—"

"I don't want to have this discussion."

"—we could…" Libby trailed off as she processed what he'd said. Her face fell and she lowered her eyes. "Sorry. I didn't mean to upset you."

"I'm not upset."

"Would you rather talk about Sean?"

That made Josh laugh. "Yes. Curiously, I would."

"OK." She perked up. "He's not really, like, a proper dad, if you know what I mean. I mean, not like you and George, or Poppy's dad."

"He's not involved in Phee's life," Josh confirmed, "although she's always known who he is, and he sends her a birthday card every year."

"Wow! That's amazing."

"Why?"

"He forgot his own birthday last year."

"What I should have said is, he sends her a birthday card when I tell him to."

"Which means she didn't get a card for fourteen years or however long it was you weren't talking," Libby reasoned.

Josh laughed, which was a bit foolish with the cup to his mouth. Milk foam sprayed his face, and through her giggling, Libby fetched him a paper napkin. He carefully set his cup down again—the coffee was too hot anyway—and wiped his face dry. It was true, what she'd said about the birthday cards, or it would've been if Josh hadn't sent Sean an email annually to remind him, irrespective of whether they were talking to each other. He also wondered—briefly, before concluding it was yet another Sean–Shaunna confidence—how Libby knew about their long-term estrangement.

"You're gonna have to get used to sharing an office with him again," she said. "Or it might be another fourteen years."

"We've never shared an office, only a house—I say *only*. Sharing a house with Sean was no easy feat, and I imagine he felt much the same about sharing with me. He's having the storeroom."

Libby gaped at him in horror. "He can't go in that storeroom. It's too small!"

Josh was joking, but she was right again. The dimensions in his head had been wildly inaccurate: the storeroom was too small and his ex-consultation room was too big, as was the hallway at the top of the stairs. Even without converting the loft into a group therapy space, which Andy assured him could be completed within a couple of weeks, it would take some serious construction work to turn the first floor into two or maybe even three similarly sized consultation rooms. And there he'd been thinking with a lick of paint they'd be ready to open to the public in the summer, when their university contracts terminated. It was disappointing to say the least.

"I could be your receptionist," Libby said, for the time being thwarting his growing despondency.

"Only in the school holidays," he pointed out. She might be in her last year of high school, but then there was sixth form, and university after that. If Josh had any say in the matter, Libby would be in education for the next ten years.

"Whatever." She sounded flippant even though she loved school and wouldn't need coercing into staying on, not that he'd ever do that. "So should I call them?" she suggested.

"The Ghostbusters or Jeffries and Associates?" Josh asked with a grin that belied how spooked he was by the mysterious noises, which—typically—had come soon after he'd acknowledged his happiness at moving back into his surgery. Could the explanation be that simple? Subconscious sabotage? "I think we imagined it, Lib."

"But we both heard it."

"We can explain that through the power of suggestion. Maybe I acted as if I'd heard something, or as if I expected to hear something."

"If you say so."

She sounded as convinced as he was, which was not at all, but he liked the alternative even less.

***

"Hi. You both home?"

A mini gust whipped along the hall from the open front door, lifting the practice exam papers Libby had spread across the kitchen table. Two took flight; Libby caught one, Josh the other.

George appeared in the doorway, rubbing his hands. "Yes, then," he confirmed with a frown. "*More* practice papers?"

"I'm done now." Libby took the one Josh was clutching and gathered the rest into a pile. "My exam's in—"

"Four weeks and three days," Josh and George finished in unison.

Scooping up her pile, Libby stuck out her tongue at George and squished past him. "Your dinner's in the microwave. Sausages and mash. Two minutes."

"Thanks, Lib."

She continued on her way, calling down as she reached the top of the stairs, "Josh has something to tell you."

George looked up the stairs. "What?" Libby didn't answer. "Do you?" he asked Josh.

"Erm...not really?" Heat shot up his cheeks so fast he went into an immediate sweat and attempted a surreptitious beeline for the microwave to avoid George's scrutiny. "Two minutes. Let's see..." He fussed with the timer—

"Joshua..."

—and pushed the start button. "It's nothing important. How was art therapy?" He turned to George but didn't dare meet his gaze.

"Good," George answered, still watching suspiciously. "We talked about Jess."

"Oh. That's...interesting." Josh focused on the seconds counting down. A coincidence? It wasn't as if they never spoke about her, but twice in the same afternoon in two completely different settings and conversations?

"Yeah. Gabby was shocked to hear she had topless photos."

"Was she?" Josh attempted indifference.

"I thought they were mates at uni—Gabby and Jess," George went on as if he were oblivious to Josh's inner war. "Didn't they live in the same halls?"

"Not for long. Gabby moved to our halls when she defected from law to psychology."

"That's right. She told me that." George joined Josh in watching the countdown. "So they weren't friends?"

"They were...friendly. More than acquaintances."

"Uh-huh?" George nodded. The microwave pinged, but he made no move to open the door.

Several agonising seconds passed before Josh relented and opened it for him. "Would you get to the point, please?"

"I don't have one." George grabbed the plate and moved to the table, tucking in right away and fanning his mouth. "Hot."

"You should leave it to stand."

"Too hungry." George scooped up another forkful of mashed potato and blew on it. "Jess didn't chase boys at uni, then?"

And let it go, Josh thought but didn't say. "A bit, I suppose. After Simon, she mostly gave up and kept her nose to the grindstone."

"Who?"

"One of the law students. Jess and Simon were an item for the first couple of weeks. He wasn't good for her work ethic."

"Hmm." George shovelled in more mashed potato, following up with half a sausage. "What did Sean think of that?"

"I couldn't say." Josh handed him a knife. "You're so uncouth sometimes. I'd blame your mother, but I know better." Any poor table manners George had developed came from borderline living rough at uni and then on the ranch. To his credit, he cut a more sensible-sized chunk off the sausage the next time, and while he ate, Josh finished clearing the kitchen around him, hoping but not believing for a second that they were done with the Jess conversation.

"So," George said, rinsing his plate and handing it to Josh to put in the dishwasher, "in conclusion—"

"George…"

"OK, OK. One question."

"Go on."

"D'you think…Simon, was it?"

"Yes."

"D'you think he was responsible for the things Jess did?"

"No."

"You said he wasn't good for her work ethic."

"He was filthy rich by birth and bone idle, but he didn't have the brains for the kind of con Jess pulled off."

"Is that why they broke up?"

"You said *one* question."

"Same question, part b." George grinned hopefully.

Josh huffed. "No. They broke up because Simon was gay and asked Jess to marry him so he could keep his inheritance. She persuaded him to tell his parents the truth."

"Then he might not be filthy rich anymore," George reasoned.

"Who knows? And who cares? I don't." Josh's overplayed shrug fooled no-one. He grabbed the dishcloth and started wiping the kitchen counters. "What else did you and Gabby cover today?"

"You first. What was it you had to tell me?"

"Libby thinks the surgery needs bright colours. I said it was bright enough, but we're a long way off decorating. My room's too big for one thing, and—"

"Josh." George's hand landed on top of his, stilling the swish of the cloth over the already spotless surface. "It can't be that bad. Come on. Talk to me."

Josh shook his head. No. It wasn't bad. It was nothing. *Nothing.* But that nothingness spun and spun and became a vortex, stretching twenty-two and a half years into the past, and it was taking all of Josh's strength to not cross the event horizon, stay in the present.

They'd broken in, taken down his blinds, hung them up again, stolen his shoes, cut the power to his light…insisted his room was haunted, and then, when it was all over, when he and Sean had finally dug down to the bottom of it and proved it was a hoax, the inexplicable had happened, that single incident neither of them could dismiss as part of some ill-thought-out research project. A group hallucination derived from suggestion? Josh was not, nor had he ever been, suggestible; for the most part, he'd have vouched for Sean in that regard too. *And there's no such thing as ghosts.* Not then, not now.

"Come again?" George said.

"What?" Josh hung the dishcloth back on the drainer. "I didn't say a word."

"You said something about ghosts."

Sometimes life seemed little more than one big, elaborate praxinoscope because they'd had exactly the same conversation last time he thought he was being haunted. "Just imaginations in overdrive."

"Yep. I *imagined* you said something about ghosts."

"That's not what I meant, George."

"Then what did you mean?"

As if she'd spontaneously transported from her room to the kitchen, Libby appeared, minus the exam papers, in their place a tower of textbooks. "He means…" She struggled across to the table, dumped the books, turned and, with an apologetic glance at Josh, said, "There's a ghost in his surgery, and he doesn't know what to do about it."

4: Most Haunted

"F OR REAL?" GEORGE stared at Libby, then at Josh, who held eye contact for as long as he could but had to abort when he admitted—to himself only—that what Libby had said was true. While she'd been occupied with her past papers, he'd mentally worked through every theory he knew, and not one of them explained to his satisfaction their experiences that afternoon.

"What the hell happened?" George asked.

"Nothing—" Josh started at the same time as Libby launched into a full account, which he punctuated with the same unconvincing arguments he'd given her earlier. By the time she was done, George's eyes were as wide as if he'd witnessed the incident firsthand.

"Whoa. That's unbelievable."

"Precisely," Josh said, "which is how we can be sure our minds were playing tricks on us."

"But we were both there!" Libby argued. "I heard what you heard!"

"Or, like I said, you were susceptible to my suggestions."

"Or, like *I* said, Jess is trying to tell you something and—"

"Enough!" Josh snapped.

Libby gasped in surprise, then her face crumpled and she fled the kitchen, swift feet thundering up the stairs into the bathroom. The door slammed shut, followed by the sharp click of the bolt driving home.

Josh stared after her, guilt and frustration waging war on his anger, although it was more like a sizzling wet cloth thrown over a pan of burning oil. He was vaguely aware of George saying, "Hey," and asking if he wanted a hug. Josh shook his head, or thought he had but couldn't be sure.

"No," he answered for good measure. Above him came the muffled honk of their daughter blowing her nose. He shifted his gaze upward. "But someone else could do with one, by the sound of it."

"She gave you a hard time today, huh?"

"She's been fine, mostly. She wanted to know about Sean's daughter, of course, so I had the Spanish Inquisition for a while, then she critiqued the surgery. She'd be sketching the redesign now if she wasn't so fixated on her exams and..." He couldn't bring himself to say it.

"The ghost?" George finished for him, adding before Josh could argue 'not a ghost', "You used the word first."

"As part of the statement 'there is no such thing as'. Do you think I'm wrong?"

"No, but something's got you rattled, and if it's not a ghost, what is it?"

"I don't know, which is why, first thing tomorrow, I'm going to call Dan and ask him to look at the electrics. Meanwhile—" Josh grimaced at a second bang of the bathroom door. "I have an apology to make." He moved to leave, but George stopped him with a hand on his arm.

"Give her some space."

"I shouldn't have shouted. None of this is her fault."

"If you try talking to her now, you'll end up having a row, and I don't want to get caught in the middle."

"I see." Josh advanced, lifting George's arms and positioning them into the hug he'd offered. "Saving your own neck, Morley?"

"Can you blame me?" George pulled back so that Josh's kiss missed on the first attempt. On the second, Josh gripped him by the ears and kept hold until the deed was done. It was no more than a peck, but it was enough to ease Josh's frazzled nerves.

After that, they moved to the living room, on George's recommendation, and chatted about his therapy session—an excuse to play with paint, as his mum called it. Last time, Gabby had asked him to sketch a house that wasn't modelled on a real-world location, which, given that George's paintings were artistic interpretations of people, animals and places he knew, had been a tough assignment. Today, he'd begun filling in the details, and he'd found it easier, he said, although he still couldn't see how it would help his dissociative disorder. As per usual, Josh offered to explain, and—as per usual—George rejected that offer.

"I'd be happy if I could get the door to look right," he grumbled. "And the roof. And the windows."

"And the walls and chimney stack..." Josh tormented.

"Yeah," George agreed ruefully. "It's all a bit askew right now."

"That's a matter of perspective, surely."

"Joshua..."

"Well, it is. Capturing a three-dimensional representation through a two-dimensional medium..."

George grunted and turned, head only, toward the TV. Josh smiled to himself, perpetually amused both by George's resistance to understanding the theory behind his therapy and by how, when they'd bought a sofa large enough to seat three, he was squashed up at one end while George was stretched full length with his head in Josh's lap. Still, it was a comforting normality, and he felt ready to deliver his apology, but it seemed he'd left it too long, as Libby was on her way down the stairs. Josh tapped George's shoulder to get him to sit up, which he did, and Josh drew breath, words at the ready. *I'm sorry I shouted. I was being unreasonable.*

"Where d'you think you're going?" was what he said instead, and that *was* reasonable at eight-thirty in the evening. Her coat and the enormous bag dangling from her side had already given him his answer, but he waited for her to say it.

"I'm going to stay at Shaunna's."

"Are you now." Not a question.

"If it's OK with you." And that was an afterthought.

"How are you getting there?"

"Andy's picking me up."

"You couldn't ask us for a lift?"

"Shaunna said he's just left the Red Lion, so he's coming past here anyway."

Josh glanced at George, who shrugged, leaving it to Josh. George would support him, whatever he decided, but he wasn't sure how to handle this. If it were a simple case of Libby being upset by his outburst, he'd have told her to go and have fun and to call him if she needed a lift home in the morning.

Or maybe it was that simple.

"Did you tell her what happened?"

"That you bit my head off, you mean?"

"No. The reason why I...bit your head off." He'd always hated that phrase—more so now when the cap fitted him so snugly.

Libby's expression was grim bordering on tearful. "I said we'd had an argument. Am I not allowed to tell her?"

That was a hell of a question. He trusted her enough to know that if he asked her not to share what had happened, she'd abide by that. *Ask a childhood abuse survivor to keep a shared secret?*

"You can tell her if you want to."

"Thanks."

"No problem." *Huge* problem. There was also a car with a huge engine idling outside their house.

Hearing it too, Libby scurried over to the sofa and leaned down to hug George, then Josh. Her bag slipped, knocking Josh's glasses onto the floor. "Oops!" She picked them up and put them back on his face. "Thank you for letting me go to Shaunna's."

He didn't say 'you're welcome' or anything of that ilk. She was sixteen years old and could leave any time she wanted. "Have a good evening."

"You too." Libby straightened and hoisted her bag back onto her shoulder. "It might not even come up."

It would. "Call when you're ready to come home. I'll come and get you."

"OK. Bye!" The front door opened and closed. The Mustang's purr became a growl, became a distant rumble.

For a few minutes after she'd gone, Josh watched the TV screen, and he could hear accompanying voices, but they didn't register as more than an annoying buzz.

"You did good," George said at last and got up from the sofa. "Coffee?"

"Are you having one?"

"Nope. I'm having hot chocolate."

"I'll join you, then."

"OK." George shook his head and sauntered from the room, muttering, "Strange man."

"Married you," Josh called after him.

"Yep," George called back.

Josh repositioned his glasses and unlocked his phone to send Shaunna a message, purportedly to thank her for always leaving her door open for Libby, but he was aware also of his desire to tell his side of the story. Not the argument part, although it dawned on him that they'd somehow bypassed his apology; he rectified that with a quick call to Libby, and it really was quick.

"Hey, Lib. I'm sorry I shouted."

"It's OK. I'm sorry I kept going on about it. Gotta go. Love you!" A blast of rock music was the last thing Josh heard as Libby ended the call.

If he hadn't known better, he'd have thought she was in the car of some irresponsible teenage boy. Well, he had the 'car' and 'irresponsible' bits right. He opened a text message to Shaunna and managed to type *'Hey. Thanks for this evening. I just…'* before an incoming call cut him off. He didn't recognise the number and almost dismissed it, but curiosity was, as usual, his worst enemy, so he hit answer.

"Hello?"

Silence.

"Hello?"

Still nothing.

George returned with the hot chocolates.

Josh quickly hung up and backspaced his message to Shaunna to the full stop, finishing off with 'You're a star. x'. He took one of the mugs from George, who re-joined him on the sofa but stayed upright with legs crossed, his mug balanced on one knee.

"Who were you talking to?"

"Nobody. They didn't speak."

"Or they'd accidentally muted themselves. I do that all the time."

"All the time? You don't even look at your phone, never mind use it."

George grinned but offered no defence.

Josh sipped his hot chocolate, the sweet heat gradually working its magic, releasing the tension in his neck and shoulders until he was saggy as an old cardigan. Laughter from the TV drew his attention to the two guys ad-libbing a client–therapist scene, predictably featuring a chaise-longue. It bore little resemblance to a real modern-day therapy session—there would be no chaise-longues in his new surgery, just as there had been none in his old one—but the skit was quite funny in places.

"Like parenting, isn't it?" George nodded at the screen. "Completely made up on the spot."

Josh laughed. "All my experience, all those adolescents I've counselled, yet I've never been so out of my depth as I have this past year. I feel terrible about today."

"That's the first time you've raised your voice to her," George pointed out. "And she does push it."

"She hit a sore spot. A few, actually. She thought Sean might be playing a practical joke."

"Unlikely. Did you tell her what they did to you at uni?"

"No. We were rudely interrupted by a self-propelled toilet roll. I will tell her at some point, though, but there's more." Josh swirled the mug between his palms, even now struggling to talk about it, and this was the man with whom he had shared every facet of himself, the good and the bad, the brightest and the darkest. "Remember the night after Jess died, when I went back to her house?"

"Did you?"

"Yes! How do you not..." Josh's mind fast-forwarded through the days following Jess's passing and his grief-triggered hypomanic episode, during which he'd done a few things he'd rather not have George remember. "Never mind. I mustn't have told you, but that was when Jess's mum asked Shaunna and me if we'd scatter the ashes."

"I always wondered about that. So they were both at Jess's place too?"

"Her mum was. Shaunna turned up a bit later. I was sitting in the garden. I couldn't bring myself to go inside the house." He felt it best to skip that he'd had a packet of cigarettes in his hand and had almost started smoking again. "I'd been crying, I think, and I could see next to nothing, but I heard a noise. A door closing. It came from the house, and the lights were off, although the sky was brightening, so it must've been around five-thirty, six o'clock by then."

"How long were you there?"

"I left here just after midnight."

"Six hours? You sat in Jess's garden for *six hours*?"

"Yes, and it was bloody cold and wet, I can tell you. But that's by the by. Someone called my name, and because, clearly, I was not in a rational state of mind, I thought it was Jess." He chewed his cheek, elaborated. "Her ghost."

"But it was Jess's mum."

"They sounded so alike. I told Jess that once, right back when we first became friends. She disputed it—vehemently. She'd bring it up at seemingly random moments, citing examples of words she and her mum pronounced differently, or her mum would say some phrase or other, and Jess would insist, 'You'll never hear me saying that,' then catch herself doing exactly that."

"Yeah. I know that feeling," George muttered, which, in spite of the topic, made Josh smile. It didn't happen often, but there were certain things George said and did that he'd picked up from his mum, although he didn't swear half as much as she did. There were dockers who swore less than Iris Morley. "So it wasn't Jess's ghost?" George asked jokingly—a gentle push for Josh to keep going.

"Obviously not, but the thing is, George, when I heard my name, I wanted so much for it to be her that even after I'd followed her mum into the house, in my mind, it *was* Jess, and I'd have given anything for it to be her. This afternoon, after we adjourned to the coffee shop—that sounds so calm and casual. We *fled* to the coffee shop, which was when Libby suggested Jess could be haunting my surgery. She wasn't serious, or I hope she wasn't, but it threw me back to that night in the garden."

"You wanted it to be true again."

"I did, but at the same time, I was afraid. I couldn't tell you if that was more for the possibility of it being a practical joke or for the whole situation kicking off another cycle after I've been stable for so long. Libby was good, though. She realised what she'd said bothered me, and she quickly switched the subject back to Sean and Phee, which wasn't a vast improvement, but it kept me from ruminating."

"Yeah, right," George said with a knowing sideways glance.

"OK. From ruminating too deeply," Josh conceded. He noticed again the hot chocolate in his hands and took a long drink. He was ready to admit it now but didn't rush to move the mug away from his mouth. "In conclusion..." He swallowed the last powdery dregs with a shudder. "I wish I knew another grief counsellor I could trust the way I do Sean. I can't work through this on my own."

"That's a first!"

Josh elbowed George lightly in the side. "Watch it, or I'll be booking couples sessions with Gabby." George acted horrified by the idea, but that emerald twinkle in his eye said he wouldn't mind if Josh were serious, which he wasn't.

"Why not Sean?"

"Because of the way he felt about Jess. He was in love with her, but he was too scared to tell her."

"She could be scary."

"I don't disagree. Of course, Sean's never outright admitted it was fear that stopped him. They were both too busy with their careers, or at different points in their lives, or married in his case, and on and on—and he has the audacity to advise me on how I should be handling *my* grief." Josh gesticulated his annoyance, flinging the dregs from his mug over the back of the sofa.

George disarmed him and set the mug on the coffee table. "Sean's broken heart aside—"

"Not aside."

"You don't know what I was gonna say."

"What's your wager?" Josh asked, smugly confident.

"Hmm…I'll make the coffee for the next month."

"And if you win?"

"I never win this game."

"Perhaps this is a night of firsts."

"Perhaps you could get on with it and tell me what I was gonna say."

"You were going to ask if I think bereavement counselling will exorcise my ghost."

"Damn you, smarty-pants."

Josh grinned.

"So do you?" George asked.

"I think it's worth a shot—for Sean as well as me, but that's a fight for another time. He has enough to contend with."

"His secret love child…"

"She's not."

"And yet no-one knows about her."

Josh patted his lap, inviting George to resume his usual position. George obliged and blinked up at him expectantly.

"Fine," Josh relented. "The potted version—when we were at uni, Sean registered as a sperm donor because he needed the money. One of the law students asked him to make a direct deposit. Imogen Rowan. She was really rather beautiful, and uncommonly nice for a law undergrad." An image came to mind of Imogen sneaking out of Sean's room early one Sunday morning, shoes in hand and false eyelashes stuck to her cheek. She was halfway down the first flight of stairs before Josh drummed up the courage to tell her about the eyelashes, and he chased after her, then pointed mutely at her face. He blushed at the memory; he'd been so shy back then, but he could laugh about it now.

George was eyeing him curiously, so he finished off with, "Phoenix is, shall we say, the interest on Sean's investment."

"Right. That makes sense. Sort of."

"Which part doesn't?"

"If he was just a sperm donor, why is she here?"

"That, ma moitié, is a very good question."

5: Uneventful Vigil

GENIE HISSED AND clamped a palm to the back of her head, hardly daring to breathe. The jolt of pain dulled to a throb, and she tried again, a gentle bend of the knees, searching with fingertips for the last piece of music, which had drifted under the sofa during the madness of the previous evening. The rest was in a heap on the piano; Margaret must have tidied around post calling an ambulance. Xander had remained with Genie until the doorbell rang announcing the paramedics' arrival, when he'd bolted faster than a spooked colt. She'd neither heard from nor seen him since.

Treading gingerly so as not to further jar her brain, she carried the sheet music to the piano and set it with the rest, much of it crumpled from the scuffle with the poltergeist—or whatever she was supposed to call it. Genie knew a smattering of French but no German whatsoever, although the internet reliably informed her *poltergeist* translated literally into 'knocking spirit', which was on the nose from her perspective. From Xander's, who knew? He'd acted as if the term were a supernatural slur and had yet to satisfactorily explain why.

Still, the knock on the head had supplanted yesterday's sheer terror that had seen her calling him 'out of the blue' after two decades of avoiding contact with her peers. Or not them specifically; she'd avoided her family and anyone closely connected to them, including Xander, his cousins Gabby and Andrew, and *darling* Simon. She missed them dreadfully—even Simon—but like her privilege, she'd left their friendships behind to start anew.

For all of that, she didn't regret calling Xander, despite the high chance of him and her father running into each other at Westminster, which was why she'd pressed the issue of confidentiality. She'd not endured all these years out of her father's reach to present him with an excuse for re-establishing his hold over her life—and Phee's—and he would take it if it were offered.

A quiet *ahem* sounded from the doorway. "Sorry to disturb you, my lady."

"It's all right, Margaret. I was..." Genie blinked a couple of times, bringing the music score and her thoughts back into focus. She'd been on the cusp of playing out an entire imagined scenario that began with finding her father and sister on her doorstep and heartily embracing them both. Now that *had* to be due to the concussion. "Sorry, Margaret. What do you need?"

"If you recall, I have an appointment this morning, so I'm preparing lunch now. Should I cater for His Lordship and Jonathan?"

"I'd say so. Have you seen either of them this morning?"

"I haven't, but I'll make sandwiches so the lunch doesn't spoil, if that's acceptable?"

"Yes, that's perfect."

"Can I get anything for you now, my lady? Some fruit and yoghurt, perhaps?"

"Good Lord, no, but thank you."

"A cup of coffee then?"

Genie's stomach clenched at the prospect. "I'd say yes, but I don't think I'll keep one down. Is it usual to feel so queasy after a concussion?" Queasy, dizzy, and an intermittent sensation that her head was shrinking, but before she could voice her concern at being left to fend for herself for half a day, Margaret interjected.

"I've asked Victor to come and take a look at the dishwasher," which was to say, Margaret had asked her partner to look after Genie in her absence.

Tempting as it was to protest, Genie could only muster a smile of gratitude as, with a nod, Margaret retreated to the kitchen.

Genie gathered the pile of music and stooped to open the stool—not her wisest move, resulting only in a sharp inhalation and cramp in her neck. She paused and tensed; the cramp intensified. Eyes shut to stave off the whirling of the room, she turned her head ever so slowly to the right until the cramp eased and, when she felt safe to move again, lowered herself onto the stool with little regard for the possibility that a ghost child had sat there the previous evening. May well still be sitting there for all she knew.

Xander would have been able to tell her, of course, and she wondered if she should wake him, but perhaps that was a task best left to Jonathan, assuming the two hadn't fled Rowan Mews in the night. It was awfully strange that the men were still sleeping. Granted, the day was young, but new house guests generally rose early then loitered like…well, like unwelcome ghosts until someone tended their needs. They'd brought all that equipment, so in all probability they'd had a late night—should she instruct Margaret to forget about preparing lunch in favour of a hearty dinner? Were there any foods Xander wouldn't eat? She couldn't recall.

"I'm off now, my lady." Margaret stood in the doorway, fastening the buttons down the front of her wine-red mackintosh. "The sandwiches are in a Tupperware box on the island, and there's a jug of orange juice in the fridge. I should be back by two."

"Take your time, Margaret, and thank you again."

Margaret nodded to acknowledge she'd heard, but where usually she'd have departed, she remained where she was, fussing with her collar and adjusting her cuffs.

It occurred to Genie that if she asked what the appointment was, her assistant would tell her out of a sense of duty, but beyond her concern for Margaret's well-being, it was none of her business. Still, the woman seemed reluctant to leave.

"Is there something else?" Genie asked.

"No…I don't think so, my lady. Why do you ask?"

"You seem a little out of sorts, and I don't wish to pry, but… are you unwell?"

"Oh!" Margaret laughed uncomfortably and turned pink. "I'm in good health, I can assure you. It is not a medical matter."

She cleared her throat and took a step forward. "I have an interview." She surrendered the information as if under interrogation.

Genie reeled, taken completely by surprise. What could she say to that? She could hardly demand to know why Margaret hadn't told her she was looking for another job. Was she unhappy? Did she want more money? More time off? Those matters could be resolved easily, if only Margaret had said something before. An interview didn't necessarily mean she would be leaving her post, but it spoke of her desire to do so.

"I'll write you a reference, of course," Genie said diplomatically but couldn't help adding, "I wish you'd told me."

"I'm sorry, my lady. I didn't feel I could."

"I understand. I do hope it goes well for you."

"Thank you." Margaret backed out of the room, and Genie was glad. The conversation was becoming more excruciating by the second. A moment later, the front door closed.

"Well," Genie said, endeavouring to wear a brave face. "That's that, I suppose." Talking to herself helped, she'd found, and she continued to do so as she returned the music scores to the stool and set off for the kitchen, where she eyed the Tupperware box in dismay. It was absurd to feel so betrayed by Margaret's secrecy, but it wasn't just that. She'd had no inkling Margaret was looking for another job, and after twelve years, she'd imagined she knew the woman well enough to pick up on something being off.

She wondered, too, how their relationship would fare should Margaret's interview prove unsuccessful when the mere fact of it was already a stubborn tarnish that even the very best replacement would have trouble polishing away. When Margaret had asked for reviews of her salary in the past, Genie had always obliged and had given her a substantial pay rise after Jess passed. Not once had she refused to grant Margaret leave, irrespective of whether it coincided with the end of the tax year or the festive season, both of which times Genie needed help the most. In all matters of managing the house, Margaret was forthright, and she seemed satisfied by her work.

What was left? A complete change of career? Personal conflict?

Before Genie could further tie herself in knots, there came the sound of footsteps and male voices descending the staircase, and Xander then Jonathan appeared before her. Jonathan was showered and clean-shaven and carrying a leather Filofax-type organiser clamped to his chest as if it were the Bible; Xander was empty-handed and had the appearance of a drunk who had spent the night in a police cell.

"Good morning, gentlemen," Genie greeted them cheerfully. "How was your vigil?"

Jonathan opened his mouth, but Xander answered.

"It was not a *vigil*."

"Oh. Sorry. Then what—"

"How's the head?" Jonathan asked, and Genie smiled in gratitude at his intervention. Xander was pricklier than usual this morning, which was saying something.

"Sore but bearable. Can I offer you both breakfast?" She turned away and checked how much coffee was in the jug, discovering there was none. "I'll put on some—"

"No more for me, thank you," Xander said, thereby explaining the empty jug.

"Something else? A glass of juice or milk? A cup of tea?"

"No, thank you."

"Perhaps I could make the coffee, Your Ladyship?" Jonathan suggested. "Sorry, *Genie*," he added solemnly as if he hadn't done it deliberately to highlight the inappropriateness of a lady serving a staffer. It was a very long time since Genie had cared about that kind of nonsense etiquette, though she could imagine Xander being quite a stickler for it, so for the sake of peace, she bowed out, left Jonathan to perform his duty and took a seat on a stool at the island.

"What are your plans for today?" she asked generally, unsure who was most likely to answer. She'd have tried a more specific query, but she was a novice whose vocabulary on spiritual matters was derived from TV ghost-hunting, and every faux pas not only patently irritated Xander but also served to prove how far out of her wheelhouse she was.

"Excuse me. I must take this call." Extracting his phone from his organiser, Jonathan strode from the kitchen and out of the side door.

Genie eyed the dormant coffee machine, contemplating her role and Jonathan's and whether he'd forgive her if she did what she'd planned to in the first place, but her defiance drive was lower than usual—another consequence of the conk on the head?—so she decided to give it another minute. Then she realised how ridiculous that was in her own house and acted decisively.

Several minutes later and with no sign of Jonathan, Xander said, "Collecting more data."

"That's handy, having someone to do the legwork for you."

Xander pulled a small notebook from his inside pocket, set it down on the island and unfastened the elastic band holding it shut. The book sprang open at a place marked by a nub of a pencil. "You asked what my plans are for today. I plan to collect more data. Would you like to read it?" He briskly tapped the page.

"You don't mind?" Genie asked.

"I wouldn't make the offer if I did." He nudged the book in her direction.

Resuming her seat, Genie glanced down at the book, but she had a question about the previous evening. "You said we had to leave."

"Yes."

"Why?"

"The boy." Xander stared at her, the effect intensified by his glasses, strong-lensed and round with tortoiseshell frames. She'd never known him to wear any other design. He blinked twice, and she found herself blinking twice back, but if it were some kind of signalling system, she was clueless to its meaning.

"You say the boy…"

"He was screaming. A horrible noise. Gurgling…perhaps he drowned." Xander's gaze turned inward, his features harrowed in palpable distress. Genie felt selfish for thinking it, but she was glad she didn't share his gift.

"I'm sorry."

"Why?"

"I brought you here."

Xander bobbed his head in agreement. "I have heard and seen more awful things. Are you going to read now?"

"Yes." Genie focused again on the book, expecting a struggle to read without her glasses but having no such problem. Dark, bold numbers were pencilled down the left margins of both pages, each denoting a time at thirty-minute intervals from 22:30 through to 08:30. Next to 02:30 was a series of abbreviations and the time 02:42.

"What's this?" she asked.

"You have mice."

"They're a permanent fixture," Genie said ruefully. Such was the country life.

"You should use humane traps."

"Phee says that too. They're kinder, I know."

"And quieter," Xander said. He tapped the page again. "The snap of the spring sets off the microphone sensor."

"Oops. Sorry about that." Guiltily, Genie pushed the book back. "I'll make sure the traps are gone before you begin again tonight."

"Ghosts don't wait for nightfall. Those *vigils* you mention are for entertainment, the séances of the twenty-first century. Ghosts are imprints of human energy, which persists with no respect for the hour, or else they'd all be asleep when those TV shows film their vigils."

"That would be an improvement," Genie muttered dryly.

"I've had no cause to watch them." Xander closed the notebook and returned it to his pocket. "The traps can stay where they are. We're not trying to catch ghosts. We're ruling out physical causes, and I worry the equipment is malfunctioning. Then a rodent assures me it's working perfectly well. They're fascinating creatures, rats."

"Rats?!" Genie's nausea, which had abated somewhat, returned in full force.

"Not here," Xander said, matter of fact. Genie let out half a sigh of relief before he added, "Or none that I saw."

"Xander, please stop!" Genie implored, at which his lips twitched in amusement. He was terrorising her. That was new, or at least, she'd never picked up on it before. Xander behaved differently in company, both less talkative and more brusque when he did speak. Perhaps she was different too, as when Jonathan returned, the conversation ground to a halt until he gave it a jumpstart.

"You made the coffee," he accused.

"You were...occupied," Genie explained, then gave herself a ticking off. This was her house, and she'd make the coffee if she damn well pleased.

"For which I can only apologise. Perhaps I could pour for us?"

"Now look, Jonathan. You're my guests—both of you. If Margaret were here, I'd still pour the coffee. I can't abide standing on ceremony, especially so early in the day, so please, sit down and shut up!"

Jonathan's eyebrows formed a harried 'M' across his forehead, though the rest of his face remained remarkably stoic as he inclined towards Xander, who gave him a nod of permission, and finally, Jonathan sat.

"Good!" One small victory. "How do you take it?"

"As it comes, Your—Genie."

"You're incorrigible!"

"I try."

"No doubt! Xander, are you sure you don't want one?"

"Positive." He was already on his way out of the kitchen. "May I take another look at the piano?"

"You carry on."

He left. Genie poured herself and Jonathan coffee and carried both over to the island.

"Thank you." He picked up his cup right away, but barely had it touched his lips before Xander called his name.

Genie offered him a sympathetic smile. "Take it with you."

"I shall."

Soon after, the drawing room door closed with Xander and Jonathan on the inside, followed by the sound of someone— Xander, she could but hope—playing the piano. She didn't recognise the piece, but it was light and melodic and afforded her a few minutes of normality with her coffee and the daily newspaper. Indeed, considerably longer than a few minutes had passed when a light rap on the window signalled Margaret's partner had arrived.

"Good morning, Vic."

"Morning, Missus," he greeted as he stepped in the back door, plonked down his tool bag and wiped his feet thoroughly on the mat, which wasn't overkill on his part. Whenever he came here, he did so via the woods, drifting in on a blast of air so fresh and natural it was enough to lure even an indoorsy type like Genie out into the Shropshire wilds. Boots clean, Victor toed them off before he came in proper, his heavy steps muted by itchy-looking woollen socks.

"Coffee?" Genie offered.

"No, ta. I've had a pot of tea already this morning. Besides, shouldn't you be resting?"

"I'm fine, Vic. Really."

"Right, well. I said I'd take a look at that dishwasher of yours. Marg says it's not emptying fast enough, so likely a blockage in the waste pipe. I'll keep the noise down. Mind you..." He paused to listen. "That a CD I hear?"

"No. My friend Xander."

Victor's nod was approving yet also managed to convey 'not my kind of music'. Genie chuckled.

"I prefer something a little rockier myself." For which she had her alumni to thank. Sean had introduced her to political folksy rock, Jess to the heavier, dirtier stuff she'd listened to because Andy did. Genie's entire social life at university could be mapped out by a soundtrack she'd been trying to rebuild since graduation, some songs bare snatches of memory, a few notes or a hook line that was impossible to pin down, others she'd listened to until, as the saying went, she'd worn them out.

Victor had wasted no time getting started, but he was slow and steady, each plod back and forth between the utility room and his tool bag an opportunity to check on Genie's well-being.

That was Margaret all over. If the hospital decreed that Genie needed someone with her for twenty-four hours, then that was what she would jolly well have.

"God, I'll miss her." The sentiment escaped aloud, fortunately between Victor's walk-throughs, but she couldn't just let Margaret go like that. She had to try to fix it.

Typically, now she'd decided to act, Victor didn't come back for some time, and she almost lost her nerve, knowing what she was about to do was unfair on him *and* Margaret.

"Vic, may I ask you a question?"

He crouched over his tool bag but glanced her way. "I know that tone." And back into his bag. "If it's about Marg…"

"It is, and I hate to put you on the spot, but I need to understand. Have I upset her in some way? Could I make it right?"

Tools clanged together out of sight, and he chewed on nothing. She couldn't decide if he was giving her a chance to retract her request or figuring out how to respond. Either way, she was about to apologise and tell him to forget she'd said anything when he finally straightened, a large screwdriver in his hand.

"It's not my business how you keep order in your house, Missus, but it's nothing *you* did. Now, if you wouldn't mind…" He waved the screwdriver and made a speedy plod towards the utility room before she could interrogate him further.

Nothing I did? Then who? Phee was hardly ever home, and it worked to Margaret's advantage, as she took her annual leave during Phee's school holidays and got far more than she would with any other employer. If not Phee, then it had to be Paul, but that seemed equally unlikely. True, he was terribly messy, but he was polite and always expressed his thanks for his ironed, folded and put-away laundry. Genie couldn't imagine him ever doing anything bad enough for Margaret to resign; still, she'd ask him when he came home at the end of the week. Until then, she had no choice but to let the matter rest.

6: Another Morning

Tierney Residence
Present Day
Tuesday, 16ᵗʰ April

A NOTHER FAILED NIGHT of intimacy. Sean didn't even need to open his eyes to confirm he had the bed to himself. There'd be a message somewhere—on his phone, maybe, or on the pillows next to his—telling him she didn't want to wake him as if she were doing it for his benefit only. He understood. It would have resulted in yet another post-mortem of his making, and those were getting them nowhere.

Of course, he'd awoken with an erection, and it was comforting to have the physical confirmation of what his GP had told him: there was no medical reason for his lack of sexual appetite nor his inability to sustain an erection when an opportunity for love-making presented itself. If Sophie hadn't already left, they'd have made the most of the involuntary bodily response, which was fine by him, but eighteen months without release, Sean was past any attempt at self-pleasure when the thought alone had deflated what little interest his body had shown.

The alarm clock got in two bleeps before he silenced it and heaved himself to the side of the bed with a sigh. Tuesday morning, three hours of clinic, followed by—

"Ha-ha! It's Tuesday morning!" Sean bounced to his feet as his thoughts about the day ahead finally coalesced with the realisation that this particular Tuesday morning would be his last marred by three hours of appointments too short and prescriptive to be of use to him or his patients. He whisked the curtains open and grinned out at the dreary April showers tumbling from a leaden grey sky. None of it could darken the sunny feeling within.

He grabbed his dressing gown from the hook on the door and exited, peering in on Dylan as he passed. "Wake him now? No. I'll sort me out first—" on to the bathroom, a pee, shower running "—breakfast, daycare, clinic—" toilet flushed, under the water "—Jesus!—" and out of the scalding spray while the cistern refilled. "Did I ask Melanie to send that referral? God, I hope so…" And on and on with the mental list of things to do, things that should have been done, things that might need to be done, all of which would be forgotten before he left the house… until Sean was back in his room, dressed and running a comb through his hair.

"Daddy, Daddy, Daddy, Daddy."

"Hold on. I'm coming." Sean threw the comb down on the windowsill and kicked his dressing gown aside on his way out of the room. "Good morning, fella."

"Up, up, up!" The tiny prisoner in a saggy-bottomed teddy jumpsuit gripped his cot bars with both fists and shook, releasing only when Sean lifted him to liberation. "Toast!"

Sean laughed. "Shall we get you dressed first?"

"Toast. Please."

It was as broad as it was long, so Sean relented and carried Dylan down the stairs, setting him on the ground to close the safety gate.

"Finx," Dylan shouted, and he was off to the kitchen, where Sphinx was cleaning his paws in a play of indifference when he'd be wanting his breakfast as urgently as Dylan. Sean was undecided on the best order to tackle the hungry beasts.

"Don't—"

With a half-hearted hiss of protest, Sphinx jumped onto the coffee machine and out of reach of grabby toddler fingers that could never resist a snatch at that bushy tail. Sean hoisted Dylan up and into his high chair, strapped him in and inspected his hand. "Let me see that. Oh, you're fine. Right, tea…toast…"

The usual breakfast routine ensued: kettle filled, bread in the toaster, cat food in the bowl. Sean marvelled at how accomplished he felt now that it was second nature to him when not so long ago it was a mammoth effort to get just himself up and out the door in one decently assembled piece, and by quarter past eight, Tierney and son were both standing outside the house with their respective bags, waiting for the taxi to arrive.

Twenty-five past eight, they were *still* standing outside the house. Sean called the taxi firm.

"Busy morning. Should be with you within ten minutes."

"OK. Thanks."

Twenty-five to nine…

"Good morning, Sean."

"Morning, Victoria," Sean greeted his next-door neighbour.

"Still waiting for your taxi?"

"Aye." Sean took out his phone and called the firm again as his neighbour drove away towards her shop, which was in the opposite direction from the university and hospital. They'd had the discussion before.

"It's on its way," the taxi firm claimed.

"From where? Birmingham?" Sean did his best to sound jovial, though his patience was wearing very thin indeed.

Quarter to nine…

"Come on, Tierney." Josh clicked his key fob, remotely unlocking his car, and got in before there was any argument, although Sean could see a taxi—potentially theirs—in the distance and getting Dylan's car seat into the back of Josh's three-door hatchback was a pain in the neck. Deciding it was safer to risk upsetting the taxi firm, Sean secured Dylan, pushed the front seat back into position and climbed in beside Josh.

"Thanks very much."

"No problem. I need to see personnel." Josh signalled and pulled away from the kerb.

Sean looked him over. "You're not dressed for a meeting."

"I'm hoping they'll get the message once and for all."

"They might at that."

Josh was wearing what for him passed as scruffs: a light-blue and white rugby shirt with iron-creased sleeves, washed-out jeans and navy suede loafers. A self-conscious smile flickered across his lips when he sensed Sean's continued perusal of his attire.

"I'm going straight to the surgery," he explained.

"Ah, right." Sean was about to say he'd go there after he was done with clinic, but his thoughts skimmed over 'more faffing with taxis' straight to a decision made with no need to think. "I'm going to get a car."

"Good idea," Josh said. "No offence intended."

Sean laughed. "Liar."

"All right, I won't dally around it. I don't mind giving you a lift from time to time, but this is getting ridiculous."

"You don't have to tell me that, but you won't be doing it for much longer, will ye?"

Josh stopped at the traffic lights and brushed a speck of dust from the dashboard. "What will you get? Something flash?"

"God, no. Just a runaround like this."

"Hm." The traffic lights changed, and Josh pulled off again.

"You're not taking that as an insult, I hope."

"No."

Sean wasn't sure if he was imagining it or the radio was getting steadily louder.

"Yes, actually, I am," Josh said. "I've had this car for six years, and whilst I appreciate it's not exactly top-of-the-range, it more than suffices for my needs. Yet people insist on passing comment. What would you have me drive? One of those low-chassis sports models? Have you seen the potholes in the university car park? Never mind that I *won't be doing it much longer.* The roads are just as bad. Sunken grids and speed bumps and—"

"Hey!" Sean interrupted. "I didn't say anything other than implying—"

"Stating."

"All right, *stating* it's a runaround, which, by the car industry's standards, it is. And there's nothing wrong with that. Not at all. Christ, Joshy."

The radio volume returned to where it had started, and the journey quietly continued for several minutes. They were not good early morning travel companions, even though they'd been car-sharing for the past two years. But where Sean normally sat back out of the way of Josh's sniped complaints and knew better than to engage him, he was frustrated—with the taxi firm, the lack of transport, the three hours of clinic ahead of him, Sophie, Phee—

"I'm sorry if I overreacted," Josh mumbled.

"Aye, you did." Sean was out of gracious acceptance, and they were already at the university, so he saw no reason to put on an act.

"Do you need a lift to the hospital?" Josh asked as he stopped the car outside the day-care nursery's one-storey building. It had once borne an enormous, rainbow-coloured sign that shouted UNITOTS across the campus, but it had been removed for safety reasons.

"Thanks for the offer, but I'll walk." Sean got out and collected Dylan and their bags but left the child seat, slamming the door with a "See you later" that cut off Josh's "Are you—" The car was still idling after Sean had pressed the buzzer and been admitted into the building.

"Hello, Dylan," one of the nursery nurses greeted with an exuberant smile. Dylan's feet touched the ground, and he was immediately away to play.

"Oh, right, bye, then," Sean called after him, more disgruntled than he should've been.

With a laugh, the nursery nurse took Dylan's bag. "He's claiming the sandpit before Alicia gets here," she said. "He's here for the day, isn't he?"

"Yes, if that's all right with you?"

"Absolutely. I'm just putting the lunch orders together."

"Fair enough. I should be back around…" Sean took out his phone and activated the screen, ignoring the new message from Sophie in favour of opening his diary, such use as that was. He scratched his head. "I don't know, to be honest. Before five, though."

"No problem." The nursery nurse frowned. "Are you all right?"

"What, me?" Sean tapped his chest with his finger and pulled up a grin. "I don't know me backside from me elbow this morning, but I'm fine." He was touched—and worried—she'd noticed he was out of sorts. "Thank you for asking. See you later."

Once he was outside, Sean paused to gather his thoughts, tempted to stop by the university café for a shot of something, but there was a good chance he'd bump into Josh. There'd be questions asked that Sean didn't want to answer, so he forwent the coffee and set off for the campus exit, keeping a brisk pace until his shins ached from the effort, at which point he slowed and took out his phone to read Sophie's message.

He hadn't told her about his visitor the previous afternoon, which wasn't to say it was a secret. He'd told Sophie he'd been a sperm donor, and about this particular 'donation', back when they were new. Seeing as it hadn't come up in conversation since—not even when they were expecting Dylan—he could safely assume it was of no concern. However, there was a stark difference between 'anonymous donor to a clinic' and 'direct donation as a favour for a friend', and it was one which he and Genie, in their youthful naivety, had overlooked. All kids, angelic or otherwise, inevitably fell out with their parents and sought allegiances with those they believed would be most sympathetic and easiest persuaded to fight their corner.

It was a hell of a corner to fight, too, and none of Sean's business, or it shouldn't have been.

"One problem at a time," he advised himself and reactivated his phone screen.

Didn't go to London. Worried about you. Working at home today – be over this evening. x

He called her. "Soph?"

"Hi. Did you get my message?"

"I did. That's why I'm calling. I'm all right."

Sophie's silence told him she didn't believe it for a second.

"All right, I'm…not all right. I've got clinic in five minutes, and…" Sean stopped outside the convenience store on the run up to the hospital. It sold alcohol, and while he was long past cracking open the whiskey at nine in the morning, he was seriously contemplating buying a half-bottle for later.

"Sean?" Sophie prompted.

"Yeah, sorry. Will you be busy at lunchtime?"

"I can take a break."

"If you could come up to the clinic for twelve, I'd be very grateful."

"OK," Sophie agreed. She'd have caught the gist of his request. A staff member's last day usually meant a bit of a celebration.

"Thanks, Soph."

"Step away from the off-licence, Sean."

He managed a laugh at her canny knack and did as he was told. "I'll see you at twelve."

"You will. Bye."

At the bleep in his ear, he moved his phone away, using the last few minutes' walk to check for email or any other messages. There were none. For the time being, he was happy to accept it was a good thing.

"Good morning, Melanie," he greeted the psych admin as he breezed through the doors, pretending he hadn't spent the past half an hour on the brink of a relapse. "How are you this fine day?"

She snorted in disbelief. "I'd wait till you see your appointments list before calling it a fine day."

"Busy?"

"Tristan's out this afternoon."

"Where?"

"Like anyone tells me."

Sean rubbed his chin in thought and realised he hadn't shaved. Well, if that was the only casualty of his absent-minded dash from the house, he wasn't doing so badly at all. If he got five minutes, he'd pop to his office and dig out his electric shaver, but for now, he needed to make a decision.

When Sean had dropped to part-time so he could set up the counselling diploma at the university, the hospital trust had taken on Tristan Morris to share the clinical post. Back then, Sean's intention had been to stick it out for another year and then resign, but in the end, he'd kept both, plus his day at the hospice, and then introduced the Master's course at the university. His reasons for not resigning were many, not least that his counterpart was young and ambitious: were it not for cutbacks across the NHS, Sean was sure Tristan would've moved onwards and upwards already.

Sean was glad of the extra work, and not for the money, although it had enabled him to drink without ever getting in debt, and he'd paid off his mum's mortgage along the way. His work was still what he loved most—clinic notwithstanding—and in which he excelled, no matter what else was going on in his life.

All of that meant, in the normal course of events, he would have volunteered off the bat to cover Tristan's clinic hours, but it would be enough of a trial getting through to lunchtime, and that was without taking into consideration that he'd promised to spend a few hours with Josh sometime this week. They still needed to finalise building adjustments and flesh out their business plan. Sean couldn't help thinking the obstacles to them doing so might be an omen.

With some reluctance, he asked, "Have you cancelled Tristan's appointments, Mel?"

She shook her head. "Not yet. I was waiting for you to come in."

"How many would you say are urgent?"

Melanie scrolled with her mouse, studying the screen. "A couple, but they're late afternoon. I can call the unit, see if someone else can stand in?"

"Don't worry about it, lovely. I'll stay."

"Are you sure?"

Sean nodded swiftly and held out his hand for the first set of patient notes. Melanie placed the folder on his upturned palm but kept hold of it. "What?" he asked.

She shrugged. "I'll miss you, Sean."

"I bet you won't miss my shocking paperwork."

"You're not too bad these days."

"Only because you've trained me so well."

"And now I'll have to train someone new." She made a sad face, although she seemed to quite enjoy bending newbies into shape. "Right, Doctor Tierney, hop to it. You're already five minutes behind." She mimed cracking a whip, and Sean jumped sideways as if to avoid it. He was still grinning as he called his first patient's name.

The morning flew by once he was into the swing of it, and it was almost eleven-thirty before he had a chance to call Josh and break the news, although he went around the houses first.

"How did you get on with personnel?"

"They sent me to the dean, who offered me another incremental rise. No-one would believe the faculty's short of money."

"They'll have even less of the stuff if their performance drops."

"I'm one of twenty-five staff, Sean. My impact is minimal."

"Tell me again how many passed your Lifestyle Behaviour module."

Josh mumbled unintelligibly.

"What was that? A hundred percent? And how many dropped out?"

"That's just one module, and it's not even mine."

"Then there's the Methods mod—"

"Anyway," Josh cut in. "Is that all you called for?"

"Ah, no. I'm not going to make it this afternoon, I'm afraid."

"Did you say you would?"

"On the way to—shite. No, I didn't get that far." He wasn't about to rehash their discussion of whether Josh's car classed as a runaround to explain the sidetrack they'd taken.

"Is there something you're not telling me, Sean?"

"There's plenty, but none of it's to do with us setting up shop. My accomplice is off again."

"Why haven't they fired him yet?"

"He's a suck-up. But now I think on, I should be done by three-thirty. Will you still be there?"

"More than likely. Dan's coming to have a look at the electrics."

"All right. I'll head straight over once I'm done here. Do you need me to bring anything?"

"A packet of cigarettes and a bottle of whiskey?" Josh suggested.

Sean laughed. "Starting as we mean to go on?"

7: The Only Way is...

T HE WIRING'S FINE, as far as I can tell. It's a new consumer unit, and nothing's tripping." Dan switched off the multimeter and set it down on the worktop in the surgery's kitchenette.

Josh vented a sigh of frustration at another potential explanation struck off the list. "Thanks, anyway."

"No problem. Are you sure it was an electrical bang?"

"No. I'm just trying to narrow down the possibilities." Josh walked over to the cubicle of a room that housed the toilet and pretended he wasn't reluctant to open the door. "One of the bangs came from in here." He stepped aside and gestured with a wave of the hand, then froze, breath held. *Cold spot? Oh, good grief. Get a grip, Joshua.*

Dan edged past, his muscular shoulders almost the width of the small room, and peered up at the ceiling, tracing what Josh presumed was the route the wiring took. "Is there a loft hatch?"

"In my—the big room." Josh led the way back through.

"Has it got a retracting ladder?"

"I couldn't say, but there's a set of stepladders in the storeroom. Do you want me to..."

Dan was already out of the door.

"It can wait, you know," Josh called after him.

"I might as well do it while I'm here." He returned with the ladders and positioned them under the loft hatch.

"You'll get dirty."

With a quick smile in Josh's direction, Dan ascended and pushed the square cover up and out of the way. "No light up here. Can you grab my meter?"

Obediently, Josh went and fetched it from the kitchenette, panic already mounting. He managed the first rung before Dan reached down and took the meter from him.

"Cheers." Back up he went. A moment later, the black void overhead filled with pale blue light.

"That's handy," Josh said.

"Yeah." Dan grunted. "Not bright enough, unfortunately. Is this your stuff?"

"No. I've never ventured up there." The mere thought made Josh queasy, but sooner or later he'd have to if they were going to convert the loft into a useable space. In the meantime, he was happy to leave the investigating to someone else, even if it was Dan, who wouldn't hesitate to use his willing assistance as leverage at a later date and was, by now, balanced on the very top of the ladder. Josh swooned and shut his eyes. When he opened them again, Dan's head had disappeared from view.

"Whoa. There's some weird..."

Silence. Josh waited.

"Dan?"

Still no response, but Josh could see Dan's shoulder muscles flexing under the fabric of his shirt, so he didn't imagine he'd been decapitated by The Loft Monster or anything equally gruesome but more believable. A couple more minutes passed, followed by a scuffing sound above before Dan descended the ladder without holding on, meter in one hand, in the other a dusty board-game box, which he held out for Josh to take.

"What's... Oh!" Josh stared down at the printed lid.

"There's loads more stuff like that up there. Are you all right, mate?"

Josh nodded dumbly and took the box, brushing some of the dust from the lid. It caked and darkened on his clammy palm. "By *more stuff like this*, what do you mean, exactly?"

"Tarot cards, tipping tables, crystal ball, pendulum, a gong—before you ask, I only recognise it because Adele's into all that psychic crap. You want me to bring any of it down?"

Josh was starting to feel like one of those nodding bulldogs. He finally shook himself out of it. "Erm, no. Not now." He offered Dan a smile, hoping it looked less feeble than it felt. Unexplained noises, objects moving by themselves...and a whole stash of spiritualist's tools in his loft, the most worrisome of them all in his hand: the Ouija board.

"I'll put these away, then," Dan said and collapsed the ladders. "How long are you here?"

"Not sure. I'm waiting for Sean." Who had consistently been on time for the past three months, but it would take far longer than that to overwrite years of Tierney tardiness.

"If you're here over the weekend, I'll come down with Andy sometime, and I'll give him a nudge about the architect."

"Thank you."

Dan took the ladders away, calling, "See you Friday."

"You will," Josh confirmed half a minute later as the outside door closed, leaving him on his own.

With the Ouija board.

Focus not on its alleged purpose...

It was hard to gauge how old it was when such things were always made to look antiquated, although the box's design was similar to those stored in the spare room at home—his grandma's old board games, with printed labels covering the top face. Some were pre-WWII, like *Jeu de L'Oie*—Game of the Goose. Ludo—his favourite—was a 1940s edition, and the box containing the Ouija board—he assumed; he had yet to look inside—was very similar to that. However, the rest of what Dan had described was the paraphernalia of so-called mediums in the Victorian era. Could it have been up in the loft all that time? Perhaps not, but Josh's researcher brain caught the scent of a puzzle and pawed the ground.

Until fifteen years ago, when the building's use changed from residential to commercial, it had been two self-contained flats. Josh knew that much from what his former landlord had told him, a fact confirmed in the deeds, and on the balance of probability, the loft's contents belonged to a previous residential tenant. He wasn't sure of the legalities, whether he was required to notify the owner, or attempt to, and give them the opportunity to collect their property. In the past, he'd have sought Jess's advice and was moderately amused by the thought that if a Ouija board did as purported, he still could have.

Given the amount of time that had passed, he could probably safely dispose of the loft's contents; nonetheless, he sent a text message to his former landlord asking if he had any contact information for the previous tenants, and then set it aside in his mind—or tried to. His priorities were the party on Friday and getting the renovation underway. He didn't need to know who owned the stuff in the loft or where it had come from.

"I don't," Josh told himself, but his curiosity was overriding his prior fears of heights and hauntings and practical jokes—on reflection, the latter scared him most—and left him wondering if he was brave enough or, more to the point, foolish enough, to take a look in the loft for himself.

"Bugger it." Leaving the Ouija board on the kitchenette counter, he collected the ladders and positioned them under the loft hatch. The ceiling was higher than the one at home, but not by much.

"I can do this," he whispered as he began his ascent, slowly, carefully, keeping his sights on his goal. Three rungs from the top, he was high enough to push the hatch cover out of the way but not quite able to see inside. He stepped up again and took a moment to make sure he was steady before he pulled his phone from his pocket and activated the LED.

Dan was right: the light barely penetrated the darkness at all, but he could see a ramshackle heap of the accoutrements of mediumship immediately to his right, extending past the cast of the LED's misty white-blue beam. Beyond those were shapeless dark masses large enough to be furniture. They could almost have been bodies, although even if people didn't notice someone's absence, they'd be hard pushed to ignore the distinctly horrendous stench of decomposition.

By now driven only by his need to uncover the mystery—not that he really thought there were dead bodies up there—Josh climbed the final two steps and hoisted himself up onto the lip of the hatch, soon after establishing two facts. Firstly, there were no boards for him to walk on, so he couldn't explore further. Secondly, and more importantly, it wasn't the going up that bothered him.

***

Fifteen years ago
February

"THIS KITCHEN IS very…small." Josh turned slowly in the narrow walkway between the two shallow counters lining either side of the square space. If he'd extended his arms, he could have touched both walls, although the room's diminutive size was its least offensive feature. To his left was a heavily scratched two-ring induction stove; to his right, hanging at an angle of around ten degrees, was an eye-level cupboard deep enough to hold two rows of mugs. On the external wall, beneath the disproportionately large window adorned with orangey-red gingham curtains and vallance, was a chipped, off-white enamel sink and draining board.

Gordon Baines, owner of this 'competitively priced, highly desirable property' and Josh's prospective landlord, waited for him to complete his rotation before saying, "You certainly wouldn't get any purchase in the proverbial swing of a cat, and it's in need of substantial modernising, which is why I switched it to commercial use." Plucking a short pencil from behind his ear and a tiny notepad from his shirt pocket, Gordon jotted something. "I've done nothing to it, as you can see."

"Yes, I can see that." Josh eyed the threadbare curtains that lifted each time the old sash window rattled with the wind. "So if I were to take on the lease..."

"Those windows would be sorted, and we could refit the kitchenette or repurpose the space."

"I'd need somewhere to make drinks for my clients."

Gordon hummed, scribbled on his pad again and gestured for Josh to follow him as they continued their viewing. "Toilet."

Josh nodded. *Fairly self-explanatory.* It was in only marginally better shape than the sink in the kitchenette.

"I'll stick in a new one," Gordon said, pushing open the next door along. "Bedroom."

Josh peeked in and was surprised to discover an ancient wash basin and clawfoot bathtub, both covered in dust but fully intact and taking up half the room. The remaining space didn't look big enough to house a bolster pillow, let alone an entire bed. "You did say this was a bedroom, didn't you?"

"I did. Keep in mind this went up in the 1850s—no inside plumbing, a shared privy out the back. I've seen worse workarounds. The dentist who's taking on downstairs is keeping the equivalent space as his wash-up room, but I don't imagine you'd need one in your line of work."

"No."

"In which case, I'll be reclaiming the bath and sink, and we can put in partition walls to give you an office, storeroom—whatever suits."

"Great!" Finally, Josh was getting a sense of what the property would look like once the work had been done, and he was cautiously optimistic. One more room to go: this would be make-or-break.

"And the sitting room or whatchamacallit."

"Consultation room," Josh said, walking ahead. "Oh, yes. This is better." It was smaller than the bedroom, and the décor was awful—curling floral wallpaper and hole-ridden lino—but he hardly saw it, his mind overlaying the view with neutral, refreshing cream-coloured walls, beige carpet, light ash desk, matching chair and bookshelves—

"What is it you do again? Hypnotist?"

"Psychotherapist."

"That's the one." The man clearly had no idea what that meant, and Josh was tired of explaining, so he didn't. A year since he'd qualified, he'd already lost count of how many times people had misidentified his career as hypnotist, astrologer, psychiatrist—at least that one was on the right lines. That or they thought he was a psychic. It was frustrating. There again, a good fifty percent of Josh's uni cohort had been clueless about what they were studying, so perhaps it was asking too much of a layperson like Gordon Baines, who, aside from not understanding what Josh did for a living, was straightforward and honest, and the rent was very reasonable for the first floor of a building so close to the town centre. It would be a stretch until he was fully established, but it would be worth it to have his house to himself.

"What d'you reckon?" Gordon asked. "Does it suit?"

"I'd say so." Josh went over and looked out the window, down into the yard at the back of the building, beyond it an alleyway accessible by a gate. "The yard's part of the ground-floor lease, I presume?"

"No. The leases relate to the building only, but you have access rights for refuse disposal and use of the fire escape."

On tiptoes, Josh could make out the thin black metal steps at the bottom of the fire escape, which was as rickety and terrifying as any he'd seen and—he reminded himself—never had to use. He turned back and surveyed the length of the room, noticing the square hatch in the ceiling. "What about the loft?"

"Also not part of the lease. Will that be a problem?"

"Not at all." With or without partition walls, there was more than enough storage space for Josh's needs. "How soon will it be ready, realistically?"

"I only do realistically, Mr. Sandison. None of that promising it'll be done in a week when there's a good month's work here. To be safe, let's say six weeks at the outside. The electrician and heating engineer will be in and out within a couple of weeks, plasterer after that. Your downstairs neighbour has already paid his deposit, so we can tackle both floors at the same time, pending your name on the dotted line, of course. No rush, Mr. Sandison. I'd rather you be sure you want it."

Josh took out his cheque book and unclipped his pen from his shirt pocket. "I want it."

***

Exactly one month later, on a bright but chilly Saturday morning, with keys in hand and a good deal of trepidation that he put down to waking in the early hours from a bizarre but not especially frightening dream about a water park, Josh locked his car and approached the two newly double-glazed front doors. The one on the right offered a dim glimpse of the dark stairs up to the first floor—his renovated, remodelled surgery, which he had yet to see in its completed state. Gordon Baines had told him he could pop in anytime to see how it was going, and Josh had hinted heavily to his friends that he wanted to show off his new acquisition, fearing he'd made a huge mistake. All he'd received in return was vague reassurance from George and complete disinterest from everyone else. In retrospect, he could have been less opaque and admitted he needed someone to come with him, thereby avoiding this paralysing anxiety about entering the building.

To give himself a moment, he studied the door on the left. In the building's shadow, it shone tungsten yellow, illuminating the words etched into the glass—*D. Giles, Dentist*—Josh's downstairs neighbour, whom he could see in the reception area, laughing and joking with a female colleague. Within seconds, the man spotted Josh and strode towards him, his beaming white smile both greeting and testament to expertise in his trade as he swung the door open and thrust out a hand.

"Good morning! It's *very good* to meet you. I'm Giles. Donald Giles, for my sins. Everyone calls me Giles."

"Morning." Josh shook the offered hand, thrown somewhat by the man's ebullience. "Sandison. Josh."

"Josh." Giles released him from the very vigorous handshake not a moment too soon. "A psychotherapist, I believe?"

That was a major point in Giles's favour. "Yes, and you're a dentist."

Giles read his door sign and grinned lopsidedly. "So I'm told. When you have a mo, we should have a quick conflab about the internet and whatnot, but I'll leave you to settle in first. Why don't you pop down when you're ready, or I can come up to you if you prefer?"

"Erm, yes, OK. I'll just go and…" Josh waved his keys at his door, hoping it was explanation enough.

"I'll see you shortly!" With that, Giles about-turned and marched back to his colleague, leaving the door to slow-close in Josh's face, for which he was thankful. It was a bit too much interaction for his first day in his new surgery.

Alas, that was only the beginning. He'd barely made it to the top of the stairs when he heard the door at the bottom click open again, followed by swift, light footsteps heading upwards. Expecting to be met with Mr. Giles's dazzling grin, Josh turned and did a double-take. Not Giles.

"Jess. What—"

"Coffee?" Shaking the jar of instant granules like maracas, she did some kind of samba move up onto the landing, following with her own double-take. "Wowzer! When you said it was 'quite spacious', I thought you were being generous. This is *massive*! Where's the kettle?" She was off exploring before Josh could respond, which meant she also found the kitchenette—"OK, not so spacious in here"—and the kettle all by herself. "You should buy a filter coffee maker," she shouted over the gushing of a tap.

There was certainly nothing wrong with the water pressure. "I'll buy you one."

"I don't need a coffee maker," Josh protested, raising his voice to be heard and then having to quickly lower it again when Jess turned off the tap. "Even if I did, where the hell would I put it?"

Jess noisily opened and closed drawers until she found the teaspoons and then jabbed one through the paper membrane covering the jar. The *pop* was disproportionately explosive. "They're quite compact, you know."

"So? There's a café about two minutes along the street."

Jess rolled her eyes. "That goes without saying. In fact, scratch the coffee maker. We should look into some kind of intravenous delivery system."

"I really don't drink that much coffee."

"Oh, you really do." Jess found the mugs and spooned coffee into two, asking on the way to the fridge, "Presumably, you bought milk—yes, you did." He hadn't, but a quick check of the date confirmed it was fresh. She left the carton next to the mugs and brushed her hands together. "So you were about to give me the guided tour."

"I was?"

"Of course! You know what they say about a watched kettle? Come on." With her arm hooked through his, she gave him little choice, although he was secretly thrilled she'd sprung a surprise visit on him.

It didn't take long to show her around, given 'quite spacious' applied only to the landing—now the reception-cum-waiting room, complete with several low chairs and coffee table, for which he'd brought a small stack of back issues of *National Geographic* and *Psychology Today*. Jess gave the storeroom, broom cupboard and toilet a cursory glance, likewise Josh's consultation room on the premise they'd be drinking their coffee in there so she could critique it at her leisure; they were back at the kettle before it had boiled.

"I am allowed to sit on here, aren't I?" Jess called pointlessly, seeing as she'd made the coffee and headed straight for the brand-new sofa in the consultation room. Josh traipsed in after her, blushing when she wriggled down into the deep cushions and moaned indecently. "This is so comfy!"

Oh, good, she approves. At last, something to put a smile on his face. "It is, isn't it?" He sat at the other end and smoothed the sofa arm, transforming the short pile from mid to light blue and back again. He'd half considered asking Gordon Baines to install a chaise-longue, but it seemed too stuffy...too Freudian, which, contrary to the teasing he'd endured since completing his undergraduate dissertation entitled 'A Neo-Freudian Analysis of Friendship', he was not. That aside, the sofa was much more welcoming and would help put his clients at ease. "So what do you think?" he asked. "Idiotic or...?"

"The sofa or the whole shebang? Because the sofa is upholstered heaven."

"And the whole shebang?"

Peering up and around the room, Jess hummed thoughtfully but gave nothing away until she finally made eye contact with him and must have picked up on his anxiety, as she reached across to squeeze his hand.

"It's amazing. I love it! I think we're going to be very happy here."

"*We?*" Josh repeated.

Jess grinned. "I'm not giving up this sofa for anyone."

8: Clocking Out

Y<small>OU DO KNOW</small> I've been here since twelve?" Sophie asked as Sean emerged into the waiting room, wiping his face with a length of blue paper towel.

"Aye, tell me about it," he grumbled. He'd overrun by forty minutes, leaving him with twenty minutes to grab lunch and buy an emergency deodorant from the hospital shop. For some unfathomable reason, the radiator was on full in the consulting room, and he'd sweated buckets in there. "Do I stink?" he asked.

Wrinkling her nose, Sophie hesitantly leaned in and took a cautious sniff. "Hmm...not stink, as such."

"Terrific. I'll see if I can cadge some scrubs."

"You do that, and I'll grab us a sandwich and drink."

"Thanks, Soph. See you at my office."

Sophie left for the cafeteria. Sean delayed a moment or so, contemplating which of his colleagues was around his size and most likely to have a spare tunic, and set off for the main corridor. He didn't even make it out of the clinic.

"Doctor Tierney!" Melanie called.

Sean glanced over his shoulder but kept moving.

"Where do you think you're going?"

"To borrow some scrubs. I'm sweating like a nun in a—" Sean stopped before the punchline. "Be right back," he said instead and made a dash for it. No more than ten steps along the corridor, he heard the *clip-clip-clip-clip* of fast-moving heeled shoes coming up from behind. Melanie rounded him and stopped with arms held wide, blocking his route.

"Mel—"

"Just five minutes. Please, Sean?" She gave him a *how could you deny me this much after all I've done for you* doe-eyed blink.

"I need to get out of this shirt."

"I can help you with that." Now, where some of the female staff may have turned the offer into a jokey flirtation, Melanie wasn't one of them, and she blushed crimson at her words. "I mean, I'll find you a tunic. I'll even give you an extra fifteen minutes before this afternoon's clinic."

Accepting he wasn't going to win, Sean relented with a sighed-out, "Fine," and followed her back into clinic, where—as he'd expected—quite a few members of the mental health team had gathered around the desk, all of them armed with disposable plastic cups, which they raised as he approached. He hated goodbyes. He was going to sob like a toddler with banged-up knees, but he donned his widest smile and hoped to God his armpits didn't kill anyone.

"Alright, team?"

"Sean." Francesca Marks, the unit manager, took a step towards him. "I know you didn't want a fuss, but we couldn't let you leave at the end of today as if you'd be back tomorrow."

"I'm not in of a Wednesday," Sean reminded her with a wink. They'd been having the same conversation for four years—since he went part-time—with Francesca convinced he changed his schedule every week. More like she was so busy she had no idea what the hell the day was.

Francesca's smile held, though she was quite emotional. "We started here the same year, as you know," she said. Sean nodded. Within a week of each other, in fact. Francesca—never Fran, she'd made that *very* clear—had beaten him to the bigger of the two offices in the then brand-new Parkwood Unit. "We've witnessed a lot of change, very little of it for the better. Remember when there were sixty permanent staff?"

"I do," Sean agreed nostalgically, noticing some of those standing behind Francesca shake their heads in disbelief. True, they had only two-thirds the patient intake of fourteen years ago, as long-term admissions had been transferred to specialist units, but they'd lost more than half of the permanent posts, mostly higher-band nurses, and those brought in to replace them were newly qualified, with healthcare assistants and agency staff filling the gaps. In the last inspection, the unit had been judged ineffective and not well led—a particularly heavy burden on poor Francesca's shoulders when she was doing the best she could with the limited resources at her disposal.

Those gathered in clinic for Sean's final embarrassment were a mix of permanent and agency staff, many of the latter as good as permanent—if one set aside the lack of employment benefits. When they were assigned good ones, Francesca was sure to ask the agency to send the same people again. Then there were the likes of Melanie the administrator and Janice the Modern Matron, both of whom had been there long before Sean and Francesca arrived like the young upstarts they were, thinking they could change the world and soon discovering Melanie and Janice had already made it as perfect a place as it could be.

Looking around the faces of the wonderful people in front of him, Sean was overwhelmed, remembering the countless kindnesses they had shown him over the years, so many incredible memories, not all of them happy, but they'd pulled together as a team—his team—and he was going to miss them very much. He was done for already, and Francesca hadn't even started.

"Come on, Ms. Marks. Put me out of me misery, will ye?" He laughed through his tears, and the team made sympathetic noises, for both him and Francesca, who was in no better a state.

"All right, Doctor Tierney. I wouldn't want to give you *a reason* to be late now, would I? Particularly as I hear your new co-pilot is even less tolerant of your tardiness than I am."

Sean laughed. "Aye, you could say that."

"We've all chipped in for a little leaving gift that might help."

"You're giving me Melanie? That's very generous of you."

Melanie muttered, "Ha, in your dreams," and gave him a sickly grin, followed by a real smile that melted into tears.

"Hey, don't you go falling apart on me. We've afternoon clinic to get through yet." Sean spotted Sophie loitering across the way and beckoned to her, hoping to take some of the heat off himself, but she stayed where she was and pointed past Sean to Francesca, who had moved while his attention was elsewhere and was now directly in front of him, holding out a large, flat package wrapped in bright-green shiny paper. Through a series of nods, raised eyebrows and rolled eyes, Francesca persuaded Sean to take the gift from her. He stared at the wrapping, letting the reflections of the lights overhead dazzle him.

"Five past one," Melanie warned.

"All right, I'm opening it already." Setting the box on the counter, he peeled away the tape and ripped the paper open, revealing plain brown cardboard with no clues as to what was contained within. He shoved the paper aside—ever-efficient Melanie immediately whisked it away—and flipped the box.

It was a wall clock, circular and around eighteen inches in diameter, green, of course. For an Irishman in England, everything was, but Sean was perfectly fine with that, and in any case was laughing so hard at the clock's set-up it could've been any colour at all. It only had an hour hand and four numbers: 12-ish, 3-ish, 6-ish and 9-ish, each approximately in the correct location. In the middle was what Sean now realised had become his catchphrase: *I'm not late, you're all early.*

"This is fantastic. Truly." Sean looked around his colleagues, nodding. "Thanks, all, so much. I'll miss yous, more than you could know."

"Even Doctor Morris?" Melanie asked wryly.

"Oh, especially Doctor Morris." They were like passing ships, and Sean begrudged having to give up his office to the man, but he supposed he would miss him in a way.

"We'll miss you too, Sean," Francesca said, advancing with her arms outstretched. He was well into the hug before he remembered he'd been sweating all morning.

"Ten past…"

"OK, Mel. Can you get me those scrub—oh, you've got them already." Sean didn't even bother asking her when on earth she'd managed to do that. She was nothing short of a miracle worker, although the tunic in question was from Paediatrics—intentionally, he envisaged—bright yellow and decorated with monkeys variously lounging on, jumping over and riding giant bananas. "Right. I'll get changed and scoff some lunch. Thank you again, you amazing people." Clutching his clock and his vibrant scrubs, he back-stepped away, bowing, and then quickly marched off towards Sophie, calling, "How long, Mel?"

"Ten minutes."

"Ten minutes, right…" Sean smiled at Sophie. "Have you seen this?" He held up the clock. Sophie lifted it so she could read the words and laughed. "It's going in my new consultation room," he said as the two of them set off at a good pace for Sean's office. It was a couple of minutes away, and by the time he made it there, changed and ate, it would be time to come back again, but he was desperate for a bit of peace away from his watchful, soon-to-be ex-colleagues.

"How's this morning been?" Sophie asked.

"Not too bad. Francesca asked me not to tell the patients I was leaving, which I wasn't happy about."

"Why did she do that?"

"I don't know. It's not like the majority could afford private treatment."

"Maybe she's hoping you'll change your mind," Sophie speculated.

"I doubt it." More likely, she'd be asking him to cover clinic on a casual basis if Tristan Morris kept getting up to his tricks, although Sean had been in on the interviews for his replacement, and he was satisfied they'd made a good decision.

As soon as he and Sophie were inside his office, Sean unbuttoned his shirt and then bashed his forehead. "Damn, I was going to buy—"

A can of deodorant materialised in front of him.

"Soph, you're a wonder." Off came the shirt. He sprayed generously into both armpits and all across his chest, turning the dark hairs white where the powder collected on them. "What's it smell like?"

"Deodorant," Sophie said, twitching her nose. "You should stop now." She opened and closed her mouth to dispel the taste. Sean put the lid back on the can and pulled on his yellow tunic, flexing his arms in a muscleman pose. Sophie laughed. "That's a good look for you."

"D'you think so? It's a wee bit like the Hawaiian shirts I used to wear before I came to work here." Sean smiled at the memory and the realisation he was almost free of the NHS again, though he doubted he'd get away with the arty attire of his younger days, certainly not without Josh passing comment.

Sophie handed him his sandwich and sat in his chair. "So, what happened?"

She was asking about his minor meltdown first thing. "I'm not sure. A bit wobbly because of the change, maybe?"

"It wasn't about last night?"

Sean nibbled at his sandwich. "No, I don't think so. It's not like it was different to any other time, is it? But there's something I need to talk to you about." He perched on the corner of his desk so he was partly facing her. "I had a visit yesterday from the daughter of an old friend. Biologically, she's my daughter too."

"Phoenix?"

"Aye, in the ashes phase, I'd say."

"I didn't realise you were in touch."

"We're not in general. She's always known who I am, and I've seen her a few times. She's sent me a couple of letters over the years, and she knew I worked at the uni, as she called my office.

Genie—her mum—and I haven't spoken in a good long while, but I got the impression Phee's giving her a hard time."

"Is Genie on her own?"

"No, and therein lies the problem. She's been with this guy Paul for about six years. I met him once, when they first got together. He must've only been twenty."

Sophie pushed a bottle of water across the desk to him. "I think I know where this is going." Sean could see from her expression that she was on the right track. "How bad is it?"

"Phee's pregnant."

"Oops!"

Sean chuckled ruefully. "You could say that."

"How old is Phee?"

"Coming up on eighteen. She's sitting her A' Levels, and she's adamant she's having the baby."

"Does Paul know? Or Genie?"

"No. That's where we got to yesterday. I told her to go home and talk to them—either of them. She had no intention of doing so and was expecting me to let her stay for a while. I did my best to talk her round, but…" Sean shrugged. He'd tried everything he could to get Phee to go home, short of borrowing a car and driving her there himself.

"Where is she now?"

"I booked her into a hotel for the night. She asked if she could stay at my place, and I'd have offered to sleep on the couch and let her have my bed, but it didn't feel right, you know? So I told her I didn't have the space."

"You don't," Sophie said.

"I didn't like leaving her to fend for herself, not with what she's going through. Of course, if I'd known she was coming, I'd have cleared out the attic for her. She could stay as long as she liked then."

"Next time, eh?"

"If there is one." Sean was undecided whether he wanted there to be. "We swapped mobile numbers, but I haven't heard a peep from her, and she's ignoring my calls and messages. Before you ask, I know she's OK—she's been online and she's still up here, even though she said she'd be getting the train back today. I don't know what to do for the best."

Sophie blew out a long breath and then offered Sean a sympathetic smile. "I can understand why you're struggling. Why didn't you tell me last night?"

"No real reason other than it's not something we've talked about in the past, and it shouldn't be an issue now."

"That makes sense."

Sean was grateful as ever for their down-to-earth, no-nonsense relationship. So much of it was good and healthy because they rarely became caught up in jealousy or comparing themselves to other partners, past or—theoretically—present. Sean hadn't been involved with anyone else, although he was fairly sure Sophie and her PhD supervisor had something going on. They'd been an item a few years back, and Sean had told Sophie he didn't want to know or, rather, he didn't expect her to tell him.

"When you say she's almost eighteen…?" Sophie asked.

"Her birthday's next month, which means she'll be free to do as she pleases—or it would if she were a commoner. Her grandfather is a marquess."

Sophie gave a weary eye-roll. "What's with all the nobility all of a sudden? Isn't George's art therapist a viscountess or something?"

"She will be. She and her younger brother asked permission for the two of them to share the title when their father dies. It caused a bit of a hoo-ha."

"Tell me again how you're not an Oxbridge graduate," Sophie joked, not for the first time. She'd always said Josh was too snooty to have studied at a commoners' university. Quite where a scruffy Irishman like Sean fitted into that picture, he had no idea.

"Our uni was redbrick—one of the best for law, I'll have you know." He wasn't sure why he was defending the institution or its faculty of law; the law undergraduates were some of the rudest, least considerate people he'd ever come into contact with—bullies, really—with one or two notable exceptions only. "Gabby and Genie were quite close back then," he intentionally mused aloud, smiling at the vivid images called to mind of the halls-warming party on his inaugural weekend when Gabby had introduced him and Genie, and the night the two girls had stayed over at his and Josh's place after an entirely innocent evening of Trivial Pursuit, and the far less innocent ones he and Genie had shared with Jess when Josh was in hospital. There had been a few more occasions of just him and Genie after she'd moved to London, the last of those being when she'd told him she was pregnant with Phee.

His recollection arrived at the morning-after fry-up— or throw-up in poor Genie's case—and his belly rumbled, prompting him to do something about the sandwich in his hand. He took a big bite and mumbled around it, "They might still be close, I suppose." It hadn't come up in conversation with Gabby, and he hadn't spoken to Genie in five years, although there was every likelihood they'd be catching up soon.

His mind drifted back to his present dilemma but got stuck in a loop that offered no solutions. He finished off the first half of the sandwich and swigged his water. "What do I do, Soph?"

"How long has it been going on between Phee and Paul?"

"Only a few months, she says."

"So she was seventeen when it started, and he's…twenty-six?"

"Somewhere around there."

Sophie unscrewed the cap from her bottle of water, took a mouthful and swallowed. Sean waited. "You want to know what I'd do in your situation, don't you?" she said. Sean nodded. She stared into the mid-distance, absently tapping the bottle against her teeth. The sound set him on edge. Still, he kept his mouth shut. "OK. Well, you don't have parental responsibility, so on that score, you'd be justified in keeping out of it. You could even argue the case for practitioner-client privilege. That said, she's a minor, so you might have to disclose—"

"Right, I know all this, Soph."

"I was getting it straight in my head."

"Fair enough."

"I think what I'd do…" Sophie leaned back in Sean's chair and twisted a few inches from side to side.

"That chair's a bit rickety," Sean warned at the same time as the back-adjustment spring dislodged. Sophie gripped the lip of the desk and sat forward. The chair sprang upright, hitting her in the back.

"Gee whizz, this thing's lethal."

"Why d'you think I let you sit in it?" Sean said mischievously, not that he could've stopped her.

"Have you reported it? The chair, I mean."

"Probably?" He couldn't remember if it was on the two-page list of faulty and broken equipment he'd given to site maintenance, seeing as it was six months ago and everything else was still faulty or broken. "You were saying…" he prompted.

"Yeah. I don't know Phee, obviously, but at her age, I had my head screwed on, and from what you've said, she has too. Did she swear you to secrecy?"

"Not at all."

"Or ask you not to tell her mum?"

"No."

"Hmm. Maybe she's hoping you will, which could be because she's scared—and maybe the boyfriend is culpable—or she's trying to stir trouble to break up the relationship." Sophie met his gaze. "You need to talk to her again, make a risk assessment."

"Treat her as if she's a patient? Is that what you're saying?"

Sophie nodded. "Do you want me to tag along?"

"Haven't you got to get back to London?"

"Not this week. I'll let Grant know something's come up."

"You don't have to—"

Sophie raised her hand to stop him. "Lunch break's over. I'll give Grant a call when I get home. You call Phee after clinic and make the arrangements." Sophie got up and put her sandwich wrapper in the bin on her way to the door. "You can have the car for the rest of the week too, if you're OK keeping hold of Dylan so I can still get some work done."

"Sure!" Sean agreed. Sometimes he wondered what he'd do without her.

"Come on," she encouraged in the same tone she used to get Dylan into his pushchair.

Sean removed the other half of sandwich from the plastic wrapper, threw the wrapper away and obediently followed her over to the door. "Thank you," he said sincerely.

She reached up and affectionately rubbed his stubbled cheek. No words needed, she opened the door, waited for him to close and lock it behind them, then accompanied him back to clinic, where she left him in Melanie's capable hands for his final stint.

9: Best Behaviour

Off Campus
Twenty-one years ago
November

WAKEY, WAKEY! RISE and shine!"

The curtains whisked open, spilling distressingly bright sunlight across the bed. Genie pulled the duvet over her face, but it didn't stay there.

"Oh my god, Jessica!" She grabbed her pillows, covering her bared boobs with one and flinging the other at Jess, who grinned and skipped from the room.

"Get up, Genie. It'll be worth your while, I guarantee it."

"I'm going to kill you, I swear!" She launched the second pillow after Jess. It hit the doorpost and plumped soundlessly on the floor next to the stolen duvet. "Bitch," Genie muttered. Already shivering, she swung her legs off the bed and sat, swaying and woozy. The night before had ended at four a.m., and it was Friday, therefore no lecture until the afternoon, although the way she was feeling, she wasn't sure she'd be sober enough to attend. Like she had the luxury of choice with Jess in full-of-beans mood. She'd drag Genie to the lecture theatre by her hair if that was what it took, never mind that they'd been as drunk as each other five hours ago, so said the alarm clock's faint, blurry numbers caught in the brash, low sun. It was a commendable effort for a November morning but did nothing to warm the biting chill of their crappy rented house with its non-existent insulation and next-to-useless central heating.

"Are you having a shower?" Jess shouted unnecessarily from the small landing.

"Are you asking or telling me?"

Jess reappeared in the doorway. "Actually, I was warning you that I'm about to do the dishes so you don't freeze your tits off."

"*You're* doing the dishes? Let me guess… Josh is coming over."

"On a Friday? You've got to be kidding. He'll probably meet up with us over the weekend, though."

"Ah! So your mum and dad are visiting." That gave Genie the impetus to get up off the bed. She liked Jess's parents, more so her mum than her dad, who wasn't creepy and had never looked at her the way most men did, but he was still a man, and experience made her cautious.

Jess unhooked the bathrobe from the door and held it open while Genie slid into it, then reached around her to fasten the belt. "Wrong again."

"About…?"

"Not my parents."

"I love how you waited until you had me where you wanted me."

Jess giggled, kissed Genie's cheek and released her. "Any time, any place, anywhere—except for here, this weekend." She followed up with a hopeful smile.

"Oh, Jess, don't make me leave. I feel like shit." Genie made a sad face, at which Jess rolled her eyes. They had a standing arrangement to keep out of the way if either of them had a hot date staying over, and killer hangover or not, Genie would abide by it. Still, it begged the question. "Anyone I know?"

"Nope. Someone from home. I might've mentioned him, though. He's just bought a new car, and he wants to take her on a good run."

"*Her.*"

"According to Andy—"

"Ha! 'I *might've* mentioned him,' she says…"

"OK, so I *have* mentioned him."

"Only once or twice—every bloody day."

"Not true!"

"Let's see, now. This *is* Andy with the massive—"

"If I may interrupt, Your Honour, my learned friend is referring to hearsay."

"Interesting name for it. What else? Hmm. Oh, yeah. Andy's into grunge like he's still fourteen or something but at least he eventually remembered what soap is."

"I did not say that!"

"Might I remind the defendant she is under oath?"

"OK. Fine," Jess relented. "Maybe you *should* stay somewhere else this weekend. You'll tell him I talk about him all the time, and he's already full of himself."

"What if I promise to keep my mouth shut?"

Jess folded her arms. "I'll believe that when I see it."

Genie sighed and squidged through the narrow gap between Jess's elbow and the doorpost, fake muttering, "Guess I'm bunking in with Gabby," but she was getting no sympathy here, not even when she added, "It's like being back at school," as she pushed the bathroom door shut and plonked down on the loo.

"You could always go stay with Sean. Isn't that what you usually do?"

"When you're not staying with him, you mean?"

"And there's another reason to kick you out," Jess said. Her footsteps receded down the stairs. "I'll vacuum now and do the dishes when you're finished in there."

"OK." Genie wiped and flushed and turned on the shower, all with one eye shut. She was getting a headache, which was maybe for the best. She might be past the hangover in time to spend the night squashed up in a single bed with Gabby or Sean. Neither option appealed, but it was fair when it was usually Genie asking Jess to make herself scarce. It was also infinitely preferable to watching Jess get up close and personal with some guy who supposedly meant nothing to her yet genuinely did come up in conversation on an almost daily basis.

Genie's thoughts spiralled further as she stood under the lukewarm water that had her washing so vigorously she grazed her belly—with a sponge! How was that even possible?—and with shampoo in her eyes, she managed to slash both shins speed-shaving. No matter that she kept telling herself it was only for the weekend; if Andy now owned a car, there was nothing to stop him coming to visit any time he liked, which would put an end to their girls-only fun.

And that, really, was the heart of it. Somewhere along the line, it had become more than 'fun' for Genie. Jess was still adamant there was no space in her life plan for a relationship, however much she loved Genie. When Genie pointed out they were too young to be thinking long term, Jess had shushed her and told her not to ruin the good thing they had before poking the shushing finger between Genie's lips, in and out, and into her own mouth as she slid onto Genie's knee, astride, hips rocking, back arched to push her breasts into Genie's face, impossible to see past or ignore.

There was only one place they could go from there, and all the while, Genie weighed up whether she could settle for keeping what they had, the gentle morning kisses and easy love-making on tap, or if she should move out and hope they stayed on speaking terms for the remainder of their studies—a miserable eternity or a glorious flash in the pan.

Satiated and without reaching resolution, Genie had fallen asleep in the middle of that balmy late-spring afternoon; when she awoke, sunlight draped silken gold across the room and Jess's supine, perfect, naked form, and she decided not to decide, but to wait until the decision was made for her.

So sure that time was nigh, Genie dressed in a hurry, relishing the wet, stinging chafe of her jeans against her wounds and pulling on a sleeveless top as, still barefoot, she descended the stairs under the cover of the vacuum cleaner's one-note song and swept a hand across Jess's back to startling effect. The note changed pitch. Jess stopped staring at Genie and held the hose between them. Genie tugged a spotty sock from the end and carried it through to the kitchen, laying it on the counter delicately, as if it were made of that same silken gold in which Jess was swathed in the image Genie's mind had captured and which she revisited so often it would reside within her for as long as she had breath. The vacuum cleaner powered down; the plug clattered as Jess rewound the cable. Abandoning the precious sock, Genie filled the kettle and switched it on, turning with a light-hearted smile and a question.

"Will he be jealous?"

"Who?" Jess's counter-question came with gaze averted and a bloom of pink across her cheekbones. "Oh! Andy, you mean?" She affected a laugh. "Jealous of what? Us? He'll think it's hot."

"What about the others?" Genie pressed. "The boys you've slept with since you've been here?"

"Yes, he'll be jealous." Jess glanced up, eyes narrowed in a challenge. "Are you planning to sabotage my weekend?"

Genie laughed as if it were a joke, as if she wasn't astonished Jess had asked. "Yeah." As if she wasn't the one who was jealous. "Cup of tea?"

"Please." The word carried a stealth sigh of relief, and as Jess turned and went back upstairs, muttering something about straightening her hair, it dawned on Genie that Jess really was afraid she would somehow ruin this weekend for her.

"Actually, you'll have to make it yourself." Genie overtook her on the landing. "Sorry."

"Where are you going?"

"Meeting with my personal tutor. Just remembered." It was the first excuse she'd thought of and an easy one to prove false, but she'd worry about that later. Right then, she needed to get away from the house and from Jess. Socks, boots, jacket on, she threw her books into her bag and dashed from her room, holding her breath as she passed Jess's slightly open door lest the tantalising warm-hair smell gripped her in its tendrils, down the stairs and from the house, not slowing until she reached the high street. That was when the whole muddled mess of emotions hit her, yet she kept walking, through her jealousy and rejection and anger and arousal because it *would* have been hot, the two of them and Andy. She'd never even seen a photo of him, but he would be a looker. They always were, and sharing Jess—with her career or other lovers—was never the issue. Losing her was.

It wasn't so much autopilot as self-preservation that steered Genie towards Cassandra's café and the promise of respite from cold sweats and nausea. There were only two customers, sitting at different tables, and Sean was working. She hadn't known he would be. In the drinking and laughter of the previous evening/early hours, it hadn't come up in conversation, and she hated him a little for his cheery-as-ever grin. Was she the only one suffering?

His grin faltered as Genie approached the counter, and she pulled on her reserves, offering a contained, demure smile.

"Good morning, Sean."

"Morning, lovely. Are you all right?" He wiped his hands on his apron and adjusted the 'today's special' miniature sandwich board on top of the display cabinet. *Chocolate fudge cake.* Genie suppressed a shudder.

"A little hungover," she said. "You?"

"Dead on my feet," he admitted. "How's Jess?"

"Unscathed, apparently."

Sean's eyebrows disappeared beneath his copious dark-chocolate curls. "Have you had a fight?"

"Oh, nothing like that. But I do need to ask a favour."

"Ask away."

"Can I stay at your place this weekend?"

"Sure you can!"

"Josh won't mind, will he?"

"To be honest, I doubt he'll even notice. Half the time he forgets I live there, and then he'll spot me and look at me like he's thinking, 'Who are ye and what're you doing in me kitchen?'" Sean winked, but added, "I'll ask him when I'm done here for the day. How's that?"

"Thank you, Sean. I owe you one."

He tapped his temple. "Logged for later. Now, can I get you anything? Tea? Coffee? A bit of cake?"

Genie's oesophagus gave a pre-emptive clench. "No, thank you, but I ought to buy something." She surveyed the contents of the glass counter—fruit scones, butterfly cakes, strawberry tarts, decadent three-layered fudge cake with a piece missing...

"How about a round of buttered toast?" Sean suggested.

Her stomach offered a small growl of reluctant agreement, and Genie nodded carefully. "I'll give it a try."

"Go take a seat, and I'll bring it over. I might join you if that's all right?"

Genie shrugged her consent and selected a table butted against the mutely yellow side wall, her gaze drawn to the watercolour print closest to her. It was of a lone house on a dark, desolate clifftop, the backdrop a choppy, grey sea and overcast skies, a perfect summation of her present state of mind, from which she was briefly lured by the plate of toast that appeared on the table in front of her.

"Miserable, isn't it?" Sean said, taking the seat opposite. "Though I may have persuaded Cass to brighten the place up a bit."

Genie picked up half a slice of toast, taking a small bite from the corner. The salty smoothness of the melted butter coated her taste buds, comforting, soothing. She swallowed and took another, slightly bigger bite, chewed, swallowed and sagged gratefully when it stayed down with no ill effects. "She should keep the yellow walls."

"Do you think so?" Sean looked around the small café, prompting Genie to do the same. It was a bit off the beaten path and not the kind of place that catered for students, but on the two previous occasions she'd been in there, she'd stayed for hours, reading, oblivious to the world beyond the steamy windows that obscured the peaceful, homey atmosphere of this pocket of the past.

"Those odd little animals." She indicated the high, narrow shelves, eight in total, each holding three miniature porcelain figurines of dogs, cats, rabbits and so on, all eyeless or too small and far away for their eyes to be visible, making them pretty ghastly despite their small stature. "Those need to go. The paintings…" She was again captivated by the foreboding seascape over their table.

"Right. I have an idea about that," Sean said. "I was chatting with one of the art students who's after exhibiting his work with a view to selling a few pieces. He's in the same boat as me, you see."

"He's Irish?" Genie guessed.

"I mean he's skint."

"Oh!" That brought her back to reality with a jolt.

"So here's how it'd work…" Sean continued, and as he did, she reappraised her perception of him. The slightly too long hair, beard scruff, faded T-shirt and threadbare jeans, she'd assumed were stylistic choices. After all, everyone had one or two of those relatives who lived as if they were on their uppers when in reality they were sitting on a fortune. Not that she'd ever thought Sean was minted, but she hadn't realised until now that he was, in fact, destitute.

She tuned back in as he came to the end of his explanation, but she'd caught the gist.

"What d'you reckon?" he asked. He looked so earnest, even if she'd thought it was a terrible idea she couldn't have told him so, but she didn't think that.

"It's brilliant, Sean."

"Thanks. That means a lot coming from yourself."

"Me? What do I know? I'm a cossetted aristocrat."

"You're more savvy than you let on, Genie. So, we still need to figure out how much to stick on the price tags, and there's no guarantee Cass'll go for it."

"Well, *when* she does, tell her I'll take this picture off her hands."

Sean leaned back and studied it for a moment. "You like that?"

"Today, I do."

"Ah." He straightened up and looked her in the eye. "Want to share?"

"Not really," she said, then spilled everything, from Jess's attempt at being casual about Andy's visit right down to the fantasy image that lived in Genie's head, which was, she realised as she talked, what she was in love with. At first, it was mortifying, as if the words were being leached from her without her conscious permission, yet the longer Sean listened without judgement or comment, the less vulnerable and disheartened she became. The hangover was easing too, she noticed as the rambling stream slowed to a trickle, which was as well. There were customers waiting to be served. The lunchtime rush had begun, it seemed.

"Oh my goodness! Look at the time. I'm so sorry, Sean." Genie rose, as did he.

"No need, lovely." He beckoned her into a hug. "I offered you my ear, so I did."

"So you did." She kissed his cheek.

"How are you feeling?"

"Better. Thank you." She clung to him a moment longer, wishing she didn't have to go, but he had work to do. She stepped away and raised her hand in a wave, turning to leave.

"Hold on." Sean fished in his pocket and pulled out his keys, freeing one from the rest of the bunch. "I'm going straight to uni from here, and Josh'll already be at the library, so if you want to make yourself at home, no problem."

He held out the key, and Genie stared at it, not sure what to do. On the one hand, it felt like taking liberties. On the other, it meant she could avoid seeing Jess until lover boy had gone home.

Sean pressed the key into her hand and closed her fingers around it. "I'll see you later, OK?"

Genie nodded, pushing out a husky "See you later" on her way to the door. His kindness had left her tearful.

From the café, she went straight to Sean and Josh's house and waited until after the law lecture had started before she called home and left a message on the answering machine so Jess wouldn't worry where she'd gone. Assuming Jess gave it any thought at all.

*****

Genie didn't know Josh well, this in spite of having mutual friends in Sean and Jess. What she did know was Josh wasn't one to hold his tongue, which made it all the more surprising he managed to do so until Saturday morning, when they crossed paths outside the bathroom.

"Sorry if this is a rude question, but how long are you intending to stay?"

"Only tonight—if that's OK with you, of course."

"Of course." Josh's tight-lipped smile told a different story, and he marched back into his room before she could tell him she'd make other arrangements. She hated when people cut her off like that and advanced on his door, fist raised to knock, but then lowered her hand. He had a right to be miffed, and she could afford a night in a hotel instead of imposing further on him or anyone else.

She returned to Sean's bedroom, her intention to grab her things and go before he awoke, but one look at him curled around the crumpled space in which she'd lain and she changed her mind and got back into bed. He draped his arm over her, awake or in his sleep, she couldn't tell and didn't care. Here with him, she was warm, safe and wanted, and her mind drifted into a daydream-like state, alert to every sound in this strange house—Josh clomping down the stairs, taps running, crockery landing heavily, cutlery jangling…a knock at the front door and an interchange that burned all hope of pretending, if only for a bit longer, that she was OK.

The conversation downstairs was loud and joyous, and it was clear from the way Jess spoke that she didn't know Genie was there. Or perhaps she did know and that was why she was spelling out her and Andy's plans for the day—just the two of them, unless Josh wanted to join them? Genie didn't hear his reply, and she didn't need to. Plainly, she had become an unwelcome obstacle in Jess's single life. She moved to get out of the bed, but Sean tensed his arm, clamping her to him.

"Stay here," he murmured.

"I can't." She fought him half-heartedly, and he lifted his arm away so she could leave if she wanted to, but she didn't want to. She wanted to hide forever in this dim room filled with his scent and his things and no trace of Jess.

"What are you going to do if you go down there now?"

"Have it out with her." Tears were coming. She swung her legs around and sat on the edge of the bed, but it made no difference. "What am I supposed to do, Sean?" He moved to sit next to her, and she leaned against him and swallowed, the tension in her throat turning it into a raw gulp.

"Ah, Christ, Genie. Come here."

Then she was back in his arms, sobbing into his chest hair in anger and frustration with herself because Jess hadn't led her on and none of this was her fault. An awful and somewhat conceited thought occurred to her, and she sniffed and cleared her throat as best she could to ask, "I'm not making you suffer like this, am I?"

"How d'you mean?"

"Like with Jess and me. For her, it's just friends with benefits, for me…"

"Ah, right. I get you now. No, other than drowning me, you're not—"

From bad to worse, Sean's assurance was cut off by a familiar series of three short raps and Jess's voice. "Sean? Are you awake? Can I come in?"

He mouthed *shite* and got up, signalling for Genie to keep quiet. "Hold on, Jessie. I'm…er…coming."

"Ugh. I didn't need to know that. I'll be downstairs when you're done. I'd like you to meet a friend of mine."

Sean scrambled into his jeans and bolted from the room. Genie crawled back under the duvet and pulled it right up to her chin, listening like a terrified teenager in a scary movie. Sean must have caught Jess on the landing, but his voice was a deep rumble, and Genie couldn't make out the words. Whatever they were, Jess said, "OK. Seven o'clock then?" Sean repeated the time and Jess went downstairs. The bedroom door opened, and Sean stepped in, leaning back against it and running his fingers through his dark mess of hair. "How're you doing there?" he asked.

"Better," Genie said and threw back the covers. "Bloody wonderful, in fact!" She snatched up her clothes from the floor and dressed in a frenzy. "So it's just me she's ashamed of."

"I don't think that's—"

"She brought him round to see Josh. She wants to introduce him to you. But I'm supposed to fuck off for the weekend?"

"Why does that mean she's ashamed of you? Maybe she's worried you'll unknowingly drop her in it."

"And you won't? No. It's bullshit, and what was that thing about seven o'clock?"

"She wants to meet at the SU. And—"

"Great. Well, I hope she's not expecting a peaceful evening."

"I'm not going, Genie."

"Of course you're going. You're *always* in the SU on a Saturday evening."

"Not this Saturday. I have plans." Sean pushed off from the door, into Genie's space. "Plans with you." He lightly grasped her arms, but she shook him off.

"I need to have it out with her."

"You need to cool off, not go in with guns blazing. Unless I'm reading you wrong and you don't want to salvage your friendship when this has blown over?"

"If there's a friendship to salvage..." Genie was breathless, and her heart was doing some sort of steeplechase, but it was hard to sustain her anger in the face of Sean's logic. She was raring for a screaming row, which would end everything—their friendship, their house share, Genie's time at university. It was a lot to lose, and she owed it to herself to do as Sean said and cool down, even if, in the end, there was nothing worth salvaging.

10: To-Do

The Surgery
Present Day
Tuesday, 16th April

A T HOME, IN a box in the spare room, was the keypad which had secured the external door at the bottom of the stairs that led to Josh's surgery, or what *had been* Josh's surgery before he gave up the lease. Now he owned the building, it was, in effect, his 'surgery' again. The idiomatic term had been the source of much unnecessary commentary the first time around, and he was loath to repeat that nonsense, but he had yet to come up with a more suitable name, and in any case, he had a business partner to consider this time.

Of course, whether they called it a surgery, therapy suite or something trendy and modern—*Wellness Centre? Perhaps not*—was something he should consider once he'd addressed his current situation.

Without the aid of the keypad.

Dan had installed it and later uninstalled it as per the 'return the building to its original state' term of the lease. Asking Dan to reinstall it was on Josh's to-do list—a seemingly ever-expanding entity, each subsequent addition shoving down further the redecorating he'd naively believed would have seen his surgery back in operation posthaste.

That was both the benefit and drawback of contracting Jeffries and Associates: they could do everything. A brief mention to Dan that he was thinking of remodelling was all it took to set the wheels in motion: the architect would be in touch in due course, and from his 'vantage point', Josh had no trouble visualising which walls should be demolished and where new walls should be erected to create three similarly sized consultation rooms.

As for the loft conversion...Josh was a one-to-one therapist all the way, and while he could see the benefit of having a space large enough for group therapy sessions, he was doing it for Shaunna. Well, not Shaunna per se, for the Daisy Foundation, but she was also the reason he'd agreed to become a trustee. Irrespective of the foundation being named after Jess's deceased baby sister, were it not for Shaunna, it wouldn't exist, and it was still without a base of operations.

So, at Josh's first trustees meeting, he'd offered the surgery's loft space, and Shaunna had hugged the breath out of him. Sean and Eleanor had been less effusive, but they'd been looking at property for months and hadn't found anywhere suitable, so the motion had carried unanimously.

Josh switched his phone to LED again and shone the feeble glow into the lumpy gloom. There was enough junk to fill a skip, maybe two, although some of it had if not financial value, certainly intrigue.

"No. Absolutely not," Josh admonished and switched off the LED. There were far more important things to worry about than the origins of the spiritualist stockpile in his loft, like, for instance, how he was going to get down from said loft with the minimum of fuss and embarrassment when the external door was locked and both sets of keys were in his jacket pocket.

Or perhaps the door wasn't locked after all.

Josh held his breath, listening hard. *There.* Thuds at regular intervals, so quiet he had to strain to hear them, but he was sure of it. Someone was coming up the stairs.

"Sean?"

The thudding stopped, but he received no response. Truthfully, he hadn't expected one.

"Not the wiring or plumbing," he recalled, given Dan had checked both less than an hour ago. "The building cooling down?" The day was wet and not especially warm, but he hadn't turned on the heating. With the residual heat rising from the dental practice downstairs, he'd rarely needed to. "It really is very warm up here...no cold spots." Quite why he was voicing his thoughts, he didn't know. Or, rather, he did know, but he'd be keeping that part to himself because—

The thudding started again.

Cold dread fought his mortification at being discovered, and won, sending a shiver of victory right through him.

"Is someone there?"

There wasn't, he already knew. The door *was* locked, and it was Tuesday—half-day for the dental practice—so Giles and his staff were long gone. There was no-one else in the building.

He was imagining it. He had to be. If not...

"I'm being ridiculous. There is no such thing as ghosts." Rationally, he believed it, but there was no getting away from the fact that yesterday, both he *and* Libby had heard the noises and seen the toilet roll unfurl, and he wasn't imagining that dull *thud, thud, thud.*

"Come on, Joshua, keep it together." He was nine feet up with only a flimsy set of stepladders beneath him, and he was acrophobic, so of course his pulse was racing.

Breathe in, two...three...four...

Out, two...three...four...

In— "Good God!" His phone's ring could've woken the dead, had they still been sleeping. "Tierney, you..." Taking one more deep breath for good measure, he answered the incoming call. "Yes?"

"Like that, is it?"

"Like what, Sean?"

"Never mind. Are you still at the surgery?"

"Erm...no." The lie was automatic, much like the regret that followed it.

"That's good. I know I said I was coming over, and I still can do, but if you don't need me—"

"I don't."

"Don't beat about the bush, will ye?"

"Sorry, I'm preoccupied. Is everything OK?"

"I'll come back to you on that one. I'm meeting up with Phee."

"Oh? How long's she here for?"

"I'll come back to you on that one too. How are you fixed for tomorrow?"

"Tomorrow…" *A good question.* "Yes, that's fine." He hoped.

"I'll be heading over straight from the hospice, so I'll see you about four."

"I'll be here." *Still be here.*

"Great stuff. Bye for now."

"Yes, bye."

Sean left it to Josh to end the call, and he wavered briefly, almost blurting it out before his thumb tapped the red button. Even then, he contemplated calling back, but no. They'd been here before, or not *here* precisely.

Josh replayed their interchange, brief as it was and with none of the usual Tierney gush of superfluous detail. Now he thought about it, Sean hadn't been himself earlier either, which Josh had put down to a tough last morning at the clinic. There was evidently more to it, but Sean wasn't telling. There again, Josh hadn't exactly been forthcoming, and not for the same reason he was reluctant to ask anyone else for help. That incident in their university halls of residence still defied rational explanation, and trying to find one had almost driven Josh insane—may well have contributed to his clinically diagnosed insanity.

He'd only stopped when they moved out of halls into a shared house, or not stopped. Redirected his fixation away from 'the paranormal' and toward the study of topics that would help him achieve his qualifications, but the unanswered questions, always somewhere in the back of his mind, were once more rising to the fore.

That would certainly explain why he'd lied on the phone: the last thing he needed was Sean egging him on, although the call had given him a much-needed distraction, and he felt calmer for it. Well, he was still stuck nine feet in the air, but his pulse wasn't beating retreat. He considered his options.

He could try calling George again, but it would be a waste of his phone's sorely depleted battery when he'd already sent two text messages, the first a vague *'When you're done at Ellie's, I could do with a hand at the surgery. x'*, the second a slightly more to the point *'SOS. I really need you to come now. x'*; for shame, he couldn't bring himself to type the words *I'm stuck in the loft.* He had to wonder whether there was any purpose to George having a phone for emergencies when it was never to hand in an actual emergency. OK, this wasn't one, technically, and as far as he knew, George was still at Eleanor's, so in theory, he could just call Eleanor and ask to speak to George. However, there was one *tiny* problem with that strategy.

He should never have told her their trip up the Eiffel Tower had cured his phobia. Her desensitisation programme, which consisted of dragging Josh to the top of increasingly tall structures, hadn't worked, largely because he'd refused to let it. First, there had been the dome of St. Paul's Cathedral, which, because it was interesting and despite the deathly spiral steps, had been bearable. Then there had been the ride in the cable car in Conway, which had scared the living daylights out of him. He thought he may even have passed out at one point. Finally, the Eiffel Tower—step three and...success! Or not, as getting drunk first was not a coping mechanism he'd endorse, but he would rather be stuck up in a loft for all eternity than admit to Eleanor he'd been lying all along.

So, not Eleanor, and not George.

Josh opened his contacts list and scrolled. *Adele...no. If she sets eyes on this lot*—he glowered at the loft stash—*she'll think all her Christmases have come at once. Andy...he'll have me abseiling my way out. Would that be so bad?* A quick downwards glance assured him it would. *Baines Property Services...potentially.* He mentally bookmarked Gordon Baines and continued scrolling through friends and business contacts, imagining the scenario for each, all of them horrific, leaving him with a shortlist of two, neither of whom he was eager to try.

Dan or Gordon Baines. Dan. Gordon Baines. He'd have flipped a coin if he'd had one to hand. *Lesser of two evils? Hard to say, but probably Gordon.* Embarrassing as it was to have his ex-landlord come and rescue him from the top of a stepladder of only moderate height, Josh could no longer feel his legs. He made the call.

"Good afternoon, Baines Property."

"Good afternoon. Would it be possible to speak to Gordon, please?"

"Who's calling?"

"Josh Sandison."

"One moment, please." He was put on hold—no music, mercifully—and then the same voice came back on the line. "Mr. Baines is in a meeting and asked me to tell you he'll call back shortly."

Josh held in his cry of anguish. "OK. Thank you. Please do tell him it's rather urgent."

"I'll be sure to let him know."

There was a bleep in Josh's ear. He moved his phone away and stared in dismay at the call-ended notification. The fingers of his other hand were stuck in claw formation and aching from clinging to the lip of the loft hatch, and he had cramp in his buttocks from keeping them tensed for so long because if he tumbled backwards...

"Now there's an idea." Crashing through the ceiling would certainly get him down quickly, but before he could give it serious consideration, his phone started ringing, and he nearly dropped it in his haste to answer it one-handed.

"Mr. Sandison. Gordon Baines here."

Oh, thank all that is... "Hey, Gordon. I appreciate you returning my call."

"No problem. I saw your message earlier, concerning the previous tenant, but haven't had chance to reply. Any information I had on them I passed on to your solicitor with the deeds and what-have-you."

"Right, that's useful, thanks. I was also wondering if, perchance, you still have a set of keys to the building?"

"Keys to the building…" Gordon sucked his teeth, the noise crackly and distorted. Josh moved the phone away and continued listening via the speaker. "I might be wrong, but I think I only had the two sets I gave to you. Have you lost them?"

"Erm… Not lost them, as such, more…I'm locked in."

"Oh? I had the locks checked before I put the building on the market."

"Yes, and I'm sure they're all working fine."

"Then how have you locked yourself in?"

"I, erm… It's complicated." It always worked when George said it. "Can you help me or not?" Josh was being bolshy, but he'd apologise later. *Anything* to get him out of his predicament.

"If I've got them, they'll be in the safe. I'll pop and have a look and call you straight back."

"It's OK, I'll wait on the—agh! The bloody bleep again! Please, please have another set."

Josh wasn't optimistic—about anything, ever, but particularly on this occasion—thus he had no justification for being so utterly disappointed when Gordon called back and confirmed the only two sets of keys to the first floor of the building were, as he'd said, in Josh's possession. Or, in fact, several feet down and to the left of his possession.

"Damn it!"

Back to his contacts, no more horsing around. He hit the call button. It didn't even ring out once.

"Alright, mate?"

"Dan. I need your help."

"Sounds urgent. Where are you?"

"Still at my surgery." *Yes, SURGERY. To hell with them all.*

"On my way."

"Thanks, Dan. Bring—"

It was probably as well he'd hung up. He'd know better than Josh what tools were needed to break in and then…what? Fireman's-lift him down? *The shame of it!* No, that wouldn't do at all.

Time for one last try.

He'd obviously turned around when he'd come up the ladder or he wouldn't be sitting the way he was and using it as a footrest. It couldn't be any harder to do that in reverse, or it shouldn't be, but lifting one foot without seeing what he was doing was a step into the unknown, and suddenly it wasn't a nine-foot drop; it was a bottomless chasm.

With one arm braced in front, the other behind, feet facing opposite directions, his body refused to comply, and his so-called-genius-level higher cognitive functions were thoroughly overridden by fear. He couldn't complete the turn, nor could he turn back. Or so he'd thought until the swift creak of hinges followed by a loud slam startled him. He jumped, jarring his back, and somehow—even afterwards he had no idea how—caught his toes under the top rung of the ladder, pulled it upwards and set it swaying from side to side. Scrabbling frantically, he made it back onto the lip—again, he had no idea how—startling a second time when the ladder toppled and clattered down onto the floor below.

"Oh," Josh said in the tiniest voice through almost-closed lips, terrified to move so much as a cheek muscle or blink as he cast his eyes along the ladder's length, a giant, wooden arrow pointing to the previously open, now closed kitchenette door, beyond it the box containing, according to its label, the Ouija board.

Mere parlour tricks of the Victorian nouveau riche, he reminded himself, though it mattered not what he believed. With the ladder horizontal and far beneath his freely dangling feet, he was absolutely, unequivocally buggered.

11: Privilege Is as Privilege Does

High Street
Present Day
Tuesday, 16ᵗʰ April

WHAT D'YOU FANCY? Pizza? Cheeseburgers?" Sean opened the front passenger-side door of Sophie's car, offering the seat to Phee, but she cut him dead.

"Do *you* like junk food?"

"I love it. I'm not supposed to eat it, mind, but I'm happy to go wherever you want to go."

Phee ducked her head and glanced past Sean, eyeing Sophie—behind the wheel. "What does *she* want to do?"

"Sophie," Sean provided as if it had been an innocent oversight. He had a good idea what Phee was doing. She'd been perfectly pleasant the previous day—when she'd defined the terms of engagement and had his undivided attention—and he wanted her to feel safe, but he wasn't about to let her get the upper hand. "Soph? Any thoughts?"

"Oh, you know me. I'm easy. But if you're after suggestions, how about the Chinese place along the high street? Their menu is quite—"

"Look, I don't care, all right? Just…" Phee shut her eyes and exhaled loudly.

Sean took a step back and watched her face, waiting for her to open her eyes again before he asked coolly, "Are you done?"

Whether in response to his offhandedness, he couldn't say, but she finally got in the car, closing the door harder than was necessary—not quite a slam. Sean delayed a few seconds before he climbed in behind her, focusing on fastening his seat belt and reminding himself she was under duress. Meanwhile, she sat with arms crossed, staring out of the front window. Sean cleared his throat, about to prompt her to buckle in, but apparently that was enough for her to get the message. Sophie waited for her to finish before she put the car in gear and pulled away from the kerb.

Several minutes of silence later, Phee mumbled, "I'm not actually hungry."

"All right, so…shall we go to a pub?" Sean suggested.

"And drink orange juice all night? If this is the best you can do, you might as well give up now."

"The best we can do?" Sean queried. Phee had inherited her mother's talent for biting sarcasm, but there was a playfulness to it. He might get a smile out of her yet.

"You're obviously taking me out to dinner for a reason."

"We thought you'd want to get out of that hotel room for a few."

"Yeah, of course that's all there is to it."

Sophie briefly met Sean's gaze in the mirror, and he gave her a nod, happy to hand over to the expert.

"What have you eaten today, Phee?" she asked.

"Breakfast at the hotel. Continental. Just the smell of the Full English made me vomit."

Sophie hummed, sympathetic but noncommittal.

"You've told her, I take it?" Phee peered over her shoulder, addressing Sean.

"Aye. Is that all right?"

"It'll have to be, won't it?" She turned to face front again. "And what do you think I should do, Sophie?"

"About what?"

"Being pregnant, obviously."

"What do you want to do?"

"Keep the baby."

"Uh-huh." Sophie signalled right. Sean frowned. He'd figured out where she was taking them, and it was a good choice but not one he'd have made.

A few minutes passed without further conversation and with Phee itching to speak. Perhaps they were doing her a disservice by not giving the lecture she was clearly expecting and instead taking a professional stance, leaving the way open for her to say as much or as little as she wanted.

Sophie pulled up to the kerb and turned to Phee with a smile. "Here we are."

"Here being?"

"My house."

"Yours?" Phee eyed the building in disbelief. It was a detached house, quite large and well-kept, but unimpressive to someone of Phee's social standing. "Aren't you a student?"

"Postgrad, yes," Sophie confirmed. "I live with my parents."

"But..." Phee wagged her finger between Sean and Sophie. "You have a child."

"Yes."

"You don't live together?"

"No."

"And you're still a couple? How does that work?"

Sophie turned off the engine and unfastened her seat belt. "Come in and see for yourself." She opened the car door, asking as she got out, "Who wants tea and toast?"

"Wh...?" The door closed on Phee's unfinished question.

"Soph's tea and toast is fantastic," Sean said.

"I'm sure it is, but what the hell?" Her anger was a defence mechanism and not an easy one to break down, but Sean would have to work with it.

"All right." He sat forward and casually leaned his elbows on the back rests. He'd give her like for like. "What were you hoping to achieve?"

"I don't know what you're asking. By getting pregnant? It was an accident. I didn't—"

"By coming all the way up here to see me." He wouldn't normally interrupt a patient, but, he reminded himself, Phee wasn't one.

She pursed her lips, letting the air escape in a series of little pops as she thought about her answer. Sean detected the very short moment she considered lying before she shrugged and relented. "I don't know, honestly. I think…I just needed to tell someone?"

Sean nodded to show she had his attention while giving her the opportunity to elaborate. Instead, she opened the glove box, which contained the manual for the car stereo and a baby-blue waffle blanket, right now the most fascinating objects in the world. She wasn't going to get there on her own.

"Did it matter who?" Sean asked.

"Kind of. I wanted to talk to a grown-up. Yes, I know I'm nearly eighteen. I mean a proper grown-up, someone…older. Sorry. I don't wish to be insulting."

"Well, I am getting on a bit."

A whisper of a smile sneaked past Phee's guarded resistance. "Mum says you're older than her."

"By about three years, aye." It had seemed a much greater difference when they were at university. Now they were in their forties, it was nothing, especially compared to the near decade between Phee and Paul.

"She talks about you a lot," Phee said.

"Does she now?" He was pleasantly surprised to hear that, and it must've shown because Phee gave him a wary but amused smirk.

"Usually when she's pissed off with me."

"That's not so great."

"And sometimes when she's not," Phee modified. "Apparently, I inherited your cheeky charm." From the way she was reading him, his 'cheeky charm' wasn't all he'd passed on.

"I suppose there are worse things."

Phee's eyebrows rose. "Such as?"

Too many to count, and maybe she had a right to know about some of them, but this wasn't the time. "I'll write you a list," he said. Now she was a little more at ease, Sean steered them back on track. "You said you needed to tell someone, and I'm glad to be that person, but, well, you told me and then you shut yourself away in your hotel room."

"Because you freaked out."

"I did, that's true. Which is why Sophie offered to accompany us this evening. She's not so easily scared."

"Of course she's not. She's a woman."

"You're on to something there, for sure, but there's another reason." He needed to take care with his words. "I don't know what the situation is with you and Paul—"

"It was consensual." Phee's defences went straight back up.

"I'm not saying he pushed you into anything, but he is your mother's boyfriend…your stepdad."

"No!" She swivelled in her seat and glared, less with fury than determination. "He's never been my *stepdad*. He's only eight years older than me!"

"It doesn't matter. You're not yet eighteen, and he's an adult in a position of trust. Do you understand what that means?"

"It's child abuse? I'm not a child!"

"As far as the law's concerned—"

"You're wrong."

"No, Phee, I'm not—"

"Yes, *Sean*, you are." Yanking her bag open, she pulled out her phone and poked the button, to no effect. "Shit. Can I borrow yours?"

"To do what?"

"Prove I'm right."

Sean's phone was in his pocket, but he hesitated in handing it over. What she wanted to show him might put him in an even more difficult position.

"Forget it. I'll ask Sophie." She was out of the car and away towards the house before Sean registered what she'd said.

He heard the bell ring and held back to give Sophie time to answer. She knew how to handle Phee, and it was nothing to do with her being a woman, or maybe it was, to an extent. She might only be at the start of her PhD, but Sophie had already earned herself a reputation as an excellent children's and young people's counsellor and was a better psychologist than Sean would ever be.

A brief interchange took place on the doorstep before Phee, with chin jutting defiantly to cover her uncertainty, went inside. Sophie frowned at Sean by way of asking if he was coming in. He supposed he ought, though she'd find more use in a chocolate fireguard. At least she had the decency to not laugh when he caught his foot in the seat belt and near fell flat on his face exiting the car. Miraculously, he made it inside the house without further substantiating his ineptitude, and she squeezed his arm in reassurance as she leaned around him to point her key fob at the car. *Good old Soph.* He hadn't intended to offload his troubles onto her, but he was glad she'd let him do so.

"How about that tea and toast?" She led the way up the stairs to her and Dylan's quarters. "Or I can make you something else?"

"Tea and toast is fine, thanks," Phee replied, a little fazed. "This is an apartment?"

"Kind of." Sophie directed Phee—and Sean, who'd been there countless times and knew the way but was a little fazed himself—into her living room. "My mum and dad live downstairs, Dylan and I live up here, and we share the kitchen. Make yourselves comfy. I won't be long."

"I'll make it if you like," Sean offered—reluctantly. He didn't mind doing it, and would rather that than be turned to stone by Phee's dark gaze, but he'd meant what he'd said about Sophie's toast being fantastic. She claimed it was mere luck at happening upon a decent toaster that consistently popped out beautiful squares of even golden brown. Sean remained convinced the soft yet crispy, hot but not too hot, generously buttered and ultimately delicious toast was the product of a sorcery to which only a select few were privy.

Sophie dismissed his offer with a stern, "Sit," and pointed him at the sofa. What else could he do but as he was told?

Phee loitered until Sophie had gone and then wandered the perimeter of the room, examining the photos on the mantelpiece and the certificates that hung in the alcoves to either side.

"Dylan's," she murmured, leaning closer to read his *Star of the Week* award for 'helping other children' and then brushing her fingertips over the glass covering his green-paint handprints. "I've just realised…" she said, moving on to the other alcove without finishing the sentence. She studied Sophie's certificates for a while before she asked, "Were you her lecturer?"

"For her counselling diploma and Master's degree, I was," Sean confirmed, then added, in case she was collecting ammunition, "after we got together."

Phee nodded and continued her perusal along the bookshelves on the next wall. She took her time, only finishing as Sophie came back upstairs, though Sean imagined Phee would have been hard pushed to name one title on those shelves.

Sophie set the tray she'd brought on the long, low table in the centre of the room and handed out small plates. "Help yourselves," she invited. "And say if you want more, OK?"

"Thank you." Phee collected the top-most slice of toast from the plate on the tray and took it to the armchair next to the empty fireplace.

"Thanks, Soph." Sean waited until she was settled beside him before he grabbed a piece for himself. He was gagging for a cup of tea, but the pot needed to stand a bit longer, so he sat back and picked at his toast, watching Phee, who appeared to be staring into the dark grate, lost in thought, but her eyes were turned to her left—Dylan's alcove—lending credence to Sean's interpretation of what she'd 'just realised'.

"So, Phee, how are things with your mum and grandparents these days?"

Phee shrugged and took another bite of her toast, eyes averted. "They're still not speaking."

"And your aunt…what's her name again?"

"Isla."

"That's right. I never met her."

"Neither have I." Her shudder cut off Sean's reading of how she felt about not knowing her aunt. She put the uneaten half of her toast on the plate. "I'm sorry. It's delicious and everything, but I can't decide if it's making me feel more sick or less. Is that normal?" She looked to Sophie for an answer.

"Well, they say every pregnancy is different, but it got me like that too."

"Please tell me it goes away soon." She'd become very pale.

"Mine stopped around fourteen weeks."

"Fourteen weeks?" She closed her eyes and breathed slowly and deeply.

Watching her battle the nausea hotwired Sean's brain, setting off an irrepressible surge of emotion and a need to ease her suffering, the same as he felt for Dylan.

"He's your half-brother," he said.

Phee gave a weak smile. "Yeah. It hit me before." She looked up at the green handprints. "Is he with a babysitter tonight?"

"No. He's downstairs with my parents," Sophie said. "I don't know if he's still awake. Should I go and see?"

"I'd like to meet him."

"OK." Sophie popped the last of her toast into her mouth and used gestures to instruct Sean to pour the tea on her way out of the room. He did the honours.

"If you're going to eat that, you'd be wise to do it before Dylan gets here. He likes his food, he does."

Phee took another bite and chewed carefully, making a bitter-pill face as she swallowed. She shuddered again. "Where's the bathroom?" She put her plate on the table and stood.

"Door at the end of the landing."

"Thanks." She didn't move an inch. "I think it's going away again. God, it's awful. They should tell you about this in sex ed. No-one would ever get pregnant again."

Sean laughed quietly at her joke. By his female colleagues' accounts, morning sickness was but the first trial of many in pregnancy. Somehow, he didn't think Phee would appreciate hearing that. "You have sugar in your tea, don't you?"

"Two, please."

She sat again, this time settling back into the chair with her feet underneath her. Some of the colour had returned to her cheeks. Sean finished stirring her tea and handed it to her.

"Thanks." She smiled up at him. "And thank you for not putting me straight back on the train."

"I'd never have done that."

"Or calling my mum."

"Ah, well, that's another matter."

"If you have to…"

"Legally—" Sean began, but she cut him off as she had in the car.

"I told you. Paul didn't break any laws. Does Sophie have a computer?"

"In her bedroom. Look, I don't need to see proof, Phee."

"Why? Because you *know* I'm wrong?"

"Tell me why you're not," Sean challenged.

"Paul isn't my legal guardian, is he?"

"He's still an adult with a duty of care towards you."

"No, he's Mum's boyfriend. You know? Like you're the sperm donor?"

She'd made Sean more than that the moment she'd confided in him, but he understood what she was saying. Legally, he had no parental responsibility. Genie had insisted on it, even when she was alone with a small child, no job and nowhere to live. It hadn't stopped Sean sending money when he could afford to and offering support as a friend, but his obligation was to Genie, not Phee, and maintaining Phee's confidence jeopardised that friendship. Even so, she was right about Paul; irrespective of the immorality of taking up with his girlfriend's seventeen-year-old daughter, he hadn't committed a crime.

For now, Sean was satisfied that Phee wasn't at risk, and Genie thought she was staying with a friend. There was no real urgency to act, and he could justify keeping what he knew to himself, but he was optimistic he could at least persuade Phee to tell her mum where she was and was big enough to admit it was, in part, self-serving. Of course, unless Phee planned on doing the same kind of moonlight flit her mother had, Genie would find out soon enough about the pregnancy. As for the rest—that, too, would have to wait, as Sophie had returned with their very sleepy son.

"Look, Dylan." She stopped in the doorway to give him a chance to assess the situation. His smile at seeing his daddy evaporated when he noticed Phee, and he snuggled into Sophie's neck, alternately closing his eyes and then peeping to see if the stranger was still there. "That's Phee," Sophie said. "Are you going to say hello?"

Dylan shook his head.

"Hi, Dylan." Phee's cheery tone was slightly higher than her husky speaking voice—another thing she'd inherited from her mother. Dylan scowled, unimpressed.

"It's not you," Sophie assured her. "He's always like this with new people."

Phee smiled. "It's OK. Margaret who works for my mum brought her granddaughter with her last Christmas, and she was the same at first."

Sophie came in and sat on the sofa, Dylan clinging to her like a baby macaque. He didn't even let go when she tore off a finger of toast and offered it to him.

"Must be shattered, poor little fella," Sean said, using the statement to cover that he was checking the time. It had been a long, stressful day, but he didn't want to put additional pressure on Phee. All the while, her eyes hadn't strayed from Dylan, nor his from her.

"You're a cutie," she cooed. He buried his face in Sophie's shirt. Phee sighed. "I'm going to tell Mum," she said, still watching Dylan. "But I need to talk to Paul first." Sean and Sophie gave each other a sideways glance. When Sean looked back at Phee, she met his gaze and held it. "I know what you think, but the only abuse here is of Mum's trust. I wish we'd waited until they'd officially broken it off."

"Is it on the cards?" Sophie asked.

Phee nodded. "They hardly spend any time together. Paul's got a place in London. I think they're just too lazy to—" She grimaced. "Sorry. Never mind."

Again, Sean and Sophie glanced at each other but with knowing smiles. It wasn't the first time someone had passed that same judgement on their relationship. People usually assumed they were separated and had joint custody, but they were happy living apart. They shared the burden when Dylan was giving them merry hell; they both continued to develop their careers; it was right for them.

"Don't worry," Sean comforted, as Phee was still mortified by what she'd said. She'd yet to learn to moderate her thoughts before they reached her mouth—some people never mastered it— but in the ways that mattered, she was mature and understood the consequences of her actions. Facing those consequences was another thing entirely, and Sean was reminded of what Sophie had said in his office earlier that afternoon about Phee's reasons for coming to him. "Would you like me to talk to your mum for you, or come with you?"

"No—thanks—but if she kicks me out…"

"You are always welcome, lovely."

Sophie nodded. "Yes, you are."

Dylan trumped in his nappy.

"See?" Sean said with a wink. "Even your wee half-brother agrees."

12: In Front of Every Good Man...

A SERIES OF THUMPS, dull, deep and likely emanating from a fist, echoed up the stairwell while a torrent of foul language poured out of Josh's phone.

"I can't pick this...stupid...bloody..." Another bang was followed by a muted roar. "That's it," Dan said. "I'm calling the locksmith."

"No!" The word was out before Josh could check himself. "I don't want a locksmith."

"The guy's not cheap, but he's good," Dan argued, no doubt mistaking Josh's petulance for miserliness, but the cost was irrelevant; he simply could not take more ridicule, even if that which he'd endured so far had been his own. His curiosity had made a fool of him, and his pride had ensured he'd had plenty of time to reflect.

"Have you tried shouldering it?" Josh suggested, bravado courtesy of desperation.

"Are you having a laugh? They've got flimsier doors on Fort Knox."

It was a very sturdy door, Josh had to agree. In retrospect, insisting Dan had a few more details before he came a-charging to the rescue would have been wiser, because why would he carry a lock pick or a ladder either in or on his trusty steed?

"Just call the locksmith," Josh relented.

"No need. I've got a plan."

"What kind of plan?"

"Breaking and entering with the owner's permission."

"Don't you dare involve the police in this."

"Who said anything about involving the police? No, I'm gonna…"

Dan went on, but Josh was no longer listening, his brain providing documentary-style footage of half a dozen uniformed officers arriving with a big metal rammer, battering his door down and charging up the stairs. *Hello, hello, hello, what's all this then?* Oh, how they'd laugh.

"…replace the window, but it'll be cheaper than a new lock. Won't be long."

"Wait!" Josh shouted. "Wait! Dan! Where are you going? Don't leave me here!" If he sounded panicked…well, he was, but there was the bleep of Dan's car alarm deactivating and he ended the call. He'd gone, presumably to fetch a ladder, and all Josh could do was wait.

He stared at his phone screen, his mood darkening with it, and added 'fix broken window' to his mental list. It would have to be one on the front of the building too, seeing as the gate leading from the alley into the backyard was locked, and the key was on the same bunch as the rest. *Unless I call Mr. Giles… No.* Josh was his landlord and before that shared business premises with him for fourteen years, yet he barely knew the man, which was entirely on Josh, given Giles had made every effort to befriend him.

"A front window it is. There can't be *that* many people around at this time, can there?" Josh checked: the middle of rush hour. "Just bloody perfect—actually, *how* is he going to bring a ladder here?" He was thinking aloud. "Or maybe I'm talking to you, *oh source of unexplained phenomena.*"

Structural or imagined audience notwithstanding, the fact remained: Dan's convertible lacked a roof to which a rack could be affixed. No rack, thus no means to transport a ladder, therefore a further delay in the proceedings, and Josh's need for the loo was threatening to surpass his other concerns.

There was no purpose whatsoever to constantly waking his phone. Indeed, it was counter-productive with eleven percent battery life remaining when he and Dan may need to coordinate their efforts. It was a tremendous test of his willpower, but Josh deactivated the screen and tried to think of something else—anything but his full bladder and the mute throb in his lower legs. He gingerly shifted position and searched his brain for inspiration.

I wonder what's for dinner. George and Libby would have eaten already, having assumed—entirely reasonably—that Josh had lost track of the time, and George still wouldn't have seen the messages and missed calls. Josh thought about calling Libby, an option he'd rejected outright earlier because she'd been with Shaunna and, painful as it was to admit it, he no longer trusted Shaunna to keep his confidence with Sean. Josh would tell Sean himself when he was ready.

Disliking the path his thoughts had taken, he checked his phone again—ten percent—and searched the vicinity for distractions. A few feet away, almost in arm's reach, there was a small mahogany box, an eight-inch cube. From Dan's earlier inventory of 'all that psychic crap', Josh surmised the box contained a crystal ball, and if he shuffled a little to his right, he was sure he could reach it—that or fall through the ceiling, and there was no predicting the outcome, which struck him as suitably ironic.

That was as far as his contemplation of more foolish pursuits went, his attention caught by the clangs of an aluminium ladder being placed and extended. Dan had made it back far quicker than Josh had anticipated. He couldn't see any of the front windows from where he was but listened hard, trying to discern what was going on from the type and proximity of each clang. By the sound of it, Dan was ascending the ladder; Josh counted the steps—twenty in all—with breath held, but still jumped when he heard a loud rap on the window. *This is it.* Pressing his fingers to his ears and closing his eyes, he waited for the smash.

It didn't come.

Plastic creaked as the window frame was prised apart; a tool scraped along the resultant gap. Two short, sharp clicks suggested the safety hinges had popped off their rivets, followed by the thud of something landing on the floor, or *someone*, because there were footsteps, and then—

"Hiya!"

Josh's eyes sprang open and he peered down in astonishment at his grinning rescuer. "Adele! Hey! Where's Dan?"

"Holding the ladder, or he was. D'you want me to help you down first or go and let him in?"

"I would very much like to get down."

"OK," Adele agreed cheerfully and bent to pick up the stepladder, backing up as she lifted it into a vertical position. "Aren't you scared of heights?"

"Yes. But clearly, you're not. You just climbed through an upstairs window."

"Oh, I used to do it all the time. Usually drunk." Her tone was dismissive, but then she frowned and hummed quietly, as if the danger had only now dawned on her. She shrugged it off. "What are you doing up there, by the way?"

"I came up to look at—" Josh remembered who he was talking to. "Never mind. Can we just…"

"Get you down," Adele finished for him.

"Please."

"Hmm. Let's think." Steadying the ladder with one hand and tapping her teeth with the vibrant pink index fingernail of the other, Adele studied the loft hatch for ten seconds or more, or probably less, but Josh's patience had departed some time ago. As he reached the point where leaping to freedom and using Adele to cushion his landing seemed his best chance of escape, she said, "I've got it."

"Good stuff." He sounded positively jovial, but his pulse was accelerating and threatening to blow out his eardrums. Desperate as he was to get down, he still had to do exactly that, and he was terrified. Rather than give in to it, he focused on Adele, who was calm and in control, and in that moment, when he was depending on her to save his neck, he realised, for the first time in their thirty-six-year acquaintance, he trusted her with his life.

"Now, Josh, if you can move your feet back a teeny, tiny bit," she instructed as she extended the ladder and secured the two halves, not in their usual A-formation but in one perpendicular length, which she angled towards the opposite side of the hatch to where Josh perched, stiff-legged, as if he were sitting on a chair, but still managed to do as she said. He kept his eyes fixed on hers as she lifted, tipped and pulled the ladder back. She glanced up and smiled. "Nearly there." Josh heard the quiet buzz of a vibrating phone. "Dan," she said and huffed. "Thinks I've forgotten him. D'you know, he was going to take out the entire window? Idiot." She gave the ladder another tug. "Is it resting securely?"

"I think so?" Josh's impression was that she'd only asked him so he wouldn't feel quite so useless, and he appreciated her efforts but was more than happy to defer.

"Fab. Now, you need to lean forward and put your feet on the closest rung."

"OK." Josh took a big breath…and didn't move. "I can't."

"You can."

"I can't."

"'No such word as can't,' my dad used to say, which is silly because there is. But whatever, you can. I know you can. Remember the first time you came down your loft stairs at home?"

"Yes." He could still see it in his mind's eye—staring down those steep, metal stairs, thinking if he ever made it to the bottom, he would never, ever go up there again. But everyone had gone to so much trouble on his behalf, he'd had to try. Same as tonight. In fact, this was easier. He didn't have to step into thin air.

He could do this. He was already almost on the ladder. And then he was on the ladder. And, finally, he was at the bottom of the ladder, stepping onto terra firma, or not, but there was floor beneath his feet and that was good enough.

"See?" Adele gave him a big beaming, ever so slightly smug grin, and then squeaked under the pressure of his hug.

"Adele, my saviour! I love you. Thank you," he gushed. "Sorry. Got to go." He released her and fled the room, accompanied by her giggles.

"I'll go and let in pain-in-the-ass, if that's OK?" she called.

"Sure." He didn't care about anything other than the pure, glorious relief of making it to the toilet, and he positively relished the pins and needles in his bottom. So, he now had a method for getting down from a loft as well as getting up, but he had no plans to test it anytime soon. Or ever again. Once Dan and Andy's contractors had installed the stairs and lift, there would be no need. In the meantime, he'd ask someone else to empty the loft, but it could wait.

By the time Josh emerged, Dan was almost done reattaching the window vent through which Adele had crawled. "Thanks." Josh met her gaze as he said it; after all, she'd done the hard work.

"No worries." Dan carefully pulled the vent shut. "It's secure, but the hinges will need replacing."

"OK. I'll deal with that in the morning." It was a small price to pay and much cheaper than having to replace the entire unit.

"Our Andy could probably sort that for you. I'd volunteer myself, but I'm in Wales for the next couple of days."

"If he wouldn't mind." It would save adding it to the list, such as it made a difference by this point.

"Where do these go?" Adele asked, holding the stepladders, which she'd already collapsed.

"In the—not in there!" Josh watched, statue-like, as Adele swung the kitchenette door open.

"Sorry!" She shut the door again and turned towards him for further instruction, but he didn't get as far as issuing it and saw the moment her brain processed the visual data from the room. She turned back, quite slowly, but Josh was dumbfounded so let her prop the ladders against the wall and open the door a second time. Reverently, she advanced and picked up the Ouija board box with both hands. "Where did this come from? Is it yours?"

Josh's laughter was equal parts incredulity and hysteria. "What do you think?"

"Then whose is it?"

"I don't know, but…" Maybe she could help him. "There's more."

"Really?" She was almost hyperventilating in excitement.

Dan shook his head. "Mental. I'm gonna take our Mike's van and ladder back. See you in twenty."

"OK. Tell him thanks," Josh said. He watched until Dan was no longer in sight and then looked back at Adele. "Would you like to do me a favour?"

Adele peered up at the open hatch and back at Josh, blinking in query. He nodded. She jigged up and down—"Yay!"—and wasted no time in returning the Ouija board to its prior location and putting the ladder back in situ. Up and down she went, spritely, confident, providing a running commentary on her progress. It wasn't until she descended with the last load that Josh noticed she was wearing running shoes rather than her usual high heels. Adele was petite—five foot two in stockinged feet—but tonight she was a giant of admirable strength.

"This stuff is amazing!" She leaned a folded table against the wall and dug in her pocket. "Look at these." She walked over to Josh and handed him a pack of tarot cards. "I'll shut the hatch," she said and verily flew back up to do so.

Josh held the cards away from him as if they might explode and offloaded them as soon as Adele had put the ladders away. She hadn't laughed at him for getting stuck in the loft, but she was definitely amused by his reaction to the items she'd brought down.

"Can I open them?" she asked.

"If you must."

She pulled out the tab, carefully tipping the box so the cards slid against her palm. "Wow... Do they look hand-painted to you?"

Josh squinted at the pictures on the cards. They were highly detailed with fine lines and lots of colour, but he couldn't see them well enough without his glasses. "If they are hand-painted, that would make them valuable, wouldn't it?"

"I'd say so." Adele flipped through the pack, pausing to study a card here and there. "What are you gonna do with it all?"

"Sell it, I suppose." Until that point, the only thing he'd cared about was getting it all out of his surgery, and it was still his primary consideration, but sell it?

"I'll buy it from you." Adele fed the tarot cards back into their packet and carefully set them down on top of the pile. She pirouetted to face him, stopping before she completed the spin, her mouth a tiny, surprised 'o'.

Josh sandwiched his lips between his teeth, clamping them tightly, attempting to clear his mind of all thoughts associated with tarot cards and Ouija boards and doors slamming and self-powered toilet rolls. He almost succeeded too, but Adele wasn't fooled. She took a couple of tiptoed steps towards him, all the while with her gaze locked on his face—by now a good shade pinker than her nails.

"You don't want to sell, do you?"

"It's not that..." he began, but he couldn't do it. He couldn't bare-faced lie to Adele even if he had done so many times before, back in the days when he'd believed she lacked the level of awareness required to know he was lying to her or talking down to her or any of the other frankly dreadful ways he'd treated her and everyone else. *Josh Sandison, therapist* had not been a very nice person. Keeping the emotional dam in place had been a job in itself, and it was an unparalleled relief to not have to do that anymore. But could he trust Adele with this?

"I want to know whose it is, or was, and return it to them if I can."

Adele's perfect pencilled eyebrows rose, along with the corners of her mouth. She fought both, to no avail. She didn't believe him, and rightly so. In spite of his mini-epiphany, he was still lying through his teeth.

"Why don't you have Botox injections?" Josh asked and then gasped, horrified he'd thought it out loud.

"Pardon?" Adele blinked in astonishment.

"I just…well, I noticed…" Josh sighed. "You can frown. That's all I meant."

Back to being amused, Adele scratched her head for show. "Actually, I do have Botox, but the techniques are very advanced these days. I can frown—" she did so "—scowl—" it was a rubbish scowl but nonetheless demonstrated full control of her facial muscles "—grin like a chimpanzee—" and that was just hilarious.

"Yes, I've got it now, thank you." Josh snorted, pleased Adele was laughing too. "I'm sorry."

"Why?"

"That was really rude of me."

"I've always liked your honesty," she said, which brought him up short. All those years of avoiding him in one-to-one situations suggested otherwise. "I just don't like you looking into my head," she qualified.

Ah, yes. That. He tried not to, he really did, but it was like trying to hold back the tide, particularly with Adele. Still, she continued to surprise him.

"If you're thinking about injections for yourself—"

"God, no," Josh dismissed quickly, but then… "Do you think it's something I should consider?" He took out his phone, using the dark screen as a mirror, and made some exaggerated facial expressions. *Not too wrinkly yet.*

Adele shrugged. "It's up to you, sweetie." She hardly ever called him 'sweetie'—only when she had the upper hand. "But if you do decide to go for it, I can put you in touch with just the right person."

"Thanks." Josh was glad for the tangent their conversation had taken. He was ready to address other matters now and eyed the stash from the loft. "I *do* want to return it to its rightful owner—or descendant thereof, perhaps—but not yet. I want to research what all these props—"

"Tools," Adele corrected.

"I want to know how they work, what they're supposed to do."

"I can tell you what they *do*," Adele corrected him again.

"All of them?"

She gave the pile a cursory glance. "Yep."

"Wow. OK, well, erm…"

"Would you like me to store them for you?"

Josh nodded slowly, not a 'yes' yet; he was considering…or trying to make himself consider because he'd decided already. "Do you have room for them?"

Adele grinned. "I have a very big house."

Josh laughed at her brag. He'd yet to visit Adele and Dan's new house, but he'd seen photos, and she wasn't exaggerating. "Yes, please. I'd rather no-one knew about this."

"I won't breathe a word," she promised, even though she was forever letting secrets slip, but it was the best she had. "If we hurry, we'll get it all in your car before Dan gets back."

"Good thinking." Josh retrieved his keys from his jacket, took the cards and pendulum, left Adele with the runes and crystal ball, and went ahead to unlock the car. A second trip saw the lamps and tables brought down.

"Only the Ouija board and the gong to go," she said, poking two large, ugly brass lamps into what was left of Josh's boot space before they went back up for the last of it. "Which do you want?"

"Gong," Josh answered without hesitation. Just the thought of touching the box containing the Ouija board gave him the heebie-jeebies. He picked up the very light gong; it reverberated with each step as he followed Adele downstairs.

"Have you ever played with a Ouija board?" he asked.

"Used, yes, because it's not a toy," Adele said. "Too many times to count." They reached the bottom of the stairs, and she held the door open for him, then ushered him out.

"Why that rather than something else?"

"Well, with the tables and pendulum, you can only ask yes/no questions. The Ouija board's sort of a bit like text messaging the Spirit World."

"The original SMS," Josh mused. He waited for Adele to load the Ouija board into his car and then laid the gong on top, quickly shutting the boot when he heard the smooth, low growl of Dan's convertible approaching.

Dan drew up at the kerb and lowered his window. "All done?"

Adele looked at Josh rather than answer.

"All done," he confirmed.

She hugged him and whispered, "Come over Thursday evening. He'll still be in Cardiff."

"OK," Josh whispered back.

Adele released him and dashed around to the passenger side of Dan's car, offering a little wave before she climbed in.

"See you Friday," Dan said.

"And not before." Josh saw them off and went back inside to collect his jacket, well and truly ready for home. He was so exhausted he didn't even bother going around to check if all the lights were off and the doors and windows were shut.

But he wasn't so exhausted he missed the dark square in the ceiling formed by the open loft hatch.

13: One Man's Treasure

Lime Street Station
Present Day
Wednesday, 17th April

Now, are you sure about this?" Sean pulled on the handbrake and switched off the ignition, ducking to take in the façade of the train station beyond the windscreen. Liverpool Lime Street had undergone a few face lifts since he first laid eyes on it all those years ago. As a naïve young Irish fella newly arrived in England, it had signified the beginning of an amazing journey, and he'd relished the adventure of travelling solo, striking up conversations with every stranger who'd stay still long enough to chat. As a forty-three-year-old father about to put his seventeen-year-old progeny on an intercity train, the enormous automatic doors may as well have been the gaping maw of hell itself.

No answer forthcoming, he looked to his passenger. "Are you all right?" A daft question whenever it was asked but especially at this ungodly hour and asked of a woman running the gauntlet with morning sickness. Nevertheless, Phee deigned to give him an answer, in the form of a short nod and hum in the affirmative through clamped lips. "If you'd let me drive you, we could stop for a break whenever you want."

"Thanks, but no."

He'd hoped to wear her down, having offered the same several times since last night, after she'd sent him the text to say she'd booked onto the first train to London Euston, but she was sticking to her guns in a spectacular demonstration of *what goes around comes around*. Now he knew how his mother had felt, watching her youngest son leave for a strange new land, and it was damned difficult to stop himself making the same demand of Phee. *Promise you won't go to London. Go home to your mum where I know you're safe and loved.* But she was going, and he could like it or lump it.

"Did you get a hold of Paul in the end?"

A short head shake.

"So he doesn't know you're coming. What if he's not there?"

"He will be, don't worry."

Sean chuckled ruefully. "There's no chance of that, young Phee. Well, come on, then. Let's get you safely on that there train." He was out of the car before she could protest that he didn't need to accompany her onto the platform. Just as he couldn't change her mind, she wouldn't change his.

The doors swished open to admit them, and Phee strode confidently ahead, her eyes on the Departures board. She slowed to read it, then turned on the spot, scanning the platform numbers until she found hers, sparing a scowl for Sean as she set off again. "You can leave me here. I know where to go, and I'm sure you have a lot to do."

"That I do." He strolled along beside her, pretending he wasn't getting the measure of the other folks heading for the London train, mostly commuters dashing, heads down, single-minded and oblivious. "But I won't be doing it until I've seen you on your way."

"Is it a private clinic, where you work?"

"No. A hospice."

"Won't they mind if you arrive late?"

"I'm not in until ten, but I'm hoping to put in a couple of hours at home first, sorting out the junk in my attic, just in case."

"In case you want to buy more junk?"

Sean glanced sideways at her. "My door's always open to you, Phee."

"I bet you say that to all the girls."

"Honestly? I say it to everyone. And I mean it too." He held eye contact with her until she broke away.

"What do you do at the hospice?" she asked.

"I'm part of a team—doctors, nurses, carers, counsellors—who provide end-of-life care."

"Is it stressful?"

"It can be, but it's very fulfilling." He wished they'd started this conversation two days ago when there was time to do it properly. "Do you have any thoughts on a career yet, or are you leaving your options open?"

"Law."

"Following in your mum's footsteps."

"I am," Phee said, and she sounded proud to be doing so. "I've already learnt tons of useful stuff, not just from Mum. From her friend Jess. She's a family solicitor—or she was. She's dead now. That's what I want to be, but I don't know if I can anymore. I was supposed to start uni in September."

Sean's heart was still going like the clappers at the mention of Jess. Genie mustn't have told Phee that Jess had been one of his friends too, and a lot more than that. Were it not for Jess and Josh's friendship, Sean might never have met Genie, and Phee's conception wouldn't have happened. Sean would've liked to share that with her; he thought she'd appreciate the insight. But again, it wasn't the right time, so he returned to what she'd said about uni. "You still could go, you know. Sophie—"

"I don't want to." The abruptness of her interruption was startling but, as Sean had learned over the past two days, not out of character. She was a straight shooter when she chose to be, so he pushed a bit harder because a lot of younger people weren't aware that it was possible to be a parent and pursue a career at the same time.

"Can I ask why not?"

"I want to do it right—have the baby, study, then my career. I have it all planned out. Kind of."

"Is that so?" Sean wasn't sure what to make of that statement. Had she planned to get pregnant? It put a very different slant on things if she had, yet she'd been adamant it was an accident, so perhaps they were talking at cross-purposes. That was too deep and contentious a discussion to have in a train station, particularly as they'd reached the barrier, and it was more important they said goodbye on a positive note so Phee felt she could count on his support in future.

He glanced along the platform and consciously relaxed the deep frown that had him gozzy-eyed from trying to see past his eyebrows. Good, strong eyebrows they were too, which Shaunna was itching to attack with her wax strips—'just to tidy them up a little'. She'd have to strap him to a chair first. He'd tried plucking them once, way back, when he'd cared that he was a scruffy gorilla in contrast to his well-groomed peers. He'd still got the jobs and the women, though he'd never fully understood why, but his looks had mattered less to him as time went on. These days, he was mostly happy with his lot, bushy eyebrows and all.

He gestured to the snazzy new train Phee would be boarding imminently. "That's like Cinderella's carriage compared to the old steam locomotive I got from here when I came to study."

"Really?"

"Aye. Well, not the steam bit. It wasn't that long ago. Twenty-two and a half years..." On mornings like this, when the air was cool and dewy, with all the same sights and sounds, it felt like only yesterday. "I got shocking drunk on the overnight ferry and fell asleep just before we docked. If the crew hadn't woken me up, I'd have ended up back in Belfast."

Phee laughed and then shuddered. "There's no chance of that happening to me on this train."

"A good thing," Sean said. "So what's your plan?"

"Plan?" Her eyes went startle-wide, and Sean's gut clenched. He had an awful feeling he'd been right about it not being an accident, but he'd meant in the short-term and clarified as such.

"Today. You're going straight to see Paul, are you?"

"Oh! Yes. His offices are near Euston—a five-minute walk. I'll tell him about…" she rubbed lightly over her abdomen "…and that I'm giving him a chance to talk to Mum before I do."

"Right. So you'll be heading home after you've seen Paul, will you?"

"God, for a sperm donor, you're a seriously overbearing father."

Sean winked. "I'd do the same for anyone." It was true, but there were deeper motivations at work on this occasion. His commitment to Genie, for one.

The guard at the barrier gave a last call for passengers.

"I'd better go," Phee said.

"All right. Will you call me to let me know you've arrived safe and sound?"

"In London or back home?"

"Both."

"See? Overbearing." Phee's twinkly-eyed grin was one Sean knew well. He'd seen it in the mirror often enough.

"Cheeky, you." He wanted to hug her, but he settled for giving her a firm but hopefully not too businesslike nod and then grunted in surprise when she threw herself at him and squeezed fiercely.

"Thanks for everything," she said.

"You're welcome."

She released him and moved off, walking backwards. "Thank Sophie for me?"

"I will. You have a safe journey."

She nodded and smiled, a little tearfully, Sean thought. Within seconds, she was through the turnstile and hurrying along the train to her carriage. She waved as she boarded, and Sean waved back. He waited while the doors closed, the whistle blew and the train pulled away from the platform, then he returned to the car, using the drive home to mentally inventory what he thought was in his attic rather than worry about what Phee had got herself into.

***

It was a sad fact, but ruthlessness wasn't a quality Sean possessed, which was no bad thing. Who needed a ruthless psychologist, after all? However, when it came to tackling the abundance of boxes in his attic—by the looks of it two for each of the fourteen years he'd lived in the house—a small measure of the stuff would have gone a long way.

One positive: since he'd had the stairs and skylight put in, it was a lot easier to navigate than the last time he'd been up there, when he'd spent hours digging through old issues of BPS journals, searching for an article he'd co-authored with his PhD supervisor. He could've accessed it online, but it still meant something to see his name in print.

"I could dig out the copies I want and ditch the rest, maybe," he told Sphinx, who was presently inspecting every box on the lookout for one he could turn into a temporary penthouse suite. Sean opened the box closest to him and removed the contents— a couple of old belts, a pair of braces and what looked suspiciously like lederhosen, although he had no memory of ever owning any. "There y'are, old fella." He pushed the box Sphinx's way and knelt in the space it left. Sphinx gave it a swift and dismissive look-see and prowled on, weaving between the haphazard stacks that doubled in height for every row further they were from the hatch.

Sean opened the flaps of the box to his right and then sprang back as something slithered from it and over his knees. Now, he was the first to admit he wasn't the most agile of chaps, but by God, did he get to his feet fast. It took him a moment to collect his senses and brave a look at whatever he'd set free.

"Ah, Jesus." He laughed at himself and stooped to retrieve the black tie, clamping the slippery garment between his fingers as he recalled his frantic search of the house a few months back, knowing he had one somewhere, but he'd been running late, so he'd bought a new one in the airport for three times what it would've cost on the high street. Still, his dad's widow and kids seemed to appreciate Sean and his brother's grieving-sons act, and if nothing else, he had a spare black tie now, in case, God forbid, he wore one of them out.

Coiling it and poking it into his pocket, he pulled the box closer and peered inside, trawling his hand through the multitude of ties, like a pit of deflated snakes in an array of colours and patterns—paisley, striped, polka-dot, cartoon print. He rarely wore one at all these days, having transferred his love of mad shirts to mad ties when he took the job at the hospital and later ditched those too in favour of smart-but-casual shirts with a button undone at the collar.

Boring, sure, but comfort took precedence on long days in clinic or stuck behind a desk. He wouldn't miss any of that, although he was already missing his colleagues and he hadn't been gone twenty-four hours yet. It was in the little things—the fleeting thought to tell Melanie about something or other when he saw her because she'd find it amusing and then remembering he wouldn't see her, or calling Francesca on a convoluted pretext, knowing she'd see right through it. Well, he supposed he could still call Francesca. Divorce hadn't stopped him, so why should resigning his post? He might even dig out a few of those old shirts—they had to be somewhere in one of these boxes. Sean could just picture Josh's reaction to him turning up on day one of the new surgery in orange-and-green palm-tree print, and it set him off chortling to himself as he moved on from the ties and dug in to the next box in the row.

He wasn't sure how, but he knew before he untucked the flaps what he'd find inside, and his hands shook as he did so, withdrawing swiftly when he felt a sharp edge dig into his skin. Squeezing the resulting pinprick cut, he watched the blood bead before shoving his finger in his mouth and one-handedly flipping the box open. It contained decanters and whiskey tumblers— two coordinating sets in lead crystal of differing designs. Only one casualty, other than himself, which was something.

The decanters were gifts from postgrad students he'd supervised, one of whom he still saw at conferences from time to time. The other had joined the RAF, and while Sean was aware she'd made significant contributions to the current body of work on bereavement and attention, her research was classified and would remain so long after she'd retired from active service.

Sean was both touched and horrified that those two students had picked up on his love of whiskey. Neither had known him well enough to realise his relationship with hard liquor was not a healthy one—nobody had before Sophie, although he'd always thought Francesca had suspected, even before their brief but amicably dissolved sojourn into marriage. People said managers were those who were promoted out of the way because they couldn't do the job, but Francesca had been a fantastic psych nurse in her day. She just happened to be a better administrator.

Sean moved the decanters and surviving three glasses into the box he'd emptied for Sphinx and put it and the ties by the stairs, ready to take to the hospice's shop in town. Next box: his certificates. His colleagues, in particular the immodest Doctor Norris, displayed the originals on their office walls, but Sean's had been photocopies, since his GP's had been stolen during a break-in and the replacements had cost a fortune. Sean thumbed through the stack, glad they were individually stowed in plastic wallets, as his finger was still bleeding, smearing enough genetic matter to turn the box into a full false-identity kit: beneath his degree, diploma and fellowship certificates were his birth and marriage certificates and his first passport.

He'd been twenty-four before he'd needed a passport and even then had only used it twice. Flipping it open, he prepared for the misery of comparing his crinkled, greying self to the young, hopeful fella in the photo but was thoroughly waylaid by the other photos stowed within. A strip of four from a photo booth, taken directly after the one on his passport: Jess; Jess and Genie; Jess and him; the three of them. They looked drunk and more than likely had been. More importantly, they looked happy. Sean couldn't remember if that was also a true record, but when he thought back to that time, which he seemed to do often of late, he recalled only one dark spot. As enormous and pervasive as it had been, it had failed to blot out the good times, so yes, he could say with some certainty that with his two favourite women on his lap, his smile was the genuine article.

Three boxes down, another couple of dozen to go. Sean pushed the certificates box against the wall so he didn't accidentally send that to the charity shop and shuffled on his bottom towards the next row, stacked two high. As he was lifting one down onto his lap, from somewhere Sphinx emitted the low growl that meant he'd come face-to-face with an adversary, followed by a hiss and the sound of several boxes toppling as the cat skittered through the cardboard maze and shot past Sean and down the stairs. Sean's hand immediately went to his chest.

"Christ. That's not worrying at all," he muttered, hoping his plan to clear the attic wouldn't turn out to be the death of him because Sphinx's behaviour suggested he had company. The question was: what kind? A rat? Another cat?

Quietly, he rose to his knees so he could see over the cardboard fortress to where the scuffle had taken place. A couple of boxes were on their sides, but apart from that, there was no movement, no sound, no sign of anything that might've spooked Sphinx, leaving Sean more intrigued than he was afraid.

It took a bit of shuffling things around to reach the back wall, and in the process he located the box containing his Hawaiian shirts as well as another full of audio cassettes, but he made it to the toppled boxes at last. The one nearest was taped shut, the contents secure but pushing to escape. Sean righted it, cringing at the telltale tinkle of more breakages. And that was when he saw it. A flash of white fur that once again threw him backwards in surprise. By now, he was sweating buckets and leaving dark handprints on anything he touched. He was in half a mind to join Sphinx downstairs and call pest control before he went any further, but whatever was lurking behind the box was no longer moving.

"Come on, Tierney, get your head in the game." He took a moment to breathe and be realistic. Worst-case scenario, a neighbour's pet rabbit or similar had sneaked in when Sphinx was out hunting. Or perhaps a dove had come in through the roof and got stuck. Either way, Sean was in no danger. Still, he maintained a healthy caution as he nudged the box out of the way. The white creature moved with it. Sean stopped. The creature stopped. Sean nudged the box, and a little more. The creature matched him move for move. Not hiding. Stuck.

Taking decisive action, he grabbed the box and hoisted it into the air. The creature—which he had now identified—came with it, dangled briefly by a leg and then plopped down at Sean's feet.

A teddy bear and not so white as it had been, clutching a red embroidered heart. *Love You Always.*

"You..." Sean picked it up and looked it in the glassy black eyes. "Causing trouble again, are ye?" He smoothed the stitched message with his thumb—the same action he'd used to wipe away Genie's tears as she'd nursed that very same bear and Jess had packed up around them. "I don't know what you're playing at, turning up now, little man, or even how you got here." Sean carried the bear reverently, taking care not to drop it as he stepped over the boxes and headed downstairs. He was done for one morning and ready for a cup of tea, or was that a teddy bear's picnic?

14: Into the Light

GENIE SCUFFLED INTO the kitchen, each step across the tiles an unpleasant reminder that her mules were still beside her bed, but caffeine was more important, so she forged onwards to the coffee machine, filled it with beans and pressed the power button, all with eyes half-open. She'd had another of those nights trapped in semi-sleep limbo, unable to get comfortable with the stubborn, delicate egg on the back of her head and having too many people in the house—far more than she was aware of if she were to believe Xander.

Nothing else had happened since the sheet music and piano incident, and while she could stomach the company in the circumstances, she worried she was wasting time Xander could put to greater use elsewhere. He insisted she wasn't, and she had no reason to doubt him. Xander was nothing if not honest. Nevertheless, she'd called on him to investigate her poltergeist, and she felt as if she were retaining him under false pretences. Perhaps better that than the alternative.

At last, the grinder whirred to life, and she inhaled deeply, breathing in fresh coffee and the waft of cool, ionised air, the latter prompting her to fully open her eyes. If there was cool air, there had to be an open window or door; either her poltergeist had become claustrophobic or she wasn't the only one up early.

"Good morning, Xander," she greeted, one foot in, one out. The sun was below the treeline, yet oddly, the patio paving was warmer than the kitchen floor. "Would you like a cup of coffee? It's brewing now."

"I can smell it. I'd like a cup, thank you."

Genie nodded and began to retreat but changed her mind. The coffee would be a while yet, and she enjoyed the refreshing tingle of the misty morning air against her skin. It was also a rare chance for an open conversation with Xander without Jonathan's interruptions. He was evidently more than Xander's private secretary—his carer too, perhaps, although Xander hadn't needed help when they were younger.

"Is there something you wish to say?" Xander kept his back to her but turned his head as if glancing over his shoulder. Genie took it as an invitation to move closer and stopped on his left side, leaving a couple of feet between them.

"Not really, but we haven't talked forever."

"We had a conversation at Gabby's wedding."

"It was hardly a conversation, Xander. And that was what, twelve years ago?"

"Fourteen."

"Worse still!" Genie laughed lightly, which prompted a half-smile from Xander. "I feel awful, dragging you away from London like this."

"You didn't drag me. I came of my own free will."

"I requested your help knowing you wouldn't refuse," Genie amended. "You've been here for two days and worked nonstop."

"I like it."

"No doubt, but it's still good to catch up, isn't it?"

Xander didn't protest her claim.

"So, how have you been?"

"Very well, thank you for asking."

"Work keeping you busy?"

"It's Easter recess, but in general, I'm well occupied with research and committee meetings."

"Sounds…riveting," Genie murmured dryly, realising too late that Xander had taken her literally.

"It's not, I assure you. Still, I have my private commissions." His unease showed in the tension that drew his shoulders up towards his ears. He expected to be ridiculed. Genie's stomach lurched guiltily at the memory flashes of making fun, insisting it was all in Xander's imagination, refusing to entertain his nonsense stories of invisible inhabitants in his family's home. She was still sceptical, but she also recognised it would have been less cruel if they had left Xander to his 'flights of fancy' rather than insisting he join in their games. After all, what difference had it made to them?

Of course, they were children then—she, Gabby, Simon and Xander, not friends as such but fellow passengers through their formative years—and as they'd matured, they'd come to accept Xander's ghosts as just one of his many peculiarities. There was little point telling him they didn't exist when he believed absolutely. Out of common respect, he'd deserved better than that from his closest childhood acquaintances—those who had known him best.

"I'm sorry, Xander."

He frowned, and rightly so, as her apology had come apropos of nothing.

"I meant for not believing you."

"Do you believe me now?"

She weighed it up, still clinging to a vain hope that she'd hallucinated the entire thing. "I'm open to the possibility," she said and then nearly jumped out of her skin at Xander's single loud clap of the hands. Now he was smiling.

"Then we are ready to begin." With those words, he marched past her, back into the house, and poured himself the first cup of coffee from the jug.

Genie followed him in, surprised when he offered to pour coffee for her too. She nodded her agreement and perched on a stool next to the island, averting her eyes while Xander struggled to clamber onto the stool on the other side. He managed it, with a fair bit of grunting. Pushing a few straggling hairs from his eyes, he regained his composure and directed Genie to her coffee.

"Thanks." She took a lingering sip to give him time to settle before she asked her question. "Does my being open to the possibility of the existence of ghosts make a difference to your investigation here?"

"No."

"Oh." She waited. He didn't elaborate. "OK. Well..." She sighed, completely stumped. "You said we're ready to begin."

"Yes." Xander set aside his cup and slithered awkwardly from the stool he'd fought so hard to mount. "A test," he said.

"Of what?"

"Your openness." He stopped in front of the range and stayed entirely still other than his head and eyes, which seemed to track movement. It was like watching a mime artist whose intent Genie had yet to discern.

"Do you see her?" he asked.

"Who am I supposed to see?"

"I believe she's the housekeeper. Or a cook." He scanned the space in front of him, up and down, and shook his head. "Her attire is wrong."

"Why? What's she wearing?"

Xander paused his bizarre actions and cast a smug glance Genie's way. "I'm not telling you."

"Ah." So the test was whether her mind was open enough to pick up on the alleged presence of the spectral housekeeper. "I can't see anything at all." She hoped she sounded suitably apologetic.

"You're not trying."

She drew breath to protest but conceded. "No, you're quite right. Don't you have to be sensitive to these things in the first place? I mean, you've always seen ghosts. I've never seen one in my life."

"You said you saw your daughter's bedside lamp being thrown across the room."

"I saw it hit the mirror," Genie clarified. True, no-one else had been in the room at the time, but she hadn't seen where the lamp was beforehand, nor any sign of a potential thrower. It could've been balanced on top of the mirror for all she knew, though that, too, would have been odd.

"You dreamt of your grandmother the night after she died," Xander added.

"I...I..." Genie stammered but couldn't go on. Xander was the only person she'd told about the dream, knowing he wouldn't mock her for wondering if it held a deeper meaning than simply reflecting remorse for her defiance. Her parents had given her an ultimatum, so certain she'd do what was expected of her once she was penniless, and she may well have gone running back to them had it not been for that dream and already being pregnant with Phee.

Instead, she'd struggled on, a single mother in a flat that was little more than a bedsit, escorting wealthy men to make ends meet and refusing her father's offers of financial assistance, knowing it would come with more strings than a symphony orchestra. It had taken her five years, but she'd accrued sufficient savings to fulfil the dream's prophecy and buy her grandmother's house. Even then, her father couldn't let her be.

"My father bought the piano," she said. Half-aware of Xander's reaction—a mere nod—she continued, "We always had one— what is a manor house without?—though none of us played. My mother doesn't care for music, but my father..." Genie smiled to herself, remembering. "All he asked was that I try to learn, and I did. I tried so very hard, but I can barely sing a note in key never mind master 'Für Elise'.

"I knew what he'd done as soon as I saw the lorry at the gates. The piano came with a handwritten delivery note—a gift for his granddaughter, whom he was not permitted to meet, but perhaps I might allow her to learn what I had not."

"Has he ever met your daughter?" Xander asked.

Genie shook her head. "My parents would use any relationship they build with Phee to bring us home. My father largely seems to have given up, but my mother still tries her luck from time to time. Each birthday, Phee receives an abundance of cards from people she doesn't know—her grandparents, aunt, cousins, biological father—and I've explained as best I can.

"It's different now, of course. We have a little more say in whom we marry or whether we marry at all. I won't spoil the illusion for her, but the piano was not an innocent gift from grandfather to granddaughter. It's all the more tragic because my problem was never with my father. It was with the Hendersons. Even after Simon came out, both sets of parents insisted we should bury the hatchet."

"In each other?" Xander suggested, to Genie's surprise. He'd cracked a joke and was grinning from ear to ear. She didn't recall him ever doing either, which made it all the more hilarious. And so, despite the early hour, her myriad guests and lack of sleep, she found herself in pleats with laughter.

"Oh, Xander. I hadn't realised you're such a hoot."

"I have my moments," he said modestly.

"You certainly do," Genie agreed, settling down a little. "Now, I hope you'll forgive me leaving you to your own devices. I need to shower, and then later—assuming you're amenable—we should have breakfast while you give me a full roll call of the ghosts with whom I share my abode. What say you?"

"I'm amenable," Xander confirmed. He extracted his notebook from his shirt pocket and set it on the island, pressing it flat with his palm.

"Excellent. See you shortly." Genie stepped down from her stool, finishing her coffee on the move. She was almost at the staircase when Xander called after her.

"What should I tell Jonathan?"

"Whatever you think."

"I'll give him the morning off so you can speak freely."

Genie peered back into the kitchen, but Xander was already absorbed in his note-making. She continued on her way upstairs, stalwartly avoiding the querulous smirks common to all her female ancestors, captured in the four portraits leering down at her. The paintings had belonged to her grandmother, which was the only reason they stayed, and in fact, the only reason Genie had rehung them once Phee's night terrors subsided to a less disruptive loathing of the four pairs of eyes that watched her every step, as they were doing Genie's now.

On the two occasions Phee had taken a tumble on the stairs, she'd been convinced 'those ugly, nasty women' were to blame, and Genie had to agree—on the ugly nastiness. Bulbous noses, beady eyes, mealy mouths and nary a chin between them, her ancestors were, ironically, no oil paintings. They were also long dead and buried—in the case of her great-great-great-grandmother and namesake, Imogen Edwina Rowan nee Stewart, a hundred years ago.

Meanwhile, the portrait of her grandmother, whom Genie had adored more than anyone bar her daughter, had pride of place above the hearth. A beautiful, gregarious brunette to the day she died, Isabella Catherine Rowan—*Lady Bella*, everyone called her, Genie included—had entertained a host of beaus in her lifetime and had been a tremendous influence, encouraging Genie to 'be her own woman' and live every day to the fullest. Genie had done so, although perhaps not how her grandmother had envisaged. At university, she'd indulged in all that the student experience had to offer and dared say been a bit of a wild one, but what she'd wanted, more than the high life and a string of handsome suitors or a stoic, privileged existence in a loveless manor house, was to be a mother. No husband or tiresome civic duties; just a child and a chance to build and share a loving bond.

Largely to appease her parents, she'd graduated, but after that, she'd steered her own path. She'd become pregnant and given birth to the most beautiful girl in the world. Phoenix Isabella had brought purpose to Genie's life, and love, so much love.

Everything Genie had done since had been for Phee, and she regretted nothing, regardless of what her parents, grandmother or that sneering line of ugly, nasty women might have thought of her.

In her room, she undressed and stepped into the shower, twisting the dial so that the effect was a warm, gentle rain that did little to ease the stiffness in her neck and shoulders but, crucially, didn't aggravate her tender scalp. The past few weeks, she'd been on her own, which was quite usual with Phee at school and Paul away on business, but it was spring break, and she'd expected to see more of her daughter, though she couldn't blame Phee for choosing to spend it elsewhere. Close as they were, what kind of young woman wanted to waste her best years keeping her mother company? Genie certainly hadn't, and she didn't expect it of Phee, but she hoped her daughter was staying safe, taking precautions and above all having fun.

In truth, neither was she surprised Paul had stayed away longer than usual. Their relationship had been stagnating for a while and seemed only to continue because breaking up was an inconvenience. She couldn't say she missed him particularly, though she'd have taken some solace from his presence over the past few days.

Perhaps it wasn't remarkable that she'd found it instead in Xander and his confidence that he could get to the bottom of whatever was going on with the house. And if it all proved to be a figment of her lonely imagination, Xander would have no problem telling her so, just as he'd recognised her discomfort in talking about the alleged poltergeist in front of Jonathan or anyone other than Xander himself.

As she dried off and dressed, she interrogated her feelings. Was her willingness to open up to Xander a sign she didn't care what he thought of her? No. Unlikely as it would seem to their mutual acquaintances, all of whom were aware of Xander's accidental—and frank—exposés, she trusted him to keep her confidences.

Satisfied her trust in Xander was the genuine article, Genie gave her wet hair a quick finger ruffle and admired her reflection, pleased with what she saw. A few greys shone amidst the browns; her smile deepened the lines and expanded the roundness of her cheeks, but on the whole, she was doing all right for forty-one.

She was still smiling as she exited her room, ready to give her best efforts to seeing Xander's ghosts, but the smile quickly turned to horror as she reached the top of the stairs. All four portraits had tipped sideways; the one immediately to her left—her great-great-great-grandmother's—continued to sway until, before her eyes, it lifted free of its hook and slid down the wall. The frame broke apart on impact with the step, one half staying where it fell, the other still attached to the painting, which bounced, end over end, all the way to the bottom of the stairs. A further noise had Genie grabbing for the banister: the familiar tinkle of a small bunch of keys dropped onto the bureau.

"Hey, Mum. I'm home. Where are you?"

***

"There." Phee firmly patted the sticking plaster. Genie withdrew her hand with a hiss. "All done."

"Thank you, darling." The gash across her palm wasn't particularly deep, but it had bled profusely and continued to sting and throb even now it was clean and dressed.

Phee tidied away the first-aid kit, her mouth tiny, lips cinched like a tightly clenched bum hole. She kicked Genie's mules out from under the table and slid her feet into them, briefly meeting her mother's gaze before disappearing into the utility room. "I'm going to check you didn't miss any glass."

"Be careful," Genie warned.

Phee reappeared, dustpan in hand.

"Mother, you look like someone beat the shit out of you."

Genie managed a small laugh at that. It aptly described how she felt. "All the more reason for you to take care."

"Yeah, right." Phee exited with an eye-roll, calling back, "You still haven't told me where Margaret is—or why those weirdos are here."

"She's taking the rest of the week off, and a little respect, please." Genie heard Phee's huff over the shoosh of the brush and the scrape of more glass splinters digging into the floor—who knew a tiny fluorescent tube could cause so much carnage?—followed by the *click-click* of muled feet returning.

Phee left the dustpan on the side and held up the half-framed, bent portrait. "What do you want me to do with this? Burn it?"

"If only..." Genie murmured wistfully. "Leave it in the hall. I'll ask Margaret to take it to the shop next week." That was assuming she came back once she'd taken the requested time off to consider her options.

Phee stood the portrait, face against the wall. "That's an improvement." She came back into the kitchen grinning, although there was still a faraway glaze to her eyes, and she was terribly pale.

"Much better," Genie agreed. "Too many Jägerbombs?"

"What?"

"Have you been partying hard?"

"Oh! Yeah. I need sleep."

"How's Sarah?"

"Fine." Phee nodded. She wasn't meeting Genie's gaze now. "Why is Xander here, Mum?"

"I invited him. We haven't seen each other since you were small. You probably won't remember. We went to his cousin Gabrielle's wedding."

"I remember," Phee said.

"You do? Well, Xander was in the area, so—"

"The house is haunted, isn't it?"

"What? Where... Why on earth would you think that? Of course it's not!"

"That portrait flew off the wall, Mum. I mean, *literally* flew."

"I must've caught it with my arm."

"Right. That's totally what I saw. And the black eyes are from walking into a door or something?"

"I slipped and hit my— Hang on. I do not have black eyes!"

Shaking her head, Phee dug a compact mirror from her bag and held it in front of Genie's face. In irritation, Genie snatched it from her and moved it to a suitable viewing distance.

"Oh, hell's bells." Her eyes were ringed in black and purple, turning yellow at the edges, so she couldn't even pass it off as the result of insomnia. It didn't stop her trying, though. "I've had a couple of late nights, that's all."

"Those are bruises, Mum."

"All right, let's say they are. Why would it have anything to do with the house being haunted?"

"So you're admitting it is?"

"No! For all you know, we could've been burgled, or maybe I was mugged—"

"Or got into a fight with Xander?" Phee finished, laughing at the ridiculousness of it. "He's a ghost hunter, and there are so many cameras in my room it looks like someone's shooting a porno."

"Phoenix Rowan!"

"Come on, Mother. I'm not a child! Just tell me the truth. Have we got a poltergeist?"

"A malevolent entity," Xander said, startling Genie and Phee with his sudden appearance. "Hello, Phoenix." He took a step towards her but remained out of arm's reach. "I'm Xander, a friend of your mother's."

"I know!" Phee shrieked. "We've met before." She side-stepped around him and stomped, still wearing Genie's mules, down the hall. "Am I allowed in my room without an exorcist?"

Genie looked to Xander in panic. He gave a small, supercilious chuckle.

"Demons don't exist."

"How about vampires?" Phee shouted from upstairs. "Or werewolves?" The slam of her bedroom door sent a percussive shudder through the wall. Another painting fell. Genie burst into tears.

"Oh God. I don't know what's going on anymore." She shut her eyes against the sight of Xander's bemused stare.

"It's all right," he said in what he probably thought was a soothing tone. "Vampires and werewolves are the stuff of fiction."

"I know that!" Genie wailed. Until four days ago, she'd thought ghosts were the stuff of fiction too.

"You don't need to worry for your daughter's safety."

"Because demons and vampires and werewolves don't exist? Xander, look at me!" She held up her cut palm, indicating with her other hand her black eyes and foolishly jabbing a finger at the bump on her crown. "How can you say Phee is safe?"

"Your…poltergeist…is afraid of her." He peered up towards the heavy thud of bass now coming from Phee's room. "And with just cause."

In a tearful mess of sobs and laughter, Genie tugged a length off the roll of paper towel and blew her nose. "Are you sure she's safe?" she asked, addressing the underside of Xander's chin, seeing as he was still staring at the ceiling.

"I am." At last, he looked her in the eye. "I would like to take you and Phoenix out for lunch."

"You would?"

"Yes. It will be easier to explain what I have established and how I will solve your problem."

Genie blew her nose again. "Where do you have in mind?"

"The—"

A scream from upstairs stopped Xander mid-flow.

Genie ran, barely registering the sharp prick of a missed glass splinter slicing into her left heel as she raced up the stairs, unaware that Xander was hot on her tail until he bumped into her when she came to a halt on the landing.

Before her stood Jonathan, one hand over his eyes, the other clutching a camera, statuesque in the face of Phee's gorgon glare.

His demise would have been a relief, perhaps even comical, were it not for the realisation that crawled over Genie as she took in her daughter's underwear-clad form, framed by her open bedroom door. The babe she had nursed at her breast, the child she had bathed and dressed, the thirteen-year-old who had clung to her for strength during her first menstrual cycle, endured spots and growing pains to emerge victorious in pre-holiday bikini fashion shows...was pregnant.

15: Too Much

Sandison-Morley Residence
Present Day
Wednesday, 17ᵗʰ April

"Coffee?" Josh asked and departed back along his hall, leaving Sean on the doorstep.

"Err...yeah. Why not?" Nonplussed, Sean stepped in, shutting the door behind him, and followed Josh to the kitchen. It wasn't as if they usually stood on ceremony, but some kind of explanation for the terse *'change of plan – we'll meet at my place'* text message seemed in order.

"You were out early this morning," Josh remarked casually.

"I dropped Phee at the train station."

"That was a short visit."

"Aye." Sean wasn't in the mood for sharing, considering his first workable state of arousal in almost two years had coincided with finding the 'Love You Always' bear, a bizarre stimulus that doubled as bromide to his poor, beleaguered libido. Now he thought on, it was probably more to do with the photo memento of those sultry three-in-a-bed nights with his beautiful girls. It was stirring again. Maybe there was hope for him yet, although, with Josh's owl eyes on him, it wilted as fast as it had sprouted. Sean locked away the accompanying mental images and concentrated on the present puzzle. "Why aren't we doing this at your surgery?"

"*Our* surgery—what do you think of 'wellness centre' as a name?"

Sean shrugged. "Not much. And again, why are we here and not there?"

"No furniture."

"Right." It wasn't news and was a half-explanation at best. "So we're…what?" Sean made a face behind Josh's back when he abandoned him a second time then reappeared a moment later with his open laptop balanced on his arm.

"We're what?" Josh repeated.

Sean laughed at their ludicrous non-conversation. "Weren't we going to sketch out a floor plan?"

"Yes, which we can do here—whilst sitting on furniture." One-handed, Josh typed something, paused, frowned and handed over his laptop. "Can't we?"

"We can, I suppose, but…" Sean trailed off and squinted at the diagram on the screen. "What's this?" He indicated the 'CR1' label in the middle of a large rectangle.

"My former consultation room. The small numbers are the dimensions in metres."

From that, Sean extrapolated the rest of the abbreviations and the rooms they referred to, but he was a visualiser and he'd only been to Josh's surgery a handful of times—while sober. He didn't care to count how many times he'd staggered up to the building, intent on having it out with him once and for all, only to find it locked up and empty because it was late into the evening, which had perhaps been as well.

The flash of the coffee machine's 'ready' light caught Sean's eye, reminding him he was supposed to be looking over Josh's measurements. "I'll take your word for it that these are accurate."

Josh extracted the full cup and exchanged it for his laptop so Sean could carry his drink. "My office?"

"Sure." Sean followed him upstairs, wondering what was going on. Josh seemed stable, but Sean couldn't get a decent read on him. It was a long time since he'd had that problem.

"Of course—" Josh directed Sean to the beanbag chair, which he loved sitting in…until it came to getting out of the thing. "—we don't yet know where the lift and loft stairs are going."

"I imagine—ooph!" The chair was always closer to the floor than Sean thought, and he lost about a third of his coffee on impact. He put down his cup while he shuffled into a more upright position and took the handful of tissues Josh dangled over him to mop up his mess. "There'll be structural constraints." He dropped the soggy mass into the wastepaper basket. "Remind me to empty that for you."

With a grunt, Josh handed the laptop back to Sean and woke his desktop computer. "Switch to the other document," he instructed.

Sean did so. "I'd have brought my laptop if I'd known we were working like this. I could still go and get it."

"No need."

Josh typed, and the text on the laptop screen changed along with his keystrokes. That got Sean's attention for real, and his eyes widened until the muscles strained. "Spooky!"

Josh sighed in overplayed exasperation. "It's mirrored, the same as the monitors and projector screens in the lecture theatre."

"I didn't mean that." Sean scratched his head as if it would alleviate the itch on the inside. "Did I send you an email in the early hours?"

"No," Josh answered and then, doubting himself, opened his email software. "Did you?"

Sean switched his attention between the laptop and desktop screens. "That's not showing up here."

"I'm only sharing the document." Josh had always been the more tech-savvy of the two, which, when it came to teaching materials and research reports, served their mutual benefit while also giving Sean a complex, not of inferiority; more that he wasn't pulling his weight.

Conscious of sticking his 'big Irish nose' where it wasn't wanted, Sean went back to the document in front of him, less reading it than playing 'spot the difference'. It could be a prank, he supposed, but Josh had an aggressive aversion to practical jokes, and this would have been a terrible one.

"No emails from you," Josh confirmed.

"Good to know." Sean leaned to the side until he could wriggle his phone free from his pocket. "It's only a rough draft—not even spellchecked—but I had a lousy night. Woke up Christ knows how many times, convinced we were at the surgery with a massive blueprint laid out on the floor." No dreams about Phee, though, or none he could recall. Plenty of awake time worrying, which was why he'd wondered if he'd sent the email in his sleep—he'd done that before—but it was still in his drafts folder. Checking he had the right recipient, he tapped 'send'. "There you go."

Josh refreshed his inbox and clicked on the new message.

"Great minds, eh?" Sean said jovially, making light, even though Josh hadn't had time to take in what was on his screen. There was some truth to that: they'd studied together, worked in the same field for over a decade and taught at the same institution for the past four years. They shared the same ethos on what an 'ideal' therapy service looked like, which was how they'd ended up resigning from their salaried posts and embarking on this business venture with little to no discussion beforehand.

There wasn't much text in Sean's email, but several minutes on, Josh was still staring at it, as dumbfounded as Sean was himself. The bullet-pointed list Josh had shared, displayed on the laptop at Sean's side, was, verbatim, identical to the one in Sean's email displayed on Josh's screen.

"So we're agreed, then," Josh said and quit his email app. "About putting the group therapy room in the loft space." He spun his chair in Sean's direction. Josh was pale at the best of times, but despite his undisguised attempt to act as if all was well, he looked ready to pass out.

"Are you OK?" Sean asked.

He half-nodded. "Andy said all we need to do at this stage is put together a rough pen sketch of our essentials and desirables, and he'll pass it on to the architect when they go in to measure up properly. I gave him a set of keys—"

"Hang on," Sean interrupted, still toying with the idea of pressing Josh on the matter of the identical lists but ultimately opting for the safer challenge. "When's Andy meeting with the architect?" He unlocked his phone and opened his diary. It was desolate without all the hospital stuff.

"I don't know. Jeffries and Associates has it all under control."

"You don't want to talk to the architect yourself?" Sean was baffled, bordering on incredulous. He was confident Andy and Dan Jeffries would do an outstanding job—they wouldn't dare give Josh less than their best—but Sean feared his future was slipping through his fingers, and if he was feeling that way, Josh should have been up the wall. It was, after all, his money behind the project. More to the point, Sean had only known him to hand over the reins once, and even then he'd put up a hell of a fight.

"Do you think we should talk to the architect?" Josh asked.

"Yeah, I do," Sean said gruffly, also thinking it was as well he hadn't burnt his NHS bridges. "What's going on, mate?"

Josh's nostrils flared as they always did when Sean called him 'mate'. He hadn't done it on purpose but refused to get waylaid in an apology.

"Are you having second thoughts?"

"Of course not!" Josh laughed, and there was an underlying note of hysteria, to Sean's relief. Like working a screwdriver under the lid of a paint tin, all the while praying it wouldn't explode in his face, he could find a way in with that.

"Is this about sharing your space?"

"If it were, I'd be in trouble. I can't afford to do this on my own, Sean. Perhaps I should be asking—are *you* having second thoughts?"

"Not at all! Sure, I'm nervous. This is new for me, the private practice, but I'm excited for the challenge. Or I was. But there's something going on, isn't there? I'm not imagining it."

For a long time, Josh sat motionless, ankles crossed, hands clasped in his lap, blinks the only break in eye contact. He looked a better colour now, a little pink returning to his cheeks, and the tension in his jaw gradually eased. Finally, he nodded. "The surgery—" he swallowed, sniffed in a breath "—appears to be—" picked up his coffee "—haunted." He lifted the cup to his mouth and hid behind it.

Haunted. Sean shouldn't have been surprised. After all these years, he could predict Josh's reaction to most situations, and he'd picked up on the attempt to relinquish control, but he hadn't expected it to be for the same reason as last time. There was, according to Josh, no afterlife, no heaven, hell or purgatory, no souls to pass beyond the veil. Ghosts were 'the products of compromised minds', and he'd accepted his subsequent diagnosis of bipolar disorder as proof, or as close to proof as a psychologist could get.

"I'm not hypo, Sean."

"Did I say a word?"

"You thought it."

He shrugged. "True enough, but let's talk about it this time around, shall we? What makes you say it's haunted?"

"Same as last time, and I didn't say it *was* haunted. I said it *appears* to be. Come on. I need to show you something." Abandoning coffee, computer and beanbag-hobbled comrade, Josh left the room.

"Hang on!" Sean called after him. "Can you give me a…shite."

He tried rocking back and forth a few times, but that was getting him nowhere fast, so he resorted to a roll sideways onto his hands and knees and heaved to his feet. It was slightly easier than trying to stand straight from sitting but still an almighty effort, and he was sweating by the time he made it downstairs to the hallway, where Josh was at the front door, car keys in hand.

"What took you so long?"

"Funny," Sean muttered, glad Josh was more his usual self. Rather than ask more questions, he followed Josh outside and stood by as he remotely unlocked his car and stepped behind it, hand poised on the boot catch.

"To clarify, in the event I need to, I still don't believe in an afterlife."

"OK," Sean accepted, even though he sensed doubt in Josh's once-solid conviction.

"On Monday, after we left you with Phee, Libby and I went to the surgery. We witnessed some…mundane incidents that defied explanation."

"Such as?"

"Doors slamming, bangs with no observable cause, a toilet roll unfurling itself."

"Right, so should I give you the stupid list? An open window? An electrical fault? Subsidence?"

"None of the above. Dan checked the electrics and plumbing—all in good working order. But while he was there, he went up into the loft, which was where he found…" A catch clicked; Josh hoisted the boot open and gestured to the objects within.

Even from a few feet away, Sean had no problem identifying what he was looking at. He couldn't decide if the fact Josh had brought it home with him rather than ditching it at the recycling centre at the first opportunity was more or less surprising than his claim that the surgery 'appeared' to be haunted.

"May I?" he asked.

Josh shrugged his consent and moved around to the side of the car from where he presided distractedly over Sean's exploration.

Sean leaned in and tilted the enormous gong out of the way to get a good look at the rest of the haul. The tarot cards, crystal ball and Ouija board he recognised, the rest not so much, but it was safe to assume it was more of the same.

"It was up there fifteen years minimum," Josh said, answering what would have been Sean's next question. "When I took on the lease, the landlord said something about needing access to the loft to disconnect the old water tank, but I don't recall him ever going up there. In any case, some of this stuff is much older."

"Don't they make it look that way for authenticity's sake?"

"I thought that too initially, but look at that box." Josh directed Sean to the Ouija board. "It's 1940s' construction, not just made to look old."

Sean lifted it out and examined it more closely. It was sturdy, thin plywood rather than cardboard, held together with panel pins, and the labels were faded for real. On first inspection, Sean had to concur: the box was decades old. "Whose is it? Any idea?"

"None whatsoever. Gordon Baines had a 999-year lease on the entire row, which entitled him to compulsorily purchase the freehold on my building when the previous owner died in 1982, but he didn't change it over to commercial use until fifteen years ago. My guess is the stuff in the loft belonged to the last residential tenant."

"Are you going to ask Baines about it?"

"I already did. He said he'd passed on all the information to my solicitor."

"And?"

"And…?"

"What did your solicitor say?"

"I haven't spoken to them yet, but I will." A car passed by; Josh followed its progress into the distance. He was on edge, and Sean was curious but didn't probe. All in good time. He put the box back and shut the boot.

They returned inside, where Josh went straight to the coffee machine while Sean diverted towards the stairs with a call of, "I'll go get the cups."

"Leave them. I'll use clean ones."

"If you say so." Sean stood in the kitchen doorway, watching Josh toil intently or give the impression of doing so to avoid eye contact. There was more to this than a few unexplained noises and finding a load of spiritualist tat in the loft, and it bothered Sean that after all this time and everything they'd been through, Josh still couldn't be honest with him.

"So are you planning to sell it or dump it or…?"

"Adele offered to look after it until I track down the owner."

"You might need to use it to find them if it's as old as you say."

Josh shot Sean a look that was not of appreciation for his joke. "If I can find out who they were, I should be able to locate their descendants—assuming they have any."

"And if they don't?"

"I'll decide later."

"Maybe Adele will buy it from you."

"If it comes to that, I'll let her have it."

"All right, so..." Sean had spotted the shift from haunted surgery to the spiritualist haul when it happened—a natural one for anyone else. "Let's backtrack a bit. The things that happened when you and Libby were there—are we talking pranksters again?"

"Well, it's rather convenient, don't you think? Unexplained phenomena one day and the next I happen upon all that junk? Maybe someone else knew it was there and decided to have a bit of fun at my expense."

"Who? An ex-client?"

"No." The machine bleeped; Josh extracted the first cup and placed a second under the spout, then wiped everything down and rinsed the cloth. "Tony Baines."

"I'd swear you called him Gordon earlier."

"Tony is Gordon's son. He was there when I negotiated the purchase, and it was clear he thought he'd be taking over the business when his dad retired."

"Surely it's too late now for Tony to do anything about your place. You bought it outright, didn't you?"

"For well under market value. He could buy it back from me for more than I paid and still make a profit, and if that's his game, I'm tempted, I must admit."

Now they were getting somewhere. "You don't submit to pranksters, remember?" Sean said.

"This is different. Last time, I'd have lost out. This time, I stand to gain."

"Then you *are* having second thoughts."

"Not second thoughts, but it's risky, and I have a family to provide for. Have you any idea how much teenage daughters cost?" Josh must've realised the insensitivity of what he'd said, as he turned lead-poisoning pink.

"Not really." Sean patted Josh's arm amicably, having learned long ago not to take his tactlessness to heart. Josh only said what everyone thought, and while a few days of keeping tabs on Phee had given Sean some insight into how quickly teenage daughters could chomp through money, he didn't have to worry about her school supplies, clothing and feeding her or ensuring she had a social life.

"I'm sorry."

"No need, Joshy. You're right, I don't have much idea, and I will tell you what's going on with Phee, but let's get this sorted out first, all right?"

"OK." Josh's agreement was tentative, suspicious. He'd opened up a little and seemed willing to listen. Still, Sean would need to tread carefully.

"I have a suggestion, but before I make it, I must be frank with you, and you're free to tell me if I'm way off here. Now, you and George may well have been talking about it for months beforehand, but from my perspective, it looked like you rushed into buying the building."

Josh's expression didn't change—a blank mask but for the occasional attentive blink. Sean pressed on.

"Whether it was down to hypomania or that you couldn't stand the idea of someone else taking it on? Doesn't matter. All I'm saying is it wasn't your usual well-considered approach." Sean paused again. Still no argument.

"Then there was your most recent brush with death. I won't insult you with lessons in egg-sucking. You know the psychological impact. We tell our clients to hold off on big decisions, and sure, you'd already made it, but somebody shot you, for Christ's sake. No-one would think less of you for changing your mind. You could have put the building straight back on the market or become a landlord yourself and leased the space to someone else. You still could, and if that's what you want to do, if I'm the reason you haven't, then don't let me stop you. My house is paid for. I only have Dylan's and my day-to-day living expenses to think about, and if push came to shove, I'm sure I could talk Francesca into giving me a few hours in clinic.

"But if you're wanting to see it through...well, I know you don't want to lose the momentum, but we can slow up a wee bit. We've time on our side here. What I'm suggesting is we give ourselves six months, longer if need be, to get up and running. Any new clients come our way in the meantime, we can see them at my place or even rent an office somewhere. That way, the Jeffries lads can get on with the work without it being a rush job. We can tout for business, and when we're ready, we'll have an official opening. And if you're not wanting to deal with the architect, I'll happily take that on."

Sean gave a nod to indicate he was done and got on with drinking his coffee, leaving Josh to mull it over, play out every feasible outcome. It wouldn't take him long and ultimately might not make any difference because Josh's decisions were black and white, all or nothing. He didn't compromise; he didn't know how. But that was what Sean was offering: something between charge ahead at full speed and run like hell in the opposite direction.

Over the rim of his cup, Sean watched and waited. He was a patient man, so people said, and he had plenty for his oldest, dearest friend, whose posture had changed, a slight twitch in his cheek signifying his deliberations were complete.

Patient or otherwise, right then, mere seconds away from the verdict, Sean could gladly have wrung the neck of whoever was on the other end of that call.

As perplexed as if he'd never seen one before, Josh pulled his phone from his pocket and hit the 'answer' button.

"Hello?" He met Sean's gaze. "Hello?" He moved his phone away and checked the screen—"Still connected"—and put it back to his ear. "*Hello?*" After a few seconds of saying no more, Josh ended the call.

"Wrong number?"

"Who knows? They didn't say anything. So, I've considered what you said, and—"

"That's strange."

"It happens. As I was—"

"You get a lot of silent calls, do you?"

"Don't we all?" Josh held up his hand, stopping Sean from interrupting again, and he would've done, having convinced himself Josh was going to turn him down and sell the building from right under them, uni resignations be damned. "Yes," Josh said. "But we need to agree on a completion date."

"So we're still game on? I don't have to go cap-in-hand to Francesca?"

"Only if you want to."

"Christ, no." Sean took out his phone and unlocked it. "All right, let's see…exorcists…" He ducked and narrowly avoided a flying teaspoon.

16: The Wrong Side

Social Science Faculty Building
Present Day
Thursday, 18ᵗʰ April

"Hiya."

Josh looked up—eyes only—from his third attempt to fit everything from his desk's top drawer into the plastic crate. "Hey, Shaunna. Fancy seeing you here!"

"How's it going?" She remained in the doorway, her hand curled around the edge of the door.

"Oh...*fine*." Josh slammed the drawer shut and sat back. "I'm sick of it—I've half a mind to chuck the lot." He glared at the crate, overflowing despite his Tetris-style packing, which he'd regret later when he couldn't get any of it out again, and turned his attention to Shaunna. "Are you waiting for Sean?"

"No. Why?"

"Just wondering why you haven't come in."

"Oh!" Shaunna came a couple of steps closer but left the door open. "Can we... Is now a good time to talk Daisy Foundation business?"

"That depends."

"On?"

"How long it'll take." Josh already had a good idea which Daisy Foundation business Shaunna wanted to talk about, and the trial of *too-much-to-do vs friend-in-need* waged in his mind. For the plaintiff, this was the third interruption of the morning. *Did you or did you not waste the past thirty minutes arranging desk sundries on a desk which, as of five p.m. next Friday, will no longer be yours?*

"Not to worry." Shaunna pursed her lips and turned away from him.

Mr. Sandison-Morley, did you or—

"Wait!" If he didn't relent, she'd use his unwillingness against him in future. No, that wasn't a fair judgement. *He'd* use his unwillingness against himself and project it onto her. "What do you want to talk about?"

"Doesn't matter." She was still heading—slowly—for the door.

"Shaunna..."

"If you're too busy."

"I'm busy, but not *too* busy." He sighed. "You came all the way here."

"I was already here."

"I'm not even doing anything useful. Come in. Please?"

At last, she shut the door and turned back with a cheeky grin. He folded his arms. Of course she'd known he'd relent.

"Sean's off-site, isn't he?" he asked.

"Yep. I didn't come to see him. Guess who's been accepted for the counselling diploma!"

"Really? I wasn't aware you'd applied."

"To four different institutions. I'm sure I told you."

"I mean I didn't know you'd applied here."

"Well, I wasn't going to, with you and Sean being the course leaders, but he talked me into it."

"He's a bugger. He's still leading the course."

"And he'll still be teaching me, but he won't do my observations or mark my assignments. Your replacement will. I just had my first supervision meeting with her."

"How did that go?"

"OK. She's a bit..."

"Eccentric?" Josh suggested.

"I was going with bonkers myself."

Josh laughed. "That too." He could hardly believe it when Zara Kaminsky-Lederman's job application arrived in his inbox; by the time Sean had not only shortlisted her but also offered her the position, Josh was quite convinced he'd passed into some parallel universe where Sean and Zara didn't hate each other's guts.

Perversely, Josh liked Zsa Zsa—the nickname he'd given her way back when she'd waltzed into his new surgery, flung herself on his sofa and called him 'daahling'. She was every bit as glamorous and dramatic as the Hollywood star and no doubt would get on the nerves of some students and faculty. However, she was the most successful and longest-serving psychotherapist in their town, and since she'd taken so many of their former students on placement, she had an excellent knowledge of the course requirements. Eccentric and bonkers, yes, but absolutely the right person for the job, and she was already in post, so Josh couldn't have rescinded his resignation had his meeting with Sean gone differently.

"So you wanted—oh! Congratulations on getting onto the course." He'd almost forgotten to offer them. "And thanks again for having Libby over the other night."

"Thank you," Shaunna accepted graciously, followed by, "And we love having her over, so no thanks needed," then, "Lawyers."

"Lawyers?" That wasn't the Daisy Foundation business he'd anticipated.

"Don't worry, hun. The drop-in centre's still kind of wish-list territory. No rush." That *was*, however. "We haven't even looked at how much it will cost to run yet, and we can hold off doing anything about it for the time being."

"Bloody Tierney and his big mouth."

"Sorry?"

"It was his idea to postpone, not mine."

"I've no idea what you're talking about," Shaunna said.

"In that case, forget I said anything. At least, forget I blamed Sean. So you know, we're postponing the official opening of the surgery, but I meant what I said. I'm converting the loft for the Daisy Foundation—unless you've found a better venue?"

"No, of course not. But…" Shaunna's nose wrinkled, and she sighed. "After what happened on Monday at your surgery—"

"Electrical fault," Josh interrupted, hoping only he could see the rapid flutter of his shirt front. He usually had no trouble lying convincingly, although he couldn't recall having lied to Shaunna before. "So lawyers then," he said, reassured that his poker face was holding when she stopped giving him that patient, confide-in-me look and nodded. "Haven't we found one yet?"

"*We* haven't, no," Shaunna answered, which was a forewarning rather than a jab—he hoped, even if he'd have deserved it. His question was only marginally better than her bringing up his and Libby's ghostly adventures, and he should already have known the answer. In his defence, he was, by consensus, more a 'sleeping trustee' of the foundation, there to make up numbers and cast his vote when called upon to do so.

"Look, Josh, I know you don't want to deal with the interviews…"

"You didn't ask me," he pointed out.

"Because you're still working here and trying to get the surgery fixed up, and then there's Libby's exams and…I wouldn't be asking now if there was anyone else available."

"You don't want me involved in the interviews, do you?"

Shaunna's cheeks turned the colour of cherry blossom. She came over and sat with her bag in her lap, strap still on her shoulder. "Please try not to take this the wrong way. I love your straight talk. I value your opinion above almost anyone else's. But—"

"You don't want me to scare off your candidates."

"Yeah." She grimaced. "I'm sorry."

Josh shrugged, a little hurt, but he couldn't argue when her point was valid. "What do you need me to do?" he asked, counter to the childish impulse to sulk.

"Would you mind sitting in on an interview this afternoon?"

"Can't Eleanor make it?"

"No childcare."

"Sean?"

"Probably, but I need someone sensible on my side, and—"

"He's not someone sensible?"

Shaunna faked weighing it up. "He can be."

"Except if it relates to—"

"It's not about Jess," Shaunna interjected.

"It's *always* about Jess." The Charity Commission had recommended months ago that they appoint a legal expert to their board of trustees, and all four of them were acutely aware of the root of their difficulty in doing so.

"Not on this occasion. The thing is…" Shaunna pressed her lips together as if to spread an application of gloss. "OK, so, Sean's having…how to put it…"

"Say no more." For as much as Josh's curiosity was egging him on, he hated putting her in a position where she felt she had to breach Sean's confidence. "I'll do the interview."

"Thanks. You probably already know what's going on with him."

"Probably." The obvious issue was Phee turning up, but Sean seemed to be coping with that, which left only Jess and his as-yet-unresolved regret for what might have been but wasn't. "What's the problem with the lawyer we're interviewing this afternoon?"

"She's too cheap."

Josh laughed. "That's not something you hear often about lawyers."

"She has her reasons."

"Criminal record?" he speculated.

"No." Now Shaunna laughed—and rolled her eyes. "I bet she's never had so much as a parking ticket. She's one of those pure-as-the-driven-snow types. And recently widowed."

"How recently?"

"Last week."

"Wow. That *is* recent. Does Sean know?"

"Not yet, but it was the first thing she said after we'd done the hellos on the phone, and I know I bounce back quickly, but a week?" She shook her head. "I'm not happy about taking her on this soon after her husband died, and Sean and bereavement..."

"Is like a kid in a sweet shop," Josh finished.

"Exactly. I'm worried he'll offer her the job out of sympathy or as occupational therapy or something."

"No, he won't," Josh said with certainty.

"He's a softy."

"In his personal life. In fact, gullible springs to mind. But when he's wearing his professional hat..."

Shaunna put her hands together and fluttered her eyelashes.

"I already said I'd—ooph!" Her hug was sudden and enthusiastic. "What's this for?"

"A reward for not stamping your feet." She released him and grinned.

"As if I would!"

"As if you wouldn't!" This time, she moved off like she meant it, calling, "The interview's at one," on her way out.

***

Campion Trust Boardroom
One p.m.

"Please come through." Shaunna appeared in the doorway, gesturing with her hand and giving Josh a dubious, slightly manic smile. A woman in a mauve, A-line-skirt suit bustled past her into the Campion Trust boardroom, the Daisy Foundation's temporary—assuming Josh ever managed to set foot in his surgery again—HQ.

Josh rose from his seat to greet her. "Good morning, Mrs.—"

"Dorothy Lomax." Her face widened with her glossy-mauve smile, and a large, warm hand firmly gripped and near shook his arm out of its socket. Mauve nail varnish. Mauve shoes...

"Dorothy, this is Josh, one of our trustees," Shaunna explained on his stunned behalf. She shut the door and came around to his side of the table. "Thanks for coming in."

"That's quite all right. As I mentioned on the phone, my husband passed away recently, and I find I'm at something of a loose end. It's really no hardship."

"I understand," Shaunna said, yet her cynicism hadn't diminished. Josh, however, was intrigued; Dorothy Lomax was nothing like the grieving widow he'd envisaged.

"Perhaps it would help if I explained." She turned in her seat, directly facing Josh and once again treating him to that wide, mauve smile. "My husband had been unwell for a long time. Cancer, angina, diabetes, dementia—he had all kinds wrong with him, poor chap."

Beside Josh, Shaunna grew an inch with muscle tension.

"It's a long time since he was the strong, intelligent man I married—and a relief to be free of the responsibility, to be frank. He refused to go into a nursing home, back when he was still capable of expressing such wishes. Fortunately, his critical illness insurance covered his care at home, and we'd saved sufficient that I was able to give up work to oversee his nurses. They were marvellous, it's such a thankless task."

Shaunna nodded in agreement. "My dad has Alzheimer's."

Dorothy's forehead crinkled like crepe paper. "I'm sorry for you, pet." She stretched her stout arm as far across the table as it would reach and patted the wood comfortingly, her mauve fingernails vibrant against the polished pale beech.

"Thank you." Shaunna's voice was quiet and unsteady. She cleared her throat and sent a waft of almond breeze Josh's way as she flicked her hair over her shoulder. It was her trip switch back to business mode. "You mentioned you're a specialist in charities."

"That's correct, yes. Social enterprise more so than charities. Milton—my husband—was the expert on charity law."

"He was a lawyer too?"

"Yes, we all three were *solicitors*—Milton, my sister and myself. My sister's expertise was in inheritance law."

Josh glanced over the CV in front of him. It was on there—Lomax Barnes Solicitors, senior partner until six years ago, which matched what she'd told them, but there was something not right. Just a feeling, the kind he didn't often get because he researched in advance and was prepared for most eventualities. His failure on this occasion was nothing to do with taking shortcuts; he'd intentionally come to this interview with no preconceptions, or none beyond knowing Shaunna's opinion, and that Dorothy was a widow whose fees were substantially lower than they should have been.

"What's the catch?" Josh glanced up and caught her taken-aback blink.

"Begging your pardon?"

"Why are you charging so little?"

"The house is paid for, there's money in the bank, and no children. I have only myself to consider. And I'm bored, Mr…"

"Just Josh," he said. "May I ask, if you don't need the money—"

"Why am I charging at all?" she interrupted.

"Yes, that would've been my question, had I been allowed to finish it."

"My apologies. Do you realise how often men interrupt women?"

"Very, I imagine." It was a well-researched area of social psychology, and he'd read countless papers. Men interrupted, dominated discussions and frequently talked over their female counterparts. Josh was fully aware of the advantages of being a white middle-class man, and how poor his social etiquette could be, so he tried to be equally rude to everyone. Well, he didn't *try* to be rude at all, but he didn't think he discriminated when choosing whether to bite his tongue or say it how it was. "You still haven't answered my question."

"I don't believe anyone should work for free, irrespective of whether it's for a good cause, and supporting families after the demise of a little one is a truly worthy cause. But even trustees attract an honorarium, do you not?"

"No," Shaunna answered before Josh could get there. "We chose not to because it's a charity, and we need the money less than those we're helping."

"That's your prerogative, pet. My fees are open to negotiation, of course, but I stand by what I said. I won't work for free, nor do I think you should."

"Moving on…" Shaunna brusquely shuffled her papers, meeting Josh's gaze for a second before she looked over their list of questions, no doubt seeking out the trickiest. She was irritated and ready to give their interviewee the heave-ho, which was a shame. Josh rather liked Dorothy Lomax.

***

Three p.m.

"AND ANOTHER ONE bites the dust." Sean tossed his ring binder onto the table and leaned back, tipping his chair and sweeping his knuckles against the wall behind. "I'm sick of this feckin' boardroom. How many's that we've seen now? Twenty?"

Shaunna shut the door and returned to her seat next to his. "Hardly! That was number seven."

"Any more on the list?"

"Nope. You've successfully scared them all away."

"Hey now, I've been perfectly charming." He tried to make it sound light-hearted.

"I was joking."

"As that may be, my boss at the hospital said the same and ordered me to keep it shut when we were interviewing for my replacement. It's a good thing to keep these people on their toes— a test of resilience, you know? Are my expectations unrealistic?"

Shaunna patted his hand. "It's not you. Or not just you. Jess might not have been who we thought she was, but I don't remember her ever being as mercenary as that." She nodded after the departing applicant—a Basil Lawson who'd formerly worked for the prestigious 'This', 'That', and 'The Other' and demanded an hourly rate on a par with a professional footballer's salary. "Or not with us," Shaunna qualified.

"No, you're right. Lawyers are shockingly overpaid for what they do, but it's not so much about the money-grabbing. It's how they're presenting themselves."

"Yeah. With Jess, there was no pretence."

"Or not with us…"

At Sean's intentional borrowing of her words, Shaunna did a combined half-smile, shrug and sigh. "We never asked, did we?"

"I don't think she'd have lied to us if we had."

"Then I'm glad I didn't." She nodded as if confirming for herself the truth of her words. Whatever Jess had been, whatever she'd done, Shaunna had loved her as much as Sean had, though in a wholly different way. "I feel like we're measuring them all against someone who didn't exist," she said.

"Is that what we're doing?" Sean was interrogating his own judgement as much as hers.

"Trying to find someone Jess would've approved of makes no sense."

"Because she's not here, you mean?"

"Not even that. You know my beliefs, Sean. My mum's still a constant presence in my life—sometimes I forget only I can sense her. Well, Adele says she can too, but it's Adele, so I'm taking it with a pinch of salt."

"Isn't salt what you use to keep the ghosties away?" Sean tormented, which earned him a well-deserved toe in the shin. "Go on. What were you saying?"

"Even believing as I do that Jess is with us in spirit, she didn't set a good example, and she'd have told us that herself."

"All right." Sean flipped his binder shut with a sense of finality. "So what do we do?"

"Hand over to Josh?" Shaunna suggested.

"Tempting." Other than he had even less tolerance of lawyers than they did, although he'd been open to the possibility of giving their penultimate candidate a trial run. "You never did tell me why you brought him in for the interview earlier."

"He was free, you weren't."

"I popped out for lunch with Soph. If I'd known you had someone coming in, I'd have rescheduled."

"You didn't miss much." Shaunna fed her copies of the applications back into their plastic wallets—an evasive manoeuvre if ever Sean saw one. "But we can't afford to dismiss her purely because I don't like her."

"Why not? You're a damned good judge of character."

"Do you think?"

Sean shrugged, all faux humility. "You picked me as a friend. How much proof do you need?"

Shaunna shook her head, her hair an undulating tide of glossy red that crashed over her shoulders. Leaning in closer, she pinched his cheek to recapture his attention. "We could always readvertise."

"All right. Do you want to sort that out now, or—actually, I've a better idea."

Shaunna put her fingertip on her chin as if she were about to take a wild guess. "Take this to Milky's and get out of this feckin' boardroom?"

"You read my mind, for sure."

She shrugged and gave him a seductive smile. "It's a gift."

17: Lonely Women

Rowan Mews
Two years ago

I CAN'T FIND MY blue shirt."

Genie glanced up from her book as Paul came back into the bedroom holding a suit by a hanger, his attention on it rather than her.

"Try the hamper," she said and returned to her reading.

The bathroom light clicked on, followed by a few muffled thuds, then, "Damn it."

She sighed, awaiting the predictable outcome of his discovery—his own fault, always assuming someone else would unpack his case and launder his clothes, but also not *entirely* his fault. He was young with no responsibilities beyond his career, and routine bred expectation.

He stormed back into the bedroom. "It's not in there."

"You have other shirts, Paul." She didn't look up this time.

"They'll need ironing."

"Then ask Margaret."

With much grumbling, he hooked his suit hanger over the door and heaved his case onto the bed, the weight pinning Genie's legs under the duvet. She knew by his disgusted sneer the moment he'd found his blue shirt. "For God's sake." He threw it on the floor, followed by the rest of the dirty clothes and underwear that had been left in the case. "It reeks."

"Look on the bright side. You've only been home *a day*."

"Meaning what, exactly?"

"Meaning it would've smelled far worse if it had been longer."

"I'll have to buy one on my way to the office." He stomped off again.

"Another one," Genie muttered. He didn't hear her. She flipped the page and continued to read while he thumped back and forth, dumping old underwear and whatever else he'd found lurking in his closet into the suitcase. Not a word of the book was going in, but she'd had a late night, so she stayed put, refusing to entertain his tantrum.

She wasn't angry with him, but lately, she'd become accustomed to her own company again, and his flouncing, which she'd found easy to ignore in the past, was getting on her nerves. Other factors were at play that were nothing to do with Paul, and she was trying her hardest to not take those out on him and make the most of their increasingly scarce time together. Since his promotion, he worked away four days out of seven, and more often than not, when he was home she was out with a client at some social event or other.

Their respective work was a double-edged sword, both keeping them apart and sustaining their relationship. Indeed, it was how they'd met—at a gala put on by the pharmaceutical company Paul worked for. The CEO had hired Genie to be his plus-one for the evening, at which Paul had been one of a handful of young, buff and obscenely beautiful reps paraded as eye candy for rich, randy directors and investors. Despite the difference in their ages and that he could've had his pick of the guests, an innocent coincidence of their trips to freshen up had sparked an instant, mutual attraction, and as soon as the CEO had dispensed with Genie's services, she and Paul had taken off for his hotel room.

Had she known at the time that Paul was still a teenager, she'd have pulled the brakes before their damned hot flirting went any further, but he'd looked older—she'd have put him at twenty-eight or nine, older than he was now—so she hadn't even thought to ask. Five years on, the fifteen-year age gap should have felt less of a chasm, not more, yet every day, something rammed it home—her fortieth birthday looming on the horizon,

Phee starting her A' Levels in a few months' time, Paul's inability to deal with his laundry when all he had to do was move it from his case to the hamper and Margaret would take care of it.

Once again, Genie reminded herself that none of this was Paul's fault, or at least, he was acting no differently than usual. Excellent sales rep and lover that he was, he lacked many of the most basic yet essential life skills—skills which Genie wouldn't have acquired either, had she, like he, continued to live at home during her undergraduate years. Granted, she'd have become a stinking recluse were it not for Jess coming to her rescue whenever she ran out of clean clothes, toiletries or cosmetics. Such were the trials for one who had never had to worry where these things came from, as was Paul's lot now, but it wasn't her duty to mollycoddle him.

It was only when the front door slammed she noticed his suitcase was gone from the bed and he'd left without saying goodbye. Or had he? She'd been so engrossed in her thoughts she didn't know, and she fleetingly imagined how awful it would be if something were to happen to him and she had to live with *our last conversation was an argument.* Much as she regretted that he'd left on a sour note, it was a relief to have the house to herself again for the next thirty-six hours, when Phee would arrive home for spring break.

Oddly, that was something she didn't regret, even though she hadn't wanted Phee to go to boarding school. It had been Phee's choice, which Genie had tried not to take to heart. The independent streak was in Phee's genes, inherited from both parents, and she needed space and freedom to be herself. If Genie were ever to try to curtail that, as had been done to her, she expected Phee would treat her with the same contempt Genie felt for her parents. But she didn't want to think about them today, or any day, so she dog-eared the page and cast aside her book in favour of a leisurely shower followed by breakfast on the patio.

She was almost finished when Margaret arrived at eight-thirty with the newspaper and her customary refusal to sit and share a pot of tea with the lady of the house. Dear Margaret and her observance of custom. She had come to Genie with only three years of service behind her but with an exceptional reference from an elderly baroness whose only complaint was that Margaret was 'remarkably staid for one so young': she was only a little older than Genie yet had borne the outlook of a sixty-year-old woman from the beginning. Still, theirs was a good working relationship, which Genie had no desire to disrupt by impetuously seeking Margaret's agreement that Paul was a selfish slob, thus she settled for mentioning the heap of dirty laundry in the bedroom and let her assistant do what she was paid to do, then perused the newspaper to pass the remaining few minutes until nine o'clock.

No need for scrolling her contacts list; the number she'd called every day for twenty years never left the top of the screen. She tapped the name and put her phone to her ear.

"Hello?"

"Hi, Steph, it's Genie."

"Hi, Genie. How are you?"

"I'm well, thank you. How was your holiday?" It was a touchy subject, but better that than put Jess's mum in a position where she felt compelled to answer 'I'm fine' when she absolutely wouldn't be.

"Lovely. The weather was stunning—not *too* hot, which it can be in Florida—and I have a smashing tan. All over!"

"Oh, I say!" Genie laughed, reminded again of where Jess's sassiness came from. She and her mum were so alike. "And how's Madam?"

"Better now she's back in her own house. When did you last speak to her?"

"Yesterday morning."

"Ah. So you'll have heard all about last week's chemo then."

"Yes." Genie matched Steph's weary tone but doubted Jess had subjected her mother to the same rant about how she wished she was dead already. Somehow, Genie had staved off the tears long enough to say what she hoped were all the right, supportive things before she'd hung up, sent Phee a text that simply said '*I love you. Mum x*', then sobbed her heart out until Paul distracted her with sex, wine and dinner.

"Is she up yet?" she asked.

"She's still in bed, but she's awake. I'm just taking the phone up to her. One sec."

There was crackling on the line and muffled voices, then Jess's feeble, "Hey."

"Hey, gorgeous. I didn't wake you, did I?"

She heard Jess's mum say, "I'll leave you in peace," followed by a few seconds' silence before Jess spoke again.

"I've been awake all night, Genie. It's *awful*. I can hear her crying in the room next door."

"Oh, Jess. I'm sorry."

"I even tried listening to music, but how does anyone sleep with music playing?"

"Depends on what it is. I found those meditation CDs we used to listen to very relaxing."

"Because you were always stoned."

"I was not!" Although she'd admit to having dabbled from time to time, considerably more than that after they'd graduated. "Maybe you could try the sound of the ocean or something."

"Ugh, no. I feel nauseous as it is. On the plus side, I don't have to put up with it for long."

A prickle of something—fear, sadness, anger—crept over Genie's scalp as she clamped her teeth to trap *I wish you'd stop saying things like that*. She'd promised she'd treat Jess the same as always, but those words carried the danger of subjecting her to more 'awful tears', so she went with, "Morbid but true."

"Well, hopefully. I haven't—"

"I thought you wanted to go to your friends' wedding."

"I do. That's not—"

"And didn't the oncologist say staying positive would—"

"Imogen, please shut up a minute. You misunderstood me, as per usual."

"But…" Genie folded the newspaper and pressed it flat. She'd only ever misunderstood Jess once. Catastrophically so. "Sorry. What *did* you mean?"

"Andy's moving back in with me."

"That's a drastic measure to get your mum to leave," Genie joked, hoping pithy humour would shield her loathing from Jess's ears because it was *always* Andy.

"It's not like that, and she isn't leaving. Not permanently. Unfortunately."

"Jess…"

"I know. I'm an ungrateful cow. But how is this helping me, Genie? She talks to me like we're strangers in the street, then goes off and has a cry. It's like Daisy dying all over again."

"For her, it's *exactly* like Daisy dying all over again." That was downright mean to say, but it was the truth.

"It's not about her, though, is it?"

Genie drew breath, but Jess ploughed on.

"I'm not denying she's hurting. I just mean she needs to stop pretending she's staying here for my benefit when clearly it's for hers."

"Clearly," Genie muttered. Jess's answering annoyance came in the form of noisy huffing and puffing on the phone mic, but she didn't challenge what Genie had said. Nor did Genie expect her to understand. She wasn't a mother. "Anyway, Jessica, this isn't a purely social call. The package arrived."

"Oh, good. Did you open it?"

"Was I supposed to?"

"Not necessarily, but you can if you like. You know about everything that's in there."

"OK. Well, it's in the vault, so unless you really need me to open it…" Genie crossed her fingers, hoping the answer was no. Not that it was a crypt-type vault; more a walk-in safe at the back of the wine cellar, but there was so much old junk in there and the concomitant dust, it left her wheezy and itchy-eyed for hours after each visit.

"No, it's fine," Jess said. "Oh! There is one thing in there you don't know about, but I'll tell you another time."

"You can't leave me dangling like that!"

Jess laughed, but she wasn't telling.

"Damn you, Jessica. I'm going to have to break out the antihistamines again."

"I'll text you when we get off the phone. How about that?"

"In that case, I'm hanging up."

"Don't you dare!"

Now Genie laughed. "I was joking, although I do need to go soon. Phee's home tomorrow, and I promised we'd go away somewhere—pick up a last-minute deal."

"You'll get a better deal if you leave it till the day you want to go."

"It's too risky."

"That's what I'd do."

"I'm not you."

"Lucky for you."

Genie sighed. "I could slap you sometimes. Or hug you. I'm never sure which."

"Then lucky for me, too, that this is only a phone call."

"Actually…" Between school fees, Margaret's wages and the usual bills, she couldn't afford more than a few days away, and she'd said they'd go somewhere hot with a pool, which they would, but life was undeniably short. "Are you well enough for visitors?"

"You and Phee?"

"Yeah. It'll be the week after next."

"I'll be here."

"Great. I'll call you later and figure out hotels and whatnot."

"Andy's the man to talk to for that. He'll get you a hefty discount."

"Even better. That's what I love about you."

"I have hot friends who get you stuff on the cheap?"

"Too right!" The less said about the hot friends part, the better, although they'd never talked about what had happened. It was a long time ago, in another life, really, when Genie still had access to her inheritance and Jess wasn't terminally ill. Perhaps that was why she kept mentioning Andy now. "I'm going, Jess. Don't forget to send me that text."

"Hang on!"

Genie waited, listening for clues over the too-quiet line.

"OK," Jess said at last. "She's gone outside for a cigarette, so I can tell you now. Andy and I are getting married."

"You're *what*?"

"Two words."

"True love?" Genie sniped but again managed to inflect it as a joke. Jess falling in love was even less likely than Paul unpacking his case without prompting.

"Inheritance tax."

"Thank God! You had me worried there."

"Ha. What about you and Paul? Any danger of you tying—"

"None at all. And I'm definitely going now. I'll talk to you later, OK? I love you."

"Love you too."

"And don't forget to give your mum my love."

"Will it stop her whinging?"

"Has it stopped you?"

"I'm not your friend anymore. Bye."

Genie's phone beeped in her ear, and she laughed. Jess had hung up on her. Same as usual.

∗∗∗

Present Day
Thursday, 18th April

GENIE DROPPED THE package, still sealed, back into the crate where it slid into the gap between the deeds to Rowan Mews and her parents' wills. After Jess passed, Andy had told Genie to incinerate it, but she had so little of Jess left, she couldn't. And, of course, Andy being Andy, he hadn't come back to her to check it had been destroyed. If he had, she'd have lied, despite knowing that the documents inside the thick brown paper were an incriminating fiction she'd helped create.

That familiar prickle started on the back of her neck, raced over her scalp, down her face, arms and torso, leaving goosebumps in its wake and her nipples resembling the knobbed lids of humbug jars. It was a feeling she now recognised as grief and disillusionment—that Jess had thought it necessary to offer bribes to secure Genie's assistance. That her love and their friendship had never been enough. The irony was laughable; the contacts she'd made through her work as an escort were what made it possible for her to do what Jess asked, in return for never having to deal with those men again. Her fortune had been restored, or that was how Jess had sold it, as if she were the croupier of some ethereal roulette wheel, fixing wins in favour of the neediest and most deserving.

Genie was now a woman of independent means, and in the year and a half since Jess's death, the money had passed through so many accounts and fund managers, charity projects and property developments, it was as stain-free as a newly laundered tablecloth. She would never again have to worry about school fees or first cars or lavish holidays, all those things she had wanted to provide for her daughter without saddling them both with familial obligation, and the only way of tracing it back to Jess's transgressions was through the contents of that package, which could be ashes in an instant.

All that money and she still hadn't been able to stop Phee throwing her life away for a few minutes' pleasure with some boy.

There were photos in the vault. Old photos of her baby girl, shiny dark-chocolate curls like Sean's, the rosiest cheeks and that sweet little smile captured on camera, the accompanying giggles as clear in Genie's mind as if she were hearing them all over again. But there had been no giggles since Phee came home. No laughter, tears, arguments, recriminations. Just the daily confirmation of nausea and fatigue and a refusal to leave her Liquorice Allsorts room until Xander and Jonathan 'pack up their shit and go'.

With the folder containing Margaret's references in her hand, Genie locked the vault and returned to the main house, snagging a pinot noir on her way through the cellar, which needed a restock; like most things of late, it was too much trouble. Writing this reference, for instance: Margaret hadn't yet given notice, but if she were asking for references, it was surely a foregone conclusion, and Genie had never written one before, hence she was taking her lead from the one provided by Margaret's former employer. Perhaps she shouldn't have agreed so easily, or so readily kowtowed to Phee's demand, as once Xander caught wind of it, he couldn't have 'packed his shit' any quicker. Well, he hadn't actually packed it; Jonathan had, but the net result was the same. Come the end of spring break when Phee returned to school, Genie would be rattling around this old house on her own. Of course, Paul would be home some of the time, but that thought brought her less solace with every passing day. Perhaps she should come to an agreement with the poltergeist now: *you stick to your rooms, I'll stick to mine, and we'll get along just fine.*

Genie opened the wine and filled a glass, raising it to her unseen housemate, gulped it down as if were mere grape juice and then filled the glass again, not a care for whether it was at its best when her options were quite starkly that she could either embrace a life of solitude or she could have it out with Phee.

Alas, the decision was ripped from her hands along with the glass when the music scores that she would have sworn on her daughter's life had been in the piano stool erupted from the music stand as if propelled by an industrial fan. They were still fluttering to the floor as Phee appeared in Genie's peripheral vision. All bar one, which came to a rest in the puddle of wine around Genie's feet.

"I'm going out," Phee said, then, "Agh. Mother!"

The song played, beginner's fingers bashing at the keys, a rhythmless accompaniment to drunken voices…

Alouette, gentille alouette
Alouette, je te plumerai

…and laughter.
"Mum?"

Je te plumerai la tête
Je te plumerai la tête
Et la tête, et la tête
Alouette, Alouette
Oh, oh, oh, oh

"Fine. Ignore me then! But you'll have to deal with that cut yourself. I'll see you tomorrow."

"It's not even the right piece." Half aware of the front door opening, Genie bent and peeled the wet paper from the floor, holding it out on her upturned palm as she straightened. "See? 'L'Alouette', not 'Alouette'."

The front door closed again, but Phee hadn't left.

"Mum?" She came into the room. "What are you on?"

"The music. Listen." Genie sang along. *"Alouette, gentille alouette, Alouette, je te plumerai."* She felt the bottle slipping from her hand and tightened her grasp as Phee tried to take it from her.

"Let go, Mum. You're drunk."

Genie laughed. "But I've only had one glass!" And yet… she did *feel* drunk. She stared at the half-full bottle. "Maybe I should eat." She shifted her gaze to her daughter's eyes, ringed with exhaustion and bushbaby wide. "And so should you."

"Mum, please—"

"I know you're pregnant."

Genie's arm sprang back with the force of Phee's sudden release of the bottle. The music stopped.

"How…?"

"How do I know? I'm your mum." Genie brushed her knuckles over Phee's peach-soft cheek, wine dripping from the music score scrunched in her hand. "Come and sit with me."

"I can't. I'm going out."

"Where?"

"I'm meeting Sarah at the pub."

"Are you really?"

"For God's sake, Mum. Yes. At the Hare and Hounds. Here." Phee yanked her phone from her pocket and jabbed the screen. "Shit. Line busy. But I swear that's where I'm going. If you don't believe me, come with me."

"I *do* believe you," Genie said.

"I've never lied to you."

"Never?"

"No. And I never would!"

"Where were you last weekend?"

Phee pursed her lips.

"Ah, a loophole. All right, then tell me this. Is he your boyfriend or someone you met at a party or…?"

Phee shook her head, pleading. "Don't, Mum."

"It's OK. You're not in trouble, darling."

"I've *got to go*." Phee pecked Genie's cheek and made a dash for the door, but not quickly enough to hide the crumple of her sweet face from her mother.

"You can tell me anything. You know that, don't you?" Genie called after her desperately. Phee left without looking back.

18: To Love and Friendship

Milky's Milk Bar
Present Day
Thursday, 18th April

"Another?" Sean nodded at Shaunna's glass, empty but for the last dregs of a cherry yoghurt-not-smoothie that looked disturbingly like coagulated blood.

Shaunna gulped and shuddered. "No, thank you. I'm driving."

"You don't drive."

"I don't have a car either."

"So the Mustang's all Andy's then?"

"Ha. What do you think?"

"I think you're very generous to let him chauffeur you around."

"Generous, you say…"

"I wouldn't say no to having you in my passenger seat."

Shaunna's eyebrows arched, and her lashes swooped low. "There's more room in the back."

"You'd know better than me."

She shook her head. "I've never done it in a car."

"Really?"

"Really. Have you?"

"No. Nor does it appeal. All those sticky-out bits to work around, and there's the chance you'll get caught by some poor old lady walking her poodle."

"That's what makes it so much of a turn-on."

"The old lady and the poodle?"

Shaunna rolled her eyes, always a dramatic display, but she was hamming it up today, as if to hide how she was really feeling. On the whole, though, she seemed her usual happy self. "You knew what I meant," she said. "It's the illicitness of it, like being a horny teenager again."

Sean sat back and watched her thoughts take hold—saucy ones, by the looks of it, as her cheeks had taken on a rosy hue and she was biting her lower lip. What a joy it would have been to see inside her mind right now, to be a voyeur to the memories that had her shifting in her seat. But for all their flirting and open conversations about their sex lives—or lack of one in Sean's case—Shaunna kept her teenage antics to herself, and he didn't want to ask, fearing she'd misunderstand his intent because he knew how it would sound. Even now, with her seemingly in a mental tryst with some teen dreamboat, when he pictured her in his head—calling it 'fantasising' made it seem sordid and unsavoury—she appeared just as she was: a voluptuous, magnificent redhead in her forties.

He was no dirty old man. Not like that cheating scumbag Paul. Sean had met a few like him over the years, and he'd done what he had to, mechanically going through the motions of impartial assessment and treatment, all the while with his sights on the drink at the end that would purge his disgust. Why had he accepted Phee's word that it was consensual? Did she know herself well enough to make that kind of informed decision, especially when it affected the rest of her life?

That was what he'd have asked Shaunna if he could. She'd been through teen pregnancy and motherhood. The little he did know was that she'd put her life on hold, much as Phee planned to, until her daughter started school. Did she regret it? Would she do it differently if she could go back?

He'd stared too long, and Shaunna had escaped her thoughts before he had. Now he was in trouble. After all, her openness wasn't the only reason he'd encouraged her when she'd said she wanted to become a sex therapist. It hadn't been part of the equation at all. She could read minds as adeptly as any psychotherapist worth their salt, himself and Josh included, and the tables had turned.

She waited, giving him a chance to speak. Feebly, he came up with, "Are you sure you don't want another drink?"

"I'm sure," she said. She trapped him with her gaze—blue-eyed today, which he had a feeling was her natural eye colour. He considered asking, to shift the focus back to her, but she was on to him and jumped in first. "What's up, Sean?"

"Why d'you ask?"

"In case you want to share, but you don't have to tell me."

"That's not how this works," he said.

"How what works?"

"Us."

"Oh, there's an 'us' now, is there?" She gave him a flash of that tantalising smile, the one where her lips parted a little and the tip of her tongue rested between her teeth. Sometimes it was a deliberate play in her flirting repertoire; sometimes it spontaneously manifested. In this instance, it was deliberate, and flirtatious, but with a different goal in mind.

"All right," he said, averting his eyes. "You can stop now. I'm at ease already."

"Hmm-hmm. If your shoulders were any tenser, your arms would stick out like windmill sails."

He hadn't realised until she said it, and he tried to loosen up. On top of being stressed, lugging all those boxes down from the attic had done him no favours, and his blood pressure was probably sky high. "Will you be offering massage once your sex clinic's up and running?"

She folded her arms. The overhead light reflected off her glossy pout. "I'm not answering that until you're straight with me and tell me what's wrong. You keep offering me drinks, so you clearly want me to stay."

"Can I not just enjoy your company?"

"If you were actually enjoying it…"

He held up his hands in surrender. "Fine. You got me." Could he say it? As he knew far too well, sometimes the will was there but the flesh was having none of it. He gave it a go. "My friend's daughter is pregnant. She's only seventeen."

Her response was non-verbal, and rich. A slight arch of the eyebrows, a relaxing of the lips, eye movement down, then up, no blinking. She sat forward, elbows resting on the table, arms still folded, and looked him dead in the eye. "And?"

"And..." He didn't know where to begin, and once again he took too long figuring it out for himself.

"You're worried she's thrown her life away," Shaunna said.

"No! God, not at all. I mean, if I hadn't met you, I'd be pulling my hair out over it, but look at you. You're setting up to embark on your second career, and you excel at your first. You're shacked up with a damn good-looking successful fella. Your eldest daughter is an amazing young woman, and all three of them are beautiful—a credit to you. You're brilliant."

Shaunna's answering laughter was bashful but brittle. "You make me sound superhuman."

"I'm not ruling it out," he joked, then asked seriously, "Do you not think you're successful?"

She thought about it for a while before she answered. "I don't know. Maybe I am, but it's not as if any of it was planned, or not planned in the way they get you to write down your targets and what you need to do to achieve them."

"'They' being?"

"Huh?"

"Who had you writing down targets?"

"Oh! Doctor Lederman. We had our first supervision meeting this morning."

"Did it go all right?"

"It went fine, thank you for asking, *aaaaand* back to you." Finally, she unfolded her arms and raised a finger. "I need to pee, but I'm not done with you." She dashed off, leaving him alone at the table.

For a moment, he thought he was alone in the milk bar, but then a member of staff popped up from behind the counter and smiled at him. She was new, and while he always made the effort to learn people's names and use them, he didn't know hers yet and she was too far away for him to read her nametag.

"Are you waiting to shut up shop?" he asked.

"Not yet." She glanced at the giant clock on the milk bar's back wall and frowned.

"It's always wrong," Sean said, taking out his phone, curious himself now. Time spent in Shaunna's company whizzed by, and beyond 'the duration of three yoghurt-not-smoothies', he couldn't have said with any accuracy how long they'd been sitting there. "It's six-thirty…" He stumbled again over not knowing her name.

"Thanks," she said, still scowling at the useless clock. "We're open for another half an hour."

"Grand. If you need us to clear out, just say, all right?"

She nodded and bobbed out of sight again, continuing with whatever she'd been doing under the counter.

"So…" Shaunna said as she resumed her seat across the table. "I was thinking in the loo. I need to ask you something." She adjusted her hairclip and tucked a loose curl behind her ear. It was the low-key equivalent of the *hair down, flick over the shoulder, I mean business* Shaunna. "I think I already know the answer, and if I'm right, you're gonna hit the roof, but I still need to ask, to be sure. I've never seen you so worked up before."

She hadn't even asked whatever it was and already she'd got Sean's back up, but he could see it was both difficult and important to her, so he nodded. "Go on."

Deep breath, hold. "Did you sleep with one of your undergrads and get her pregnant?"

"What the—" A roar of fury pushed its way up his throat, and the pressure in his head was unbearable. Hit the roof? He could've blown the thing to outer space. But his defences were holding—so far—and there had to be a reason for her asking. A good one. However it seemed, this was not an accusation that he would do something so abhorrent made by someone he loved, respected and trusted and of whom he had believed those sentiments were reciprocal.

He managed to push out a gruff, "No," at more or less normal volume but didn't dare say anything else.

"OK," she said. "I'm sorry I had to ask."

"So am I." He reached behind him for his coat, intending to get out of there before he exploded or fell apart, it could go either way, but she grabbed his arm, stopping him. He shot her a warning glance, and she flinched but didn't back down.

"Hear me out, Sean. Please?"

He didn't move, and she released him, tentatively, her expression beseeching him to stay. He nodded, no promises.

She was quiet for a few minutes, weighing her words and taking great care to not offend him further. He wasn't sure that was a possibility when he was beyond offended and the only bolster against the utter devastation of his self-esteem was his rapidly diminishing anger. There was still enough in the reserve for him to tell her to get on with it, but he gave her the benefit of the doubt and waited until, finally, she was ready.

"You think I'm this powerful, intuitive goddess-like being, Sean, but I'm not. I'm an ordinary woman. A mum. A hairdresser. Yes, I'm trying to be something more, but those psychology courses I did—it was so hard for me because I'm not like you and Josh and Ellie and Jess. I'm not naturally clever. I struggle with every word. I mean, you've no idea how long it took me to get my head around Piaget. You and Josh—that's how you talk all the time, but it's like a foreign language to me.

"And it's not just that. I remember you saying I'm kind of doing therapy on my salon clients already, but sometimes I get it so wrong. Like this woman came in a few weeks ago with an awful cut, and I felt sorry for her, so I made her a cuppa and let her cry on my shoulder. She said she'd been to the big salon on the high street and one of their trainees had done the hack job, so I thought the least I could do was tidy it up, stick a tint on it, turn it into something she could stand seeing in the mirror. I only charged her for a cut.

"Then last week, one of the salons across town called to say someone had been in asking them to fix her hair because a trainee in our shop had messed up her colour. We don't even have a trainee! Thank God Hayley's an understanding boss. The woman was a con artist, and I fell for it."

"We all make mistakes," Sean said, and if the words sounded harsh, then what of it? He'd thought they knew each other better than this. Better than she knew a walk-in client.

"I'm not explaining this well."

"No?"

"No!" She reached for his hand, and he was too slow to dodge. She squeezed. "I assume the best of you, Sean. Always. I've never doubted you."

"That's not how it feels—comparing what's happening here to some woman you met the one time. How—ah." His higher reasoning skills must have been reconnecting by increments. "You doubted your own judgement."

"Right!" She relaxed her grip on him, palpably relieved that he understood where she was coming from, although there was a way to go yet. "Believe it or not, I asked because I'm trying to be a good friend."

"Yeah, I'm not seeing that. Can you explain it to me?"

"I'm trying to. The thing is, I can usually see right through you. I'm not saying you're shallow or anything like that. You're wide open to me. Intentionally, I think. But this week, especially today, you're closed off somehow, and I was trying to figure it out in the loo. Why would you be so worried about this friend's daughter when you say what I've achieved reassures you she still has a future—unless you feel culpable? Why would you care that much unless you're involved with the girl in some way?

"I'm not saying you only care about people you have a connection with. I saw how you were with Libby when she first came here, but this is different. It's deep inside you, like you're burying it, and it's dark—worry and shame and regret and disgust. So…I thought maybe you were trying to confess something awful to me, and I talked myself into being sympathetic and understanding, even though I'd have wanted to rip your balls off and choke you with them if you'd admitted what I accused you of. I'm so, so glad I was wrong."

"You and me both, lovely." The sentiment wasn't there yet, but Sean was no longer seething. "Well, what can I say? Other than it's no wonder you get it wrong from time to time. How the hell do you cope with that level of empathy?"

"I got it *really* wrong, though, didn't I? I feel awful."

"Don't. All right, you maybe went about it badly, and I can't say I'm pleased you hit me with that, but you're dead on with everything except the motivation. To tell you the truth, I'm in awe."

"In awe…of me?"

"Aye." The menu board behind the counter darkened, and the coffee machine powered down. Sean met the server's gaze and nodded to indicate 'message received'. To Shaunna, he said, "We should go."

"Yeah. I was just thinking if I stay here much longer, Andy'll send out the search and rescue. I hadn't realised it was so late." She stood to put on her coat.

Sean did the same and then walked ahead of her, holding the door open as they both said good night to the server and stepped out into the light but cool evening.

"I'll give you a lift home," Sean said.

"I can walk."

"I know, but you took the time to explain to me. It's only fair I do the same." He unlocked Sophie's car and opened the passenger door.

Shaunna stared at it for a few seconds before relenting and climbing in. "Thank you for the lift, but like I said, you don't have to tell me—unless you want to."

"It might help me shed light on some of that darkness you picked up on."

"In that case..." Shaunna fastened her seat belt. "You may begin."

And so he did, and he didn't stop until he'd told her everything—about Phee and Paul and how desperate he was to check in with Genie, at the same time wanting to give Phee time to tell her mum what was going on. By then, they'd stopped outside Shaunna and Andy's place, and they watched, in silence, the outline of Andy carrying the twins across the room and up the stairs.

"He'll be giving them a bath," Shaunna said.

"I'm fine, you know. You don't have to stay with me."

"That's not what I'm doing." She inhaled slowly, exhaled twice as long, unclipped her seat belt and opened the door. "Remember what I said about your balls? If you see him—Paul—that's what you need to do, and if you can't do it, bring him to me." And with those words and a kiss on his cheek, she was gone.

19: Unsettling Symmetry

Chateau Reeves-Jeffries
Present Day
Thursday, 18th April, evening

"DOROTHY LOMAX?" ADELE repeated with a frown as she grabbed half the stuff from Josh's boot and waited for him to shut it. "I know that name."

"You do?"

"I think so. I wonder where from." She led the way inside the house. "What does she look like?"

"Mauve," Josh said, his surroundings a blur as he followed Adele up the stairs and into one of the bedrooms—or not a bedroom, he discovered when she said, "Closet light on," and the dark space transformed into a veritable boutique of women's clothing and accessories. Josh uttered a breathless "Wow!" which had Adele beaming as brightly as the many, many LEDs in the ceiling and around the mirror that took up an entire wall.

"I'll put this lot up there," she said, looking upwards yet tapping her toe against a deep drawer at floor level. The drawer slow-opened, revealing itself to be a step, onto which she climbed, permitting her to reach the passenger-plane-style overhead lockers.

"Adele, this is…fabulous!" Josh gushed, openly covetous of the gadgets.

"Thanks!" With a grin, she took the rest of the items from him, stacking the lot in the locker. She jumped down off her step, a perfect landing in high heels, said, "Secure closet"—counting in a whisper through doors one to three—"four," and the locker door swung shut. "There. All safe and sound. How about a coffee? I'll give you the tour later."

"OK. And thanks." In a daze, Josh followed her back down the stairs.

"She left an impression?" Adele said.

"Hmm?"

"Dorothy."

"Oh! More a purple haze, I'd say. She even smelled mauve."

Adele giggled, glancing at him over her shoulder. "I know exactly what you mean. Like all those perfumes we used to wear back in school. Well, us girls, at any rate. You can still buy them in the department store."

"A heavy, fruity scent, I recall."

"Yep. And always in purple bottles. It makes sense, though, doesn't it? Purple's the colour of success and creativity—maybe that's why women my age are doing so well for ourselves."

"Maybe," Josh said diplomatically. Adele was heavily into pop psychology—dream interpretation, reading body language, feng shui, self-help, neuro-linguistic programming, parapsychology—and on occasion, he'd indulge her, but he was already under pressure from Libby to deploy some 'colour psychology' in the surgery. If she ever discovered she had an ally in Adele, they'd gang up on him, and they'd win. He dreaded to think what colour the walls would end up then.

Adele deposited him outside a partly open door and continued on her way, calling, "Go in, make yourself at home."

Josh peeked in before entering and muttered, "Bloody hell." Were it not for all the soft furnishings, he'd have heard an echo. It was a hangar of a room that diminished the two four-seater sofas and cinema-worthy TV down to normal-people size. The décor was presumably the result of compromise, as the walls were plain white, but the sofas were a deep teal, and the prints on the two walls not taken up by a TV and a double door also had teal accents. It was so tidy it was almost unlived in, but what struck Josh more than the size, the formality or the colour coordination, was the perfect 180° symmetry, as if the room were half the width and reflected in a mirror even more enormous than the one in Adele's closet. It wasn't. He'd checked.

As Josh finished his sightseeing rotation, Adele appeared at his side and handed him one of the two lattes in glasses she'd brought with her. "What do you think? Do you love it, or...?" She braced in advance of his answer.

Josh gave it another look. He'd always admired Adele and Dan for their stylishness. Between Adele's interest in fashion and Dan's love of tech, they were early adopters, often months ahead of the trends, and there was nothing wrong with the room. Yet there was something very wrong, and he couldn't work out what, beyond knowing he really didn't like it.

"I love it, Adele."

"Yay! I thought you would. The sofas are amazingly comfy." She beckoned to him, and once again, he followed in her wake, sitting where she told him—he could agree the sofa lived up to her description—and sipping his somewhat feeble latte while she explained where she had procured each item and the theory behind its placement. Symmetry was the latest fad, apparently. At least there was a sound psychological basis for that.

She reached the end of her sales pitch as Josh swallowed down the last of his beige warm milk, which was when it dawned on him that it wasn't only Dan missing from the house. They were completely alone.

"Where are Shu and Robbie this evening?"

The buzz of Josh's phone vibrating sounded before Adele could reply, and she tilted her head in query, but Josh couldn't have appeased her curiosity if he'd wanted to. He didn't recognise the number, although it was a mobile this time, not the landline that had silently called him twice this week.

He hit the answer button and accidentally put the call on speaker. "Hello?"

"Good evening. Sorry to trouble you. Am I speaking with Josh Sandison?"

"You are." He made eye contact with Adele and mouthed *I recognise his voice. Do you?* She shook her head but pursed her lips in appreciation. The guy's voice was exquisite, with a rich, round tone and a very expensive accent.

"Hi, Josh," that exquisite voice continued. "You probably don't remember me. The name's Simon Henderson. We—"

"The inbred Adonis," Josh said and immediately shoved his fist in his mouth. Adele spluttered into her latte.

"Sorry?"

"Never mind." Josh could've slapped himself. He hadn't been intentionally insulting, just *very* surprised. "Yes, I remember you. How are you?"

"Well, thanks. And you?"

"Yes, I'm well too. How can I help you, Simon?"

"We share some acquaintances."

Josh knew that. "Whom specifically in relation to this call?"

"Gabby Bowes. Or Porter-Bowes these days. I met up with her at a gallery showing a couple of days ago, and she…ah, how to put it? She mentioned you were shopping around for a legal specialist in charity work?"

Josh was quietly astonished, which was to say rendered speechless. He muted the phone and stared at Adele, not that he expected her to know what he should say.

"Who is he?" she asked.

"A guy from uni. He studied law with Jess. I hadn't realised George had said anything."

"George knows him?"

"No, I meant to Gabby."

"Who?"

"George's art therapist."

"George has an art therapist?"

"Are you still there?" Simon asked.

"Yes. Oh!" Josh scrabbled to unmute the phone. "Sorry, I was wondering why Gabby mentioned it to you."

"If I have the wrong impression, I apologise."

"Not at all. This is probably a silly question, but *do* you specialise in charity work?"

"Ah." Simon chuckled. "Had I not been fully briefed in advance, I may have been inclined to say yes."

Josh shook his head, perpetually exasperated—and perhaps a little proud—that he had the kind of reputation that preceded him. "So if you're not a charity specialist..."

"I'm a commercial barrister, mostly largescale property acquisition, but I have worked with several charitable organisations."

"Which ones?"

Simon's laughter was like an air-clearing thunderstorm rumbling into the distance. "Gabby said you'd ask a lot of questions."

"I'm not about to divulge our requirements to a cold caller."

Adele covered her mouth but still snorted a giggle.

"Of course you're not," Simon said good-naturedly. "Perhaps if I could have your email address and send my CV, you can check my credentials at your leisure."

"Yes. That's acceptable. I'll send it to you in a text message."

"Great. I'll put my offer in writing, and if you're interested in discussing the matter further, I'd be happy to meet with you face-to-face."

"I'll be in touch," Josh said, then added, "Thanks for calling, Simon."

"Thanks for answering. Take care, now."

Josh ended the call and put his phone away. "That was Simon Henderson," he said. "The guy Jess had the hots for in her first week at uni."

"The rich one?"

Josh wrinkled his nose. "The first of many rich ones, I'd say. He's landed gentry. He asked her to marry him."

"Yes! And she told him she wasn't the marrying kind."

Josh coughed, attempting to cover his amusement. "Something like that."

Adele pouted. "She told me all about it, you know."

"Did she?"

"Yes. She wasn't high enough class for his family, but they didn't get that far because he told them he was gay even though he could've lost his inheritance."

"Wow, Jess really did tell you everything!" That or Adele had overheard a conversation she shouldn't have.

"Are you considering his offer?"

"Honestly, Adele, I have no idea." A week of Shaunna et al. interviewing lawyers and still without one, Josh couldn't justify turning Simon away without good reason, but the phone call alone had agitated the stew of emotions that had been accumulating since Monday's unexplained events.

"I know what'll help with that decision," Adele said. Josh waited for her to embellish. "I'll read your tarot."

"Absolutely not."

"Or we could use my rune—"

"Seriously. Enough of the hocus-pocus."

She tittered. "I'm teasing. I know you're confident in making decisions without asking Spirit for help."

"I wouldn't say confident..." Josh argued, but what he lacked in that regard couldn't be found in 'Spirit'.

"But you don't believe in *all that spiritualist crap*." Adele smiled to sweeten her sarcasm and then gasped. "Oh! D'you remember Gavrilovich?"

"Gary the Russian medium? Yes," Josh said suspiciously, seeing as Gavrilovich call-me-Gary Ovsianikov had done a number on him at what should've been an evening of fun entertainment. "Why?"

"He passed over last Christmas. And no, he didn't see it coming." She covered her mouth, horrified by her joke, and then fell into a fit of giggles. Despite his best efforts, Josh fell with her.

"Oh, Adele. That's hilarious! Not that he died." He wiped his eyes with his thumb. "Was it sudden?"

"I'm not sure. I read about it online."

"Not in your cards?"

She lightly smacked his arm, her giggles silenced by his mockery.

"I'm sorry," he said. "I can't help it."

"I know." She swirled the last inch of her coffee and lifted it to her mouth but then moved it away again. "I don't get it. You don't think any of that stuff from your loft works and don't believe Gary could communicate with the spirits, yet you freaked out when he told you he was in contact with your mum."

"Because he manipulated my feelings and the feelings of everyone else who was there. I'm certain he wasn't talking to the dead, but it still affected me."

"Why, if you're so sure he was a fake?"

"How do you feel when I look into your head, as you put it?"

"Really uncomfortable, like you know all my secrets."

"That's how I felt at the psychic night. Gary took his cues from my reactions. It's similar to what I do—reading people's expressions and behaviour—although I try not to do it without their consent."

"But you gave Gary your consent by being there."

"Yes, that's true." Like he'd given the psychology department his consent by becoming one of their undergraduates. Sometimes his naivety dismayed him. "The thing is, it should be informed consent, and I admit I didn't know what a psychic night entailed. Suffice to say, I hadn't foreseen him telling a room full of strangers that I'm an orphan."

"Oh." Adele looked stricken. "I'm so sorry."

"Why?"

"I invited you."

"Yes, you *invited* me. And I accepted. You didn't force me to go. It's not your fault curiosity got the better of me and I let Gary cold read me. Because that's all it is, Adele. No psychic ability required."

"But even if Gary was doing that cold-reading thing, it doesn't mean it's not real. There are lots of other mediums out there."

"OK, but so far, psychologists haven't found much evidence to suggest it *is* real." Josh was conveniently overlooking the other thing Gary had said to him. Even if taken in conjunction with Monday's strangeness and what had happened in his halls of residence all those years ago, it was of no significance in scientific terms. However, it *was* significant to him, so profoundly so he'd hardly slept in days and could now hear Gary's words echoing in his memory as clearly as two years ago.

Whether you choose to believe what I say or not, your friend needs to see a doctor. It won't make any difference in the end, of course.

Josh had never told anyone about it. Or no-one but George, who wasn't sceptical as such but had inherited his mother's take-no-crap attitude and had reminded Josh that digging dirt on people wasn't his exclusive domain. If that was how Gary had gleaned the information, then he should have been working for the Secret Service because Jess's terminal prognosis hadn't been confirmed until the day after the so-called psychic night.

Still, Josh had accepted George's reasoning. Gary *could* have accessed Josh's GPS data and the oncology department's records and established he hadn't been attending an appointment himself. That would be sufficient for a starting point; the rest could be gleaned from Josh's responses on the night. It seemed a lot of effort to go to for just one audience member and impractical to do it for all sixty in attendance. Then again, clairvoyance was a lucrative business. Perhaps good old Gary had a team of minimum-wage research monkeys tapping away behind the scenes. In a just world, that would be what happened to parapsychology graduates caught with their ethical pants around their ankles, like Ali, Josh's torturer in the name of empirical study.

A polite cough at his side brought Josh out of his thoughts and alerted him that a certain blonde friend with a passion for all things psychic was doing some cold reading of her own. He met her ponderous, sideways-tilted gaze, and she smiled.

"Shall I make more lattes?"

"Yes," he answered for some unfathomable reason. The first latte had been palatable but largely devoid of caffeine, and he had work he should be getting on with, but he couldn't say he wasn't enjoying her company this evening. Or he had been until she tottered across the room that made him uncomfortable and he realised why that was. "I'll come with you," he said.

"You don't have to."

He did have to, lest he break the symmetry again with his singular presence, but she was quick, and the hallway was already empty by the time he escaped. "Adele?"

"In here!"

There were four doors, all slightly ajar to the same extent, as had the living room door been earlier, and he couldn't discern where she was from the direction of her voice. He tried the two doors closest: the first was a WC; the second concealed a narrow staircase presumably leading to a cellar. "In where?"

The answering giggle came from behind him and gave him no clearer a sense of where she was, but before he could try a third door—which would also have been the wrong one—Adele's grinning face popped into view.

"Sorry." She didn't look or sound it. "I forgot you don't know where the kitchen is."

Josh snuffed his disgruntlement and followed her into the mercifully asymmetrical kitchen, although alien abductees had never faced such blinding brightness. It was so *white and shiny*! High-gloss cabinet doors, polished marble worktops, porcelain tiles on the walls and floor. He almost asked if Adele had modelled it on her plastic surgeon's operating theatre, but her expectant blinks saved them both from his thoughtlessness.

"This is incredible, Adele," he said instead, which wasn't a lie. He liked how clean and uncluttered it was, but perhaps Libby was on to something with incorporating a little colour into his surgery renovation.

As if she'd read his mind—and Josh was ruling out nothing—Adele asked, "Is green still your favourite colour?"

He smiled bashfully, delighted that she remembered whilst still not comfortable with her having figured it out in the first place. "Yes," he confirmed.

"Hm." She handed him a full latte glass, positioned a second one under the nozzle of the coffee machine—also white—and said, "Set kitchen to emerald green." And just like that, all that shiny white turned to a rich, vibrant green.

"Wow!" Josh stared around him in wonder. "How did you do that?"

Adele grinned. "It's magic. Do you love it?"

"I really do!" It was the truth this time.

"Would you like a go?"

"Can I?"

She nodded encouragingly.

"OK. Erm…so I just say, 'set kitchen to…sky blue' and—"

Adele clapped in glee at his surprise when on his command the green faded gently into a fetching pale azure. "You could have this in your kitchen," she said.

Josh nodded in distracted agreement.

"Or any room," she said. "We have it in the kids' rooms and the gym, and—"

Josh put down his latte and planted a noisy kiss on her forehead. "Adele, you are a genius!" She staggered slightly as he released her.

"I am?"

"You are. You've just solved my surgery colour dilemma."

"Yay!" She clapped again, applauding herself. "I'm a genius!"

"So." Josh pulled out a stool at the island, sat, latte in hand, and gestured for Adele to join him. "Teach me about colour psychology."

"F…for real?"

"Yes, please."

She did a mini jump up onto the other stool and considered him through narrowed eyes. "First, you have to be honest with me."

"OK." Josh prepared for a barrage of questions about his colour preferences, the kind of mood he wanted to create and so on. He should've known better.

"What is it you don't like about my living room?"

20: By One's Teeth

Rowan Mews
Present Day
Friday, 19ᵗʰ April

"Moorhaven NHS Trust."

Damn it. "Hello…again!" Genie completed the gate doodle depicting her attempts thus far to make it past the hospital switchboard, although this operator, unlike the coarse Northerners before, had a throaty, Scottish accent that added a luscious curl to the 'r' and aspirated the 'h', reminding Genie of her old maths teacher, a slick-haired, sharp-featured little man who'd treated all of his charges with the same impatient contempt. As reminiscences went, it didn't bode well for a successful conclusion to her telephone quest. "I wonder if you could help me?"

"I'll certainly try," the operator replied blithely.

"I'm hoping to get through to Doctor Sean Tierney. He works on the Parkwood Wing. Before you ask, I know it's a big department, and no, I don't have an extension number."

"Ah. You've called already."

"Five times now," Genie sighed.

"All right, well, let's see if we can make this the last. I'm going to have a chat with the Parkwood admin office. I'll have to put you on hold for a minute, OK?"

"OK."

At least this operator hadn't connected her to a phantom extension with no phone at the end of it, although listening to the distorted 'hold' Muzak, Genie thought she might have preferred the dead-line tone. It took her a moment to realise the digital *beep-beep* wasn't part of the composition but was her incoming-call alert. Phee. *Damn.* They needed to talk, but the way Genie's luck was going, the operator would come back on the line and, deciding she'd given up, disconnect her. Placating herself that it would be better to speak to Phee face-to-face, Genie dismissed her call and went back to waiting.

Perhaps she wouldn't have been quite so irritated by this rigmarole if she could shake the feeling that Sean had intentionally withheld his new mobile number from her, but why would he? It wasn't as if she called him all the time. In fact, she couldn't remember when they'd last spoken, other than knowing for sure that whenever it was, she'd done the calling. In all the time they'd been friends, he'd never called her.

As the archived 'conversation' with a dud number showed, he'd sent texts from time to time—another trait Phee had inherited from him, it seemed, the difference being that Phee *would* call if her messages went unanswered. It had been tempting last night to not respond to Phee's apologetic '*I'm sorry I didn't tell you. I love you xx*' and force her hand, but Genie knew how to pick her battles, so she'd replied '*I love you so much – I'm here for you always xx*' and tried to get some sleep, securing a couple of hours at best.

The 'hold' music stopped without resolving, and the operator said, "Hello?"

"Hi."

"Bad news, I'm afraid. Doctor Tierney *did* work here, but he doesn't anymore."

Genie inhaled sharply in surprise—not because Sean had left the hospital, although that was surprising in itself. She coughed on the influx of suddenly cold, dry air, and then did it again when her breath misted in front of her. After the madness of the past few days, her thoughts went straight to more ghastly causes than British springtime weather, as if that weren't ghastly enough.

Unable to bring herself to move, she scanned the kitchen, shifting her eyes only, for signs of her invisible house guest, but aside from Xander's detection of a phantom housekeeper, nothing untoward had happened in there. If she really wanted to know— which she didn't—she'd have to go into the drawing room, where the piano was.

"Are you OK there?" her friendly Scots operator asked, which reinstated some reason, permitting her to consider that perhaps it was just a chilly morning, even if the sun's reflection off the tiles had been dazzling enough that she'd closed the blinds. She tweaked the cord, peeking out between the slats, and could have cried with relief at the steam rising from roofs half covered in light frost where the sun had yet to reach.

"Yes, thank you," she said. Her throat still a little tickly, she grabbed her upturned cup from the drainer and filled it from the sink tap, swallowing down a couple of mouthfuls of tepid, chlorine-heavy water before she attempted to say anything further. All the while, the operator waited: Genie could hear the hum of the busy hospital and their murmured words to someone else. When the murmuring came to a pause, she said, "My apologies. I don't suppose you have another number for Doctor Tierney?"

"I don't, but if you wouldn't mind giving me your details, I'll forward them to his colleague, who said she'd contact him on your behalf."

"Wonderful!" Genie gave her name and number and sincerely wished the operator a lovely day before they ended the call. Now she could only wait and hope Sean phoned back. Those few moments of interaction with a stranger had diminished the urgency of her need to talk to him to wanting simply to catch up and find out what he was doing if he no longer worked at the hospital. He'd given her the impression they'd have to carry him out of there in a body bag before he'd leave, but that was a long time ago.

Out of habit, Genie sipped from the cup in her hand, expecting coffee, and shuddered at the bleachy, filmy aftertaste. Tipping the water into the sink, she set off the coffee maker and popped to the loo, trying to pin down when, exactly, she'd last talked to Sean. Was it before or after Paul came on the scene? She thought she'd introduced them, but she may have merely rehearsed doing so. She knew it was before Jess became sick because Genie had been sworn to secrecy. It had been like carrying a tumour of her own, and she'd come within a hair's breadth of breaking her word, especially towards the end. No-one else knew what Jess had meant to her, nor would she have trusted anyone other than Sean to maintain the secret, but ultimately, sharing her burden with him would also have made it his, and so she'd kept it to herself, even when Jess cut contact a few weeks before she died.

She returned to the kitchen, where the coffee maker was still dripping, and she urged it on. Her reflections had taken a bleak turn, and a partisan one at that. So little of note happened in her life, often she felt as if she were on a horse trotting around the same paddock, day upon day, with loss the only, mercifully rare variation. First her grandmother, then Jess, and now she feared her relationship with Paul was in countdown. Even her daughter, whose very existence gave Genie's meaning, was causing more heartache than she thought she could withstand. Of course, she'd been there before, when Phee, aged eight, had fractured her shoulder performing a complex gymnastic manoeuvre, and again when, aged twelve, she'd shown symptoms of meningitis. Like all mothers, Genie had made it through both scares because what else could she do? She'd chosen lone parenthood and in general felt she coped perfectly well, but at times like these she wished there were someone to help carry the load.

With that acknowledgement, it came to her, clear as crystal. The last time she'd spoken to Sean was when Phee was admitted to hospital. There was no practical reason he should be any more invested than Paul in Phee's well-being, yet he'd arrived at the hospital before the blood test results were back—not meningitis, thank God, but an acute sinus infection that nonetheless needed aggressive antibiotics to send it on its way. Once Phee had settled for the night, Sean had taken Genie home and slept on the sofa until Paul rudely disturbed him the following morning.

Genie's anger had quickly dissolved into a hurt that had endured, but she refused to let Paul see it, and not because he was a poor stepfather. He was no stepfather at all. As with Sean, she'd been adamant from the start that her relationship with Paul was separate from her life with Phee, irrespective of the three of them sharing a house. It was no hardship, considering how rare it was for them all to be home at once. She'd also made it clear to Phee that Paul was not to be involved in their battles.

Genie was aware she was being contrary. The meningitis scare came when she and Paul were still fairly new, but she didn't think it was too much to expect his emotional support when her daughter had a life-threatening illness. Granted, it hadn't been what they feared, but Paul hadn't known that until he arrived home, fresh-faced and casting filthy glances in Sean's direction while asking chirpily how Phee was faring as if she'd gone to bed with the sniffles. He worked for the company who'd developed the pneumococcal vaccine, for goodness' sake. He *knew* the danger.

That was why, now, she was going to such lengths to get hold of Sean instead of calling Paul, and her actions spoke volumes. Their relationship was as dead as Xander's ghosts, and she should do the decent thing and end it. It was better to push people away—her parents, her sister, her old friends, Sean—than to let a relationship fester into something rotten, in Genie's experience. Her grandmother and Jess were the only ones she'd fought to keep in her life, and they'd left her.

The coffee had stopped dripping some time ago, replaced by the steady drip of tears she'd left unattended until her phone rang, which was timely and might just have saved her from cracking open a wine bottle before noon. Alas, it was not the call she'd hoped for. It was from Xander's office. Genie wiped her eyes and gave her nose a quick blow before she answered.

"Hello?"

"Hello, Your Ladyship, it's Jonathan Reardon, calling on behalf of Lord Etherington-Bowes."

"Genie," she reminded him. "How can I help you, Jonathan?"

"His Lordship has suggested—" He stopped when Xander spoke in the background, his voice suddenly becoming clearer, presumably now on speaker phone.

"We will come back once your daughter has returned to school."

"If that is all right with you, of course," Jonathan added.

"It should be." Between morning sickness and the emotional upheaval, Genie wasn't sure if Phee would be returning to school, but she needed to give Xander a firmer answer. "May I call you back later?"

"Ask her what time," Xander said.

"By five o'clock this afternoon," Genie answered and heard Xander grunt in the affirmative. "Sorry to dash, but I'm waiting for an important call."

"My apologies, Your—Genie. Goodbye for now."

"Bye," Genie replied, but Jonathan had already cut her off, and a good thing that was too, as her screen lit up with another incoming call. Still not Sean.

"Hello, darling."

"Why didn't you answer my texts?" Phee demanded.

"I didn't see them."

"No surprise there! You're a phone demon this morning. I've been trying to call you for hours."

"Hardly hours."

"Hours!"

Genie glanced at the clock, confirming it had been no more than twenty minutes, although a further glance at her call log also confirmed two further missed calls from her daughter.

"You *never* use your phone," Phee said, which was mostly true. Since Jess's passing, the only regular outgoing calls Genie made were to Phee. "Who were you talking to? Xander?"

"Yes. Well, briefly." Despite their text truce, Genie hesitated before she asked, "How are you feeling this morning?"

"I'm...all right. Are you?"

"Tired, but I'm fine. What time are you coming home?"

"Not sure yet. Why?" Phee was already on guard.

"I thought we could do something—go to the cinema?"

"The cinema."

"It doesn't have to be."

"Is there something you want to see?"

"I've no idea what's on."

"Knowing our luck, a rescreening of *Poltergeist*," Phee said dryly.

Whether it was because of nerves, fatigue, relief or perhaps a combination of all three, Phee's joke broke the stalemate, and they laughed as they volleyed titles of all the ghost films they'd seen together—something they'd always loved to do. A scary movie, complete with bucket of popcorn and massive drinks, was prime mother-and-daughter time when the only pressure was on their over-taxed bladders. No need to talk about difficult things.

"OK," Phee said, calling a ceasefire. "I'd really like that."

"Should I pick you up, or are you coming home first?"

"Can you come and get me now? I need to shower and change."

"Of course, darling. See you in..." Genie's phone beeped, and she moved it so she could see the screen. Another incoming call, this time from an unknown mobile number. She put the phone back to her ear. "A client's trying to call me. I'll leave as soon as I've spoken to them. Love you."

"OK, Mum. Love you too."

Genie wasn't quite quick enough to reach the answer button. She clicked on the missed call.

"Your call cannot be taken at the moment—"

She hung up and started counting, intending to call back in thirty seconds, but the caller was trying again.

"Genie?"

"Sean! Hi!"

"I got a message you'd called the hospital. Is everything all right?"

"Oh, yes! Everything's fine!" she declared bravely before, in an instant, all her false cheer dissolved into a wretched sob that rendered her incapable of further lies while at the other end of the line Sean offered quiet reassurances that he was still there. She could take her time, he said, and she did, through no choice of her own, as the emotions she'd held in, not just for the past few days but for years, rushed like whitewater rapids through her mind. It was, in the end, the realisation Phee would know she'd been crying that stemmed the flow, and still Sean waited as, for the second time that morning, she wiped her eyes and blew her nose into a rough paper towel.

"It's funny," she said. "According to Xander, people cry too loudly to hear those they miss."

Sean chuckled. "He might be on to something—if by that you mean you've missed me."

"I always do, Sean." She cleared her throat with some success. "You're no longer working at the hospital?"

"No, but I only finished there two days ago. I don't know if you remember Josh Sandison—one of the other psych students from uni?"

"Your old housemate?"

"The very fellow. We're setting up a private clinic."

"Wow. Excellent. Are you excited?"

"I am. What about you? Still looking after rich gentlemen?"

"God, no. I got out of that game a couple of years back, after—" Genie turned her abrupt cut-off into a cough, but there was no way she could bluff her way out, not with Sean. It would be unfair on them both if she tried. "Do you know Jess passed?"

"I do."

"Right. I wasn't sure you'd stayed in touch."

"We hadn't. I planned to, but you know me."

"Indeed, I do."

Sean grunted. "I'm sorry, Genie. I get caught up in work, and the time passes me by, and I think to myself, 'I should call,' but it's always too late at night, and then I forget the next day, and on it goes. But I have missed you. I really have."

"And Jess?"

"I miss her tremendously. We lived a few miles apart and worked in the same town for all those years, it's an awful shame. But we reconnected a little while before she passed."

"I'm glad, Sean." Genie carefully phrased her words. "I'm not telling you this to be cruel, but she never mentioned you."

"No, and likewise. You stayed in touch?"

"Almost to the end. That was when I gave up the escort business."

"It was a wake-up call," Sean said.

"Something like that."

"You saw the news reports, I'm sure."

"Yes." Genie had seen them, and she'd refused to read them. She'd had no need to.

"Were you surprised?" he asked.

"Not really. She was ambitious, a risk-taker."

"That she was."

"You don't seem surprised either," Genie noted.

"Not now I've made my peace with who she was and the way she kept everything compartmentalised. Like, when I think back to what you said about how mad she was when she found out you were expecting Phee…"

"Because it was with you." Genie nodded and smiled to herself. She'd taken some sordid satisfaction from getting a rise out of Jess—the closest she'd come to a display of possessiveness, except Genie knew now it was no such thing. Jess had been protecting her secrets, even back then, which was why she'd kicked Genie out of the house whenever Andy came to visit until it suited her needs not to. "Did you go to her funeral?" she asked.

"Yeah."

"Was it a good one?"

Sean laughed. "See, now, you could only say that to a Catholic boy. Aye, it was lovely, as funerals go. The wake was in a Chinese restaurant."

"That's…unusual."

"And a welcome change from where I'm standing. I've given up the booze, Genie."

"Really?" Too late, her astonishment was out there.

"Three years dry."

"Three years? Gosh! I can't imagine how hard that must be. Does it get easier?"

"I suppose it does, but I have rough days, you know?"

"I do." She was having a glut of them, and it felt like the right moment in their conversation to tell Sean why she'd made contact. "So, ah…" The right moment, but now it was here, she could barely bring herself to say it. "I've had an eventful week."

"OK." She could tell from his tone that he'd switched to 'psychologist' mode.

"Well… When… What…" Before she went through all the Ws, she paused, employing what she'd learnt long ago about constructing an argument. State the facts, then elaborate. "Two things," she said. "First, I have a poltergeist. Second, Phee's pregnant."

She waited for a response, and it was safe to say she'd received the one she'd have expected from anyone other than Sean. She'd never known him to be lost for words. Perhaps he was waiting for her to explain, or their call had disconnected.

"Are you still there, Sean?"

"I am. I'm…processing."

"OK. Sorry."

"No need. To recap, by poltergeist, are we talking stuff turning up someplace other than where you left it, or—"

"Lamps shattering mirrors, pictures falling off walls. That kind of thing."

"That kind of thing," Sean echoed. "The usual, then."

Genie's hysteria poked a finger into her side, eliciting a high-pitched titter.

"Now I understand why you mentioned Xander."

"He's looking into it for me."

"Good." Sean was still using a neutral but sympathetic tone that made it impossible to gauge his true thoughts or feelings. "And Phee—is it official or a suspicion?"

That was a good question because an '*I'm sorry I didn't tell you*' text message was no admission. "Somewhere between the two. I told her I knew. She has neither confirmed nor denied it."

"She'd make a fine politician."

"She'd make a fine anything she put her mind to," Genie said, adding in her head, *if she hasn't thrown it all away.*

"Just like her mum," Sean flattered as if he were privy to her thoughts. "All right. What d'you need from me?"

"A listening ear."

"Anytime."

"And a means to reach it."

"Are ye too posh for plastic cups and string in your neck of the woods?"

"Ha-ha. I've got your number now."

"You always did, Genie."

"Hmm." The conversation was taking a sentimental turn, and on another day, she'd have maybe indulged him, but her emotions were beyond frayed. "I need to go and collect Phee from her friend's place. We're going to the cinema."

"OK, lovely. It's been grand talking to you."

"Same here."

"And I mean it. You can call me anytime. Who knows, I might even call you again!"

"I've had more than my share of the unexpected this week."

"Next week, then," Sean said, his grin audible. "Take care, Genie."

"I will. You too." Genie ended the call and used her phone's camera to check her face. Slightly bloodshot eyes, a tinge of red around her nostrils. Better than she'd anticipated.

21: Abstinence

A Friend's House
Present Day
Friday, 19th April

"A RE YOU STILL in there?" The bathroom door handle twisted a couple of times and sprang back. "Phee?"

"Hold on." She flushed the loo and took a tiny sip of mouthwash. Her gag reflex violently ejected it.

"OK, you're scaring me now," Sarah said from the other side of the door. "*Please* let me in."

Lips clamped in teeth, Phee crossed the dizzying checkerboard floor of the enormous bathroom and unlocked the door. "I'm fine." She saw how unconvincing her carefree smile was when Sarah mirrored it back with added irony.

"Your mum's outside."

"Good. I can't wait to go home, get a shower…" Phee made a small sobbing sound, but she could've cried for real. "We're going to the cinema."

"Shower and jim-jams is what you need," Sarah advised, watching over her in a motherly fashion while Phee went around the room gathering her make-up, phone charger and purse. "You didn't even drink that much, did you?"

"No. I had two vodkas." She'd stuck to water all night. Slinging her bag over her shoulder, she followed Sarah downstairs.

"Maybe you were right, then, about Dad's cooking."

"Shh! He'll hear you, and anyway, it wasn't his cooking."

"He's gone to work. But you said it tasted weird."

"It'll be a stomach bug or something." She hated lying to Sarah—hated even more that Sarah's dad was getting the blame for something he hadn't done. She'd always loved his chicken pasanda—until last night, when she'd swallowed one mouthful and had to sprint from the dining room.

They reached the front door and hugged.

"Thanks for letting me stay."

Sarah drew back and frowned. "Why are you thanking me?"

"It's polite."

"You don't usually thank me."

"I don't usually spend half the night throwing up in your bathroom."

"Hmm." Sarah wasn't buying it. In fact, Phee was sure the entire conversation, like the one they'd had after dinner the previous evening, was a fishing expedition. Sarah was in her final year of uni, so she didn't know Phee's sickness had begun weeks ago at school, but they'd been friends a long time. She'd have picked up that Phee was hiding something, but there was no way she could tell Sarah. No way.

"Talk over the weekend?" she said, closing off the discussion.

"OK, prin. Enjoy your movie."

"I'll try."

Sarah stepped aside, and Phee left, waving on her way out to the car.

"Hey, Mum." She shut the car door and turned to fasten her seat belt, coming almost nose-to-nose with her mother's harrowed face. "What?"

"You're terribly pale, darling."

"I didn't put any make-up on yet. No point before I shower, is there?" She tilted her head meaningfully to get her mother moving, and it worked, but it didn't stop her going on.

"Have you been throwing up?"

"Not really."

"What does that mean?"

"Mum…"

"And are you eating and drinking enough? Whatever you decide to do, you still need to look after yourself."

"I am. Look, can we talk about something else or, you know, not talk at all?"

"As you wish."

It wouldn't last. To prove it, Phee counted down from five in her head. She reached two.

"We can postpone the cinema trip."

"No."

If nothing else, it meant a couple of hours without the constant questioning, which was what had prompted her to flee to Sean five days ago. Had he given her the choice, she'd have still been there, avoiding the inevitable moment when she told her mum the truth and it ruined everything forever. So however crap she felt, she'd suck it up for an afternoon at the cinema with her mum because it might be the last one.

***

Tierney Residence

GETTING A WEEKDAY morning to himself, Sean felt like he was pulling a sicky. He'd been watching breakfast telly and enjoying hot, fresh tea while the rest of the world went off to work. Then Francesca's PA had called to pass on Genie's number, bringing his leisurely breakfast to a grinding halt.

The conversation with Genie could have gone a lot worse. She didn't cope well with anything that was out of her control, and her daughter's independent streak had tested her many times over the years, each eliciting a telephone counselling session where she ranted and Sean listened and took the genetic blame blows on the 'Irish' chin that was so much more endearing on his offspring.

Ignoring the meningitis scare, a terrifying night all round, the last time had been when Phee asked to go to boarding school, and Genie had lost the plot for a while, pouring out this whole mess of things that had happened to her at boarding school, any one of which would see most people in therapy for years. But on that, like almost every other occasion, all Genie required of Sean was that he listened. It was one of her greatest strengths: once she'd talked it out of her system, she moved on.

This pregnancy malarkey, though, was a whole new level of out of Genie's control, and Sean worried for them both. Phee hadn't told her mum who the father was; that much was clear from what Genie *hadn't* said, and now Sean was wondering whether as an ignorant bystander he'd have naturally asked if there was a boyfriend on the scene. Had he given himself away by not asking? Genie hadn't picked up on it, but she'd realise in time, he was sure of it. She was as astute as they came, and she'd want to know why he hadn't frogmarched Phee straight home and insisted she tell her mother what was going on, but that wasn't Sean's decision to make.

Honesty's a good thing. He said it so often it felt like a catchphrase, but experience told him it was almost always true. Not the little white lies or minor indiscretions. The kind of dishonesty that takes root and taints every thought, feeling and interaction. However brutal or painful, laying it all out in a safe, mediated space was a chance for those involved to truly understand each other and nurture a more meaningful relationship, regardless of how much or how little time they had left.

That was what had him stumped. For the first time in as long as he could remember, he wasn't sure honesty *was* the good or right thing for Phee and Genie, and he'd floundered, sent Phee packing when he should have offered to mediate, to be their safe space. It was cowardly and futile, like hiding under a flimsy sheet while the roof caved in, because whichever way he looked at it, the fallout would be devastating. If Phee told her mum about Paul, it would destroy Genie's trust; if she kept it a secret, it would hang over their relationship forever.

And God almighty, he needed a drink. Every night since Phee turned up, he'd gone to bed, relieved to have made it through another day without succumbing to the urge and with the hope that tomorrow he'd feel different, but it was still there when he awoke, and it clung on relentlessly, infiltrating his thoughts and crumbling his resolve.

He could do some baking, although he'd used up his quota of that distraction this week. "*More* soda bread?" Soph's mum had said. "How lovely!" He'd need to do some shopping first, however, and shops sold whiskey, so that was out of the question. Cleaning, maybe? Catch up on some reading? That appealed no more than cleaning.

Downing the dregs of his tea on the way to the kitchen, he weighed up the options. Baking always put his mind at ease, so he should at least check if it was possible.

"Right, let's see…" Opening all the cupboards, he stood back. "No eggs, no flour." He picked up a pot and shook it. "Got bicarb, a bit of sugar." He closed the cupboards and went to the fridge. "Not enough milk, no butter." The cat flap clicked. "Christ, it's like Old Mother Hubbard's here, Sphinx—oh, it's you again, is it?"

Jinja hopped up onto the counter and tucked into Sphinx's breakfast. Sean shook his head, laughing because what else could he do? Tell Josh to train his cat not to walk in uninvited? He'd have more success getting Jinja to train Josh, but it wasn't fair on Sphinx. Cantankerous, independent old so-and-so that he was, he picked battles he could win, and Jinja wasn't one of them.

"Come on, out you go." Ignoring the mewl of protest, Sean scooped up the big orange tom and put him outside, making a mental note to ask Josh later where he'd bought Jinja's microchip-programmed cat flap and maybe take back his claim that it was a faddy gadget.

Sadly, the interlude with Jinja wasn't enough to shake Sean's desire for drink, and he was in his coat with the front door half open when a tiny spark of willpower gave him pause. If he left the house, he'd buy whiskey, and he couldn't trust himself to stay put. Before he could think on it further, he shut the door and locked it, removed the key from the lock and did the same with the back door. Looping both onto the same ring, he opened the living room window and threw the keys as hard as he could.

"Ah, shite." His willpower might have been weaker than a newborn kitten, but apparently his throwing arm was in fine form, as the bunch of keys flew straight over the hedge and clattered onto the pavement beyond.

***

Rowan Mews

For once, Phee was in full agreement with her mum that they needed to make a move. She couldn't get into her clothes fast enough after she heard the bottle smash. The stench of wine was vile but not the reason why she'd raced out to the car, still no make-up, wet hair dripping down her top as she fought to fasten her seat belt on the move. No, the reason for her immediate compliance was that they'd both been upstairs when the bottle, which Phee had watched her mum put in the fridge, had somehow smashed into a thousand pieces all along the hall.

"Oh my God, that beep is driving me mental! Can you stop a minute?"

Without taking her eyes from the road, her mum indicated and pulled over. As soon as she did, Phee's seat belt clicked into place and the beeping stopped. Still facing forward, her mum indicated again and re-joined the flow of traffic.

"When are you going to call Xander?" Phee asked.

"Later."

"Before we get to the cinema?"

"You told me to send him away. Now you want him to come back?"

"No, I don't, but there's a ghost in our house. It could harm us."

"I don't think—"

"It threw a bottle!" Phee leaned forward and squeezed her hair over the footwell.

"Do you have to do that?"

"Well, have you got a towel?" She opened the glove compartment, as if there'd be one in there, and shut it hard.

"There's a roll of blue paper towel under the seat."

"Argh! You could've said!"

Her mum huffed and checked the rear-view mirror.

Phee reached under her seat and found the end of the roll, pulling a length from it and wrapping it turban-style around her head. "I could call him," she suggested.

"No."

"You're driving."

"It can wait until I've parked the car."

"But it's already injured you." Phee stared at the side of her mum's head, ready to argue if she claimed she'd 'just fallen' again. "You'll never forgive yourself if it hurts me...your only child."

Her mum laughed. "Fine. You can call him. Phone's in my bag."

Phee reached behind her for the enormous tapestry thing her mother insisted on filling with all kinds of junk, which had spilled across the back seat from being thrown into the car. The phone had slid onto the floor, out of reach. Phee unfastened her seat belt, setting off the beep again, and climbed through the gap.

"That is *so annoying*!" She picked up the phone and unlocked the screen.

"It really could've waited, darling."

"Do you think?"

"Whatever it is won't hurt you. Xander said it's scared of you."

"Wh..." Phee stared at the phone screen, immobilised. The adrenaline rush of their hasty escape had kept her nausea at bay; now it whooshed up her throat in a tidal wave that erupted before she had the window fully open. Vomit splattered down the glass and along the side of the car, and the sight of it brought more. Meanwhile, her mother switched from rambling about ghosts to parroting familiar soothing assurances. *It'll be better soon, I promise.*

Phee wanted to tell her to shut up, but still the vomit kept on coming. She couldn't believe she'd been such an idiot, thinking she could trust him. Of course he was going to tell her mother, who kept looking at her through the mirror, all soft-eyed and concerned like nothing had changed, but everything had, and it was never going to get better. Not with that call at the top of the log. Thirty-three minutes, incoming, from Sean Tierney.

***

Tierney Residence

In the end, Sean called Shaunna, and there was no logical reason for it. Josh was only two doors away, and his car was outside, so he was definitely home. Sophie would have been straight over in a taxi. He could rely on either of them to keep him sober, as they'd done countless times before, but talking to Genie had stirred something deeper, more complicated, a feeling Sean hadn't experienced in almost two years. Desire.

So he'd called Shaunna, who was at work in the salon five miles away with no transport. Would she ask Andy to drive her? Call a taxi? Catch a bus? If Sean claimed he hadn't considered the inconvenience beforehand, it would be an outright lie. It was a selfish, ill-conceived and dangerous move, and worst of all, he didn't care.

Alcohol briefly lost its salience again, leaving him free to admit that that was a lie too. He *did* care, and there was the rub—and also the outline of a certain redhead approaching the front door. Keys rattled; the lock clicked. Sean set aside his self-pity and smoothed his shirt, only now thinking to check whether it was clean enough for entertaining.

Like a flash fire, she was, marching past him with barely a glance, swinging open the door to the living room where she lingered briefly, then on to the kitchen and his wee office off to the side. Most houses in the terrace had knocked the two rooms through to make a bigger kitchen, and Sean had felt the lure to keep up with the Joneses—or the Sandison-Morleys at any rate—but what use was a family-size kitchen to a lone healthcare professional/academic one slip of the bottle away from losing his shared parenting rights?

Shaunna passed him by again, paused only to deposit her coat on the banister, then up the stairs she went, same performance: his bedroom, Dylan's bedroom, the bathroom. She was longer in there; the small part of him that clung naively to his self-respect reasoned she was using the loo but surrendered at the clanging of the stairs to the attic. A minute later, she was back downstairs and standing in front of him.

"It's clear," she said. "No booze anywhere."

"I could've told you that and saved you the trouble. More trouble."

"Right. And I would totally have taken you at your word after you called and said, 'I'm desperate here. Can you come over?'"

"I only called fifteen minutes ago. How did you get here so quickly?"

"Client with a motorbike."

Now she said it, Sean noticed her cheeks were rosier than usual, and her copious red curls were constrained by a thick plait, which she duly unravelled, setting them free. Like some lush beauty in a shampoo ad, she shook her head in a swirl of shiny spirals that cascaded over her shoulders and down her back. A few strands caught around the tag of her tunic's zip, which sat just below her collarbone, its asymmetrical placement drawing Sean's gaze down, following the contour of her left breast, until she gave a shrill whistle and his attention snapped back to her face.

"I'm sorry." He bowed his head, ashamed.

"For what? It's not as if we've never looked at each other in that way before, is it? And I'd soon let you know if you overstepped, believe me."

"That doesn't give me a right to objectify you."

Shaunna laughed. "Is that what you were doing?"

"Well...no. But...ah, hell." Managing to bypass her so he couldn't accidentally ogle her again, he stared up at the ceiling. His brain was a scramble of guilt and need and relief that it wasn't the need for alcohol anymore.

"What are you thinking about?" she asked.

What to say... The truth? That he'd wished often they were both single with this set-up specifically in mind? That he felt inadequate and unworthy in her presence? After all, here was he: out-of-shape, poorly recovering alcoholic with erectile dysfunction. And here was she: drop-dead gorgeous, sensual beauty.

"Sean?" She stepped towards him, into his space. He glanced down, instantly caught in the kaleidoscope of her eyes: greens, browns, hints of blue. Contact lenses today, he acknowledged as, from one hypnotic stimulus to another, he caught the motion of her tongue flicking across her lips and quickly averted his gaze upwards again.

"Wondering whether banging me head on this wall might knock some sense into me." He bumped back against the wall behind him.

"Don't do that." She stepped closer and tilted her chin up, which had the secondary effect of bringing their torsos together, touching at the points they protruded—her breasts, his paunch. God, that was an awful word, but it was how he felt—middle-aged spread, greying hair, pallid, crinkly skin...

"What about Andy?" he blurted as if this moment, this maddeningly erotic moment, were a prelude to some glorious love-making rather than his mind trying to process the myriad conflicting messages from his traitorous body.

"Andy thinks we've been doing it anyway," she said.

"He...what?" No conflicting messages now. His mind and body were in agreement, and it was flight all the way, but that he could escape. "Andy thinks...we're having an affair?"

"An affair?" Her lips curved, not quite a smile, but certainly amused. "An affair is a secret. Behind people's backs."

"Right, so…this… This…is…" God, if he could string together a whole sentence, it'd be grand. "This, if we continued, that is…" He vented a breath and some of his tension. "What I mean is—" He laughed at himself. "Jaysus, someone help me out here."

"Are you trying to find a way to tell me you don't want this?"

"Oh, I want this, all right," Sean confirmed.

Shaunna laughed, a little breathless, it seemed, and relieved. Had she honestly believed he didn't?

But that was the thing. What Andy must've picked up on was the wanting, which was not the same as doing and was all well and good for those in a healthy relationship. There was also nothing wrong with admiring from afar, or even up close. A bit of innocent flirting could be good for the self-esteem of all involved, assuming they'd all consented.

"Do you always do this?" Shaunna asked. At Sean's puzzled frown, she explained, "Weigh up the pros and cons."

"I'm not…well, all right, I am, and maybe? I don't know. It's been a while since I've been in this situation of wanting and knowing I stand a good chance of getting somewhere. But here's the pr—" Shaunna's lips muffled the rest of the word, and he lost any that might have followed to passion.

It was a funny thing, a kiss. The fantasising of soft lips and warm breath, always perfectly fragrant, and noses didn't get in the way. Hours, he'd spent, watching her lips while she talked; she'd notice and reward his attentiveness with a seductive smile or a slow swish of tongue. Andy's descriptor of red hot was dead on; it was astonishing the plastic straw in her milkshake didn't just melt away.

The real deal was more, better than everything he'd imagined, and his mind had set the bar impossibly high. As she eased her lips from his, he inhaled deeply, sighing out the air in relief that she wasn't taking it further. All the while they'd been kissing, sex had been on his horizon and coming at him faster by the second.

"What are you thinking about now?" she asked.

"What a spectacular kisser y'are," he answered with a wink.

"Hmm…" Shaunna pulled back so she could look at him but kept her arms around his neck, her body pressed to his. "You're worried about your lack of erection."

He considered lying, but why bother when she could feel its absence between them?

"Sometimes I get it up just fine, but that's as far as it goes. Other times, like now, I'm so turned on, but I've nothing to work with, if you catch my drift."

Tenderly, Shaunna smoothed his hair back from his forehead. He hadn't noticed he was sweating. "Do you remember the conversation we had about sex therapy?" she asked.

In spite of his self-consciousness, Sean smiled. "Aye. And d'you remember I told you it didn't involve the thing itself?"

She gave him a wry grin. "I knew that, wise-ass. What I'm getting at is we can deal with that side of it, for real."

"Ah, right, so this was an intervention?" Sean said, play-pushing her away.

"Well, duh! You called me!" She laughed, as did he. "I did it to get your mind off alcohol, although don't think I wouldn't be interested."

"If I didn't have Soph and you didn't have Andy?"

"You said it."

The sexual attraction was still there, in the background as usual, but the intensity, which would inevitably have ended in the bedroom if Sean had been capable, was over.

"Look, hun, maybe I'm not the right person to talk to about this, but you do need to talk to someone. How long has it been, did you say? Two years?"

"It could be a fair bit longer than that, honestly. Between drinking and Dylan coming along and losing Jessie, I don't remember the last time both me and little Sean had our heads in the game."

"What about your relationship before Sophie?"

"Francesca?" His memories of their short, mutually unsatisfying marriage were shamefully sketchy, none of them involving sex. It might have been a different story if they'd ditched work for a week and gone on a honeymoon. They used to joke that they were bigamists, married to the hospital as well as each other, and agreed to a no-fault divorce, but that hadn't stopped Sean admonishing himself for failing to put in the effort.

"Shall I make us a cuppa?" Shaunna suggested. She must have noticed him sliding.

"That'd be smashing."

"All right." She moved to leave, but he caught her hand and brought it to his lips in a courtly rather than erotic gesture.

"Thank you."

"No thanks needed. You did the same for me when I flipped out after Jess passed. Besides…" She leaned close, her breath hot in his ear as she murmured, "One day, you'll choose sex over a cup of tea." She drew back again and blew him a kiss as she headed for the kettle. "Therapy goals."

22: Party

ONCE, MANY YEARS ago, under a moderately ancient oak tree, Josh and Gabby had a conversation. Like most of those he'd had in university, it was a one-off and all the more significant for it. He recalled with vivid clarity the skeletal dark branches creaking overhead, the damp chill of the bench soaking through his trousers, the familiar, much missed catch of cigarette smoke in his throat and, of course, every last word he and Gabby had shared that day.

He could think of no reason why that particular conversation should come to mind upon opening the gate to Shaunna and Andy's garden where in excess of thirty people had gathered, by invitation, to celebrate his and George's birthdays. Granted, Gabby was among that number, although Josh had yet to spot her, and in his endeavour to do so, everything became clear.

That day, under the oak tree, if Gabby had asked Josh what his life would look like at forty, his answer would've been long, detailed and wholly inaccurate. At seventeen, Josh had foreseen a single life, his academic career taking precedence, evenings spent reading papers, a wealth of qualifications in disciplines pursued for pleasure—a second Master's in English literature, history or mathematics, perhaps all three, and a doctorate. Had that been his lot, he would have been content, fulfilled, accomplished. But the seventeen-year-old Joshua Sandison who had, that day under the oak tree, shared a secret and in his youthful arrogance doled out advice he was not yet qualified to give, was a blueprint for a different life.

He still doubted the wisdom of the advice he'd offered, yet it had shown him an alternative path, one which meant, when mental illness intersected his planned route, he was faced not with a dead end but a fork in the road. To the left lay academia, a precarious highway beset by diversions, any one of which might have led to his final destination; to the right, psychotherapy, a life-giving bypass under heavy construction but flowing with potential. And he, a young man who loathed change and thrived on routine, stepped into the unknown, onto a path he would not have taken without that conversation twenty-two and a half years ago, a path which had safely carried him into his future and made it possible for him to be here, now, celebrating his fortieth birthday with his husband, adopted daughter and all of these people, who were indeed his friends.

"Here they are. The men of the hour!" Dan raised his beer bottle—a signal to all those in hearing range to follow his lead. Adele rushed over and hugged the breath out of George, squealing "Happy Birthday" so loudly he blinked with each syllable and once more for good measure as she deposited a big, shiny, pink kiss on his cheek.

"Thanks, Adele." He staggered upon release only to be accosted by seemingly every other woman in attendance, while Josh sneaked past. He didn't get far, brought to a halt by the realisation he was walking into a marquee so large it encompassed everyone and everything—the pagoda, Jacuzzi, pots of shrubs, even trees—transforming Shaunna and Andy's garden into a fragrant arboretum. Amid the cherry and apple blossom shone tiny pearls of creamy light; blue sparkles flittered through the water dome of the miniature fountain beneath the Japanese maple; discs like cat's eyes flanked the meandering path from the house to the rustic wall at the far end, where a banner—no, make that a mural—hung. Were it not for being so utterly overwhelmed by everything, Josh might have laughed, for it declared in oversized glittery blue and green letters:

HAPPY
18th + 21st + 40th
BIRTHDAY
GEORGE & JOSH

"Hiya!" Adele popped up in front of him, lipstick refreshed on her broad, confident smile, and well it should be. The moment he'd sent her the requested list of guests to invite, he'd essentially given her carte blanche on this party, and he'd had no qualms doing so. After all, she'd organised their wedding, and it had been perfect. Still, he couldn't help teasing her a little.

"You do know George is forty-one today, don't you?"

She tutted and lightly slapped his arm. "Do you like it?"

"I do, Adele. I love it." He glanced back towards the gate, where George had made it a few inches further under the canvas if that. The women might have been done with him, but the children were not. Oliver—almost seven and dressed identically to his CEO father—gave George a very business-like handshake while the smaller ones clung to his legs and hung off his arms. He was utterly in his element.

Birthday greeting delivered, Oliver turned and strode a few feet along the path before breaking into a dash and dodging between the adults, a young man on a mission; it took only a few seconds to figure out what that mission was.

Adele went up on tiptoes and cupped her hand around Josh's ear, although the music prohibited whispering. "Isn't he a little young to be going steady?"

Josh leaned away so he could act incredulous to her face. "Says the woman whose children's father she's gone steady with—"

"On and off..."

"—since reception class, to the man who married the boy he fell in love with when he was seven." As he said it, Oliver emerged from the crowd, a hand clasped in his, and advanced on Josh and Adele.

"Hey, Ollie. Hey, Shabina. Thanks for coming."

"We wouldn't miss it for the world," Oliver said.

"The whole, whole world?" Josh asked and was rewarded with a shy grin from Oliver and a giggle from Shabina—Oliver's best friend *in the whole, whole world*. "You look very smart." At that, the children put their shoulders back and chins up proudly. They made a beautiful couple. "I love your suit, Shabina."

"Thanks. My mum made it." She held out the hem of the top to show off to full effect the soft peach fabric with its slightly darker edges.

"Wow!" Adele said. "It's gorgeous! Is your mum a designer?"

"No. She just makes our clothes."

"She's super talented. Look at that pleating!"

Shabina gave a little twirl that sent the fabric swirling around her like the copious, delicate petals of a rose. "And she teaches the ladies in the refuge how to sew too."

"Your mum's amazing!" Josh gushed, glancing around to see if Anu was there, but no. Shabina must've come with James and Oliver, which was a shame, as the reminder of Anu's talents set Josh off thinking of all the potential, even among his immediate friends and acquaintances, for a whole host of creative therapies, but perhaps the middle of his long-anticipated birthday party wasn't the best time to explore that idea. He made a mental note to talk to Anu later and turned his attention back to Oliver and Shabina. "I hope you both have lots of fun this evening."

"We will," Oliver said, reinstating his grip on Shabina's hand, adding as something of an afterthought, "We hope you do too," before the pair traipsed off whence they came.

"All the Browns must be born middle-aged," Adele remarked, and Josh laughed. It was a fair observation, given Oliver's younger brother was slumped on Eleanor's knee, his face old-man wrinkly and grumpy from having recently woken from a nap. "Your phone's ringing, by the way."

Frowning, Josh fished it out of his pocket in time to see 'call ended'. "How on earth did you hear that?" With or without the music playing from speakers discreetly positioned in the shrubbery, Adele shouldn't have heard a thing. His phone was set to silent.

"I told you! I'm sensitive to vibrations." She grinned mischievously. "Who was it?"

"No idea." It was that same number again, and other than it having their area code, he didn't recognise it. He put his phone away. "In any case, everyone I know is here. On which note, I suppose I ought to do the rounds."

Adele shrugged. "It's *your* party—"

"And I'll cry if I want to?"

Adele looked aghast.

"It's a song," Josh explained.

"I knew that! But you can do what you want. I don't care as long as you're happy…"

"I am," Josh assured her sincerely.

"Then my work here is done." With a wave of her fingertips producing a blur of pink that matched her lips, off she went, still somehow managing to stride with purpose in six-inch wedged heels. She passed Gabby and her husband, who were heading Josh's way.

"Good evening, both."

"Good evening, Josh."

"I'm so glad you could come," Josh said as he and Gabby embraced, the only reluctance this time in releasing each other.

"Thank you for the invitation. I'm afraid Howard was called away on family business."

"Oh?" *Not her husband then.* Josh reappraised Gabby's companion over her shoulder.

"I hope you don't mind," she murmured, stepping back and gesturing stiffly. "Josh, this is my agent and very good friend Dustin."

"Hello." Dustin leaned in for a warmish, formal hand shake.

"Agent?" Josh questioned.

"He arranges my gallery shows and sales," Gabby answered.

"I see." Josh was still getting the measure of the man but offered him a quick smile. "Thanks for accompanying her this evening."

"She almost didn't make it," Dustin said.

"How so?"

"Nothing to worry about," Gabby interjected. "It's been an… unusual week. That's all." She diverted her attention to their surroundings. "This is marvellous, isn't it?"

"Unusual in what way?" Josh pressed.

"Really, it's nothing. Do you need a drink or…" She met Josh's gaze and trailed off.

"Simon Henderson called me," he said. It was a shot into the twilight rather than the dark because something—maybe the side effects of Adele's vibrational sensitivity—was telling him Gabby's 'unusual' week and his shared some common features.

"I thought he might."

"He said he'd spoken to you."

"Yes. I hope it was all right to pass on your details. It seemed serendipitous that he should attend one of my exhibitions on the same day George mentioned you were having trouble finding legal representation."

"He's the wrong kind of barrister, unfortunately," Josh said, at which Gabby's face fell. "But thank you for thinking of me. Well, of the Daisy Foundation."

She reached out and squeezed his forearm. "I know you didn't like him, but you should give him a chance. He's changed a good deal since our university days, and he loved Jess very much."

Josh clamped his teeth. 'Didn't like him' was putting it mildly. Nor had he ever seen any indication that Simon cared for anyone other than himself. However, tonight was neither the time nor place for exercises in pedantry, so Josh nodded, smiled blandly, and said, "I'll keep that in mind. Now, I really must say hello to a few more people and get that drink you mentioned—do either of you need a top-up?"

Gabby and Dustin waved away his offer and found a quiet corner to hide out under the canopy of cherry blossom. Gabby barely knew anyone at the party, and Josh didn't like leaving her to her own devices, but she smiled and nodded, which he took as reassurance that she was fine and prepared to welcome the rest of his guests.

It took little effort on his part, as mostly they came to him. First Kris and Ade regaled him with their latest chat show adventure—a forewarning that they'd given the British viewing public a potted biography of *Josh Sandison-Morley, Psychotherapist, Mind Reader and Offender Profiler* and that one of the producers seemed *very* interested in talking to him about an idea they had for a crime show. Josh was flattered and, he realised with some surprise, not averse to the idea now he was free of his university work, so he agreed to Kris passing his number on to the producer.

Next, Sean and Sophie brought him a bottle of beer and an official invitation to Dylan's baptism in six weeks' time. Josh was a 'godparent' and didn't need a bit of paper to tell him where and when it was, but he accepted the fancy card and made a show of saving the date to his diary.

After that came Krissi, Wotto, Jay and Hadyn, none of whom he'd expected to turn out for a fortieth birthday party on a Friday evening when they were young, wild and free, by comparison. Krissi was already beyond tipsy, but as always, her three companions—her fiancé, BFF and BFF's right-hand man respectively—were looking after her.

No sooner had they departed than Shaunna crept up behind Josh and murmured, "Hiya, hun," in his ear. He nearly dropped his beer.

"Sorry." She hugged him and kissed his cheek. "Are you OK?"

"Yes, astonishingly."

"Who knew you had so many friends?"

"Not me, that's for sure!" He raised his hands, gesturing to the marquee, the tables and chairs along the sides, all the lights twinkling among the foliage. "This is incredible, Shaunna."

"I'd love to take credit for it, but those Jeffries boys, you know?"

"Ha. Yes." No job too small to turn into something extravagant. "Mind you, it would be nothing without Adele's event-planning expertise or those magical green fingers of yours."

"Thanks." Shaunna looked up and around her, smiling at what she saw. A year ago, when she and Andy had bought the house, the garden was an overgrown mess, and they'd worked like Trojans through sun, wind, hail and rain to transform it into this enchanting outdoor room.

"Speaking of magic," she said, looping Josh's arm, "have you seen your cake?" She spun him 180° so he was once more facing the wall at the end of the garden.

"Not yet—oh! *Wow!*" Now he had, he didn't know how he'd missed it before. It was huge, and it was dessert rather than cake, chilling in a solid ice bowl the size of a satellite dish. Specifically, it was a super-size version of George's favourite dessert—orange sorbet and white chocolate ice cream, topped with orange liqueur syrup and flaked dark chocolate—Wotto's now infamous *Pure Bliss*. "Quick! Get me a spoon before George sees it!"

Shaunna laughed. "There's plenty more in the freezer. Actually, where is George?"

Both turned back and located him, no trouble at all, courtesy of his current swarm of fans, this time in the form of those present who were part of the Lions football team.

"I'm glad Rob made it this evening," Josh said.

"Me too. Adele wasn't going to invite him."

Josh sighed. He'd known when he gave Adele his guest list that putting Rob Simpson-Stone's name on it would cause trouble.

Like most of those at the party, Rob was Josh and George's high school alumni, and Adele had never got on with him. Over the past couple of years, her minor dislike had turned to outright scorn; that he'd been working undercover made no difference, nor that he had been hurt the most by Jess's con. As far as Adele was concerned, Rob was a liar who'd abused their trust, and once she made up her mind about someone, there was more chance of reversing the Earth's spin than changing her opinion.

"You invited him, didn't you?" Josh said.

"Yeah, I did."

"Thank you."

"Welcome. Oh, look! I can actually see your husband!"

A few of the footballers peeled away to replenish their beers, and George looked over, meeting Josh's gaze, holding it for a few seconds, perhaps as many as five, before the guys from the farm stepped in, breaking the connection.

"What did he say?" Shaunna asked.

"Hm?" Still entranced, Josh processed the question after the fact and frowned. "Who? George?"

"Yeah. That whole 'my mind to your mind' thing you and he do?"

"Neither of us have the ears for that."

"Obviously, you wouldn't be able to hear him from all the way over here."

"I mean we're not Vulcans."

"Eh?"

"Star Trek?"

Shaunna gave a few ultra-long-lashed blinks of confusion.

"Never mind," Josh said. "He was checking I was OK with fending for myself while he plays to his adoring fans."

"Hmm. Yep. I bet that's the real reason Kris dumped him in high school."

"Spotlight too small for two?"

"Exactly!"

It had been considerably more complicated, as is the way of adolescent love, but Shaunna's theory had some merit. Aside from on the football pitch, George wasn't a show-off, yet he didn't shy away from attention or admiration when it came his way, and it was doing so in abundance.

That was how it continued for most of the evening. George garnered crowds and kept them entertained, always with a drink in hand despite never making it more than a few feet from the gate. Josh wondered—but also acknowledged it was ridiculous—if their guests were conspiring to keep them apart. It seemed whenever he made any move to re-join George, someone intercepted, and so he eventually gave up and resorted to people-watching. It was no great hardship.

Of course, he'd have liked to do a good deal more than watching because he had questions, such as who Rob's date was. A police officer or soldier maybe? She had the confident, slightly pugnacious stance to be either of those. Whoever she was and whatever her reasons for being there, it was good to see Rob enjoying her company in his usual stoic way. Undercover work had cost him dearly, and there was no overlooking that Jess had been to blame for that.

There was also something going on with Krissi. Murmurings and furtive finger-pointing resolved into her storming off with Wotto in pursuit, while Jay and Hadyn loitered and then…

Josh missed what happened next when two Jeffries brothers lumbered into his line of sight. His phone was also vibrating again.

"Alright, mate?" Andy began but paused for Josh to take the call. He needn't have bothered.

"Wrong number?" Dan asked.

"I presume so." Another hang-up, same number.

"What d'you reckon, then?" Dan tilted his head, only the vaguest indication he was asking about the party set-up.

"It's awesome."

"Not *all* our doing, of course."

"No." On another day, Josh might've challenged Dan to give credit where it was due, but with Simon's re-emergence on top of what had happened at the surgery and now these mystery phone calls, his grip on rationality was slipping. It had to be Tony Baines. Had to be.

"You look spooked, mate. Are you all right?"

Josh tuned back in and tried to discern which brother had spoken. He didn't usually have that problem, but both were eyeing him like he was a misfiring engine they were trying to fix.

"I'm fine." He backed up his claim with a smile that prompted matching raised eyebrows from the not-twins.

"Can we talk shop?" Dan asked. It would have been a tactless question from anyone other than a fellow workaholic.

"Sure."

"I was telling him—" Dan thumbed in his brother's direction "—about your electrical fault that isn't."

"OK?"

"Yeah, so," Andy picked up from Dan, "I'm gonna have a gander at the timber—if it's all right with you."

"Why wouldn't it be?"

"I might have to take down some of the ceiling."

"Ah." Josh was beginning to understand why building contracts rarely completed on time. "How much of the ceiling?"

"Depends what I find."

"Deathwatch beetle," Dan said with a ponderous, slightly smug nod.

"Pardon?"

Andy's lip curled at his brother.

"They can make a hell of a racket," Dan added.

Andy squared up to him. "Who's the CSTDB around here?"

"All right, smart arse. What d'you reckon it is?"

"I won't know until I've looked into it."

Intent on deciphering the abbreviation—*Chartered Slayer of the Deathwatch Beetle?*—Josh let them bicker for a while, but they were loud and dangerously close to fisticuffs, so in the end he had to step in.

"They're not anything to do with death, are they? The beetles."

"Nah." Andy shrugged the tension out of his shoulders and backed down, but not without a killing glare at Dan. "Old superstition, that is."

Josh didn't imagine for one minute that the presence of alarmingly named insects could explain unfurling toilet rolls, but still. It was better than no explanation at all.

"OK," he said. "You have my permission to do what you need to."

"Great. I'll get in there first thing Monday. The architect's coming at noon, so—"

"Actually..." Josh interrupted, but fear hijacked his thoughts before he could follow through on Sean's advice and volunteer to tag along. He didn't need to talk to the architect. It would all be fine. "I'll send you my notes via email."

"Good stuff." Andy said, and there the discussion ended, with him sniffing the air like an overgrown Bisto kid as a delectable waft of cheesy, yeasty goodness came their way.

It turned out Krissi hadn't stormed off in a huff. She and Wotto had returned with freshly baked pizza and garlic bread, an excellent choice, to Josh's mind, and all conversations ceased as the guests descended en masse to have their fill of the delicious party food—a welcome change from cold sausage rolls and curly-crusted sandwiches—followed by a bowl of birthday dessert for those who wanted it, and most did.

It wasn't long after that when Krissi and the gang packed their equipment into a van and left. George's farm colleagues weren't far behind them, followed by most of the children.

In the midst of all the coming and going and eating, Josh's phone vibrated thrice more. The first time, he'd returned the call, ready to blast Tony Baines or whoever it was, and was miffed when all he got was the continuous dead-line beep. After the third call, he turned off his phone. Even if he hadn't promised

George he'd stop chasing mysteries, he had no real desire to go to war with a hoax caller. Not this evening when the guests had dwindled until only their closest friends remained.

The Circle. Nine friends from high school, give or take a swindling lawyer and a smug Irish psychologist. Friends who had promised long ago to give him and George the perfect birthday party, and as the two of them joined the rest around the giant ice bowl to tuck into what was left of the Perfect Bliss dessert/birthday cake, each armed with a spoon, it was safe to say they'd delivered on that promise.

23: Spa Partners

A Leisure Complex
Present Day
Friday, 19th April

S TOP DOING THE soft-eyes thing on me, Mother. I'm *fine!*"
To emphasise, Phee took a large bite of her cheeseburger, but
what some insultingly called the Rowan women's 'mealy mouths'
was as much about what went into them as came out. With no
room to chew, Phee's cheeks ballooned and she spat the chunk of
cheeseburger into a paper napkin.

"It is terribly dry," Genie justified, though she had not yet
touched her burger. Perhaps fast food hadn't been the wisest
choice, but she'd wanted so much to stick to the usual routine
of their cinema trips, hoping that doing so would act like
a reset button and delete the past few weeks. The plan had fallen
at the first hurdle, the evidence in clear sight, courtesy of the
restaurant's glass front overlooking the leisure complex car park.
The three-hour turnaround the mobile car-cleaning company
had quoted was almost up, but the two young men who'd arrived
following Genie's call were still hard at it, lugging industrial
machinery in and out of their van and clambering all over
the car.

"Mum? Hel-lo?"

"Hmm?" Genie turned away from the window and smiled at
her daughter. "Sorry. What did you say?"

"Try it without the bun." Phee waved her half-eaten naked
burger in demonstration.

"Ah. Yes, a good idea." Genie followed her example and dismantled her burger, then picked at the warmish brown patty, no appetite whatsoever. "What did you think of the film? Awful?"

"So bad! And how was that a rom com, please? I mean, her high heels breaking wasn't funny the first time."

"It *was* romantic, though," Genie argued.

"Yeah, whatever, Mother." Phee shook her head in light-hearted disparagement of Genie's soft spot for snappily dressed, blonde-haired 'totty', in this instance the female lead who had, in a modern and—as Genie knew from bitter experience—unlikely twist in the trope, got her man *and* held on to her high-powered corporate career. Of course, she and Phee would have enjoyed it more had they been rom com fans rather than two people escaping a real-life horror movie, on which note...

"I need to return Jonathan's call."

"Yes, you do."

"I know you don't like them being in the house—"

"I don't care as long as Xander gets that ghost out."

"I'm sure he will, but I think we should stay away until he has."

"Where? A hotel?"

"Yes."

"Please not the Travel Inn."

"Goodness, no!" Genie laughed. "I thought we could make a little holiday of it, drive up to Wharton Hall."

"Where?" Phee already had her phone out, researching.

"Staffordshire, not far from where I went to uni."

"Got it. Wharton Hall Hotel and Spa. 'A peaceful haven surrounded by acres of rich landscape, this Georgian mansion was home to the—'" Phee stopped reading and looked up. "The *Rowan* family?" Genie nodded. "As in *our* family?" Genie nodded again. Phee read on. "'...was home to the Rowan family until the late 1980s, when Grange Estate Management PLC renovated the property, transforming it into a highly popular retreat. Relax in our natural spa pools, saunas and Roman baths, detox in our aromatherapy, massage and beauty therapy suite or simply enjoy a walk in the fresh, open air.'" Phee scrolled. "Daily yoga in the Japanese gardens—do they have those Zen gardens where you rake patterns in sand?"

"I've no idea," Genie said. "I've never been."

"Didn't you live there in the eighties?"

"No. We've always lived in Shropshire. Your great-great-uncle Edward lived there before the Second World War, but he was killed on the battlefield as it were, and he never married or had children, so it stood empty for forty years, derelict, actually, before Grange took over managing the estate. They've made an excellent job of it, too, according to your grandfather, and he's a notoriously difficult man to please."

"Wait—it still belongs to our family?"

"Yes. Well, to your grandfather."

"And when he dies—"

"It will go to your aunt," Genie said, nodding with each word, although Phee hadn't brought up the non-inheritance in a while. She'd had no cause to since Jess died.

"We still get to stay there for free, right?" Phee asked with a conniving smirk and returned to perusing the website.

"Sadly not." Or not without Genie backing down, and that wasn't an option while Phee was still young enough for her grandparents to meddle in her life.

"Sucks. Should I fill in this online booking form?"

"Yes. Do that, and I'll phone Jonathan." Scooping up the paper burger wrapper and her largely uneaten meal, Genie dropped it in the closest bin and headed outside, her mission interrupted by an incoming call. Paul.

"Genie?"

"Hello, darling. Are you home?"

"Yes. I've been back half an hour. Where are you? Shopping?"

"No. Phee and I went to see a film. Listen, we're going away for a few days—make the most of the spring break and whatnot."

"I can't come with you. I'm flying to Germany tomorrow, remember?" Paul's tone was brusque, and it riled Genie, but she played it cool.

"Yes, I do remember, and I meant Phee and me."

"When did you plan this?"

"Spur of the moment."

"So I'm eating dinner alone. *Again*."

"I'm sorry, darling."

"It's fine." He was still snippy, but she sensed he was trying to be reasonable. "Have a good time."

"Thank you." Genie paused, not ready to sign off on the call yet. "When you get back, we should chat."

"About us?" The lack of delay and accuracy of his guess was telling.

"Yes, but I don't want you fretting over it while you're away."

"Too busy for that!"

"A good thing, too. I'll let you go."

"OK. See you in two weeks."

"You will. Bye, darling."

"Bye." No click as he hung up, the silent moment marking another step closer to the end, and Genie hadn't thought to ask about the shattered wine bottle. Margaret must have been in and cleaned it up or Paul would have mentioned it. Hoping it meant she intended to stay rather than having returned to work her notice, Genie sent a quick message of thanks to her assistant and finally got around to calling Jonathan, who must surely have had the phone in his hand, as he picked up right away.

"Hello, *Genie*."

She sniffed back her pointless annoyance. "Hello, Jonathan. Sorry I couldn't talk earlier. I'm taking my daughter away for the week, so if you can let Xander know you'll have the place to yourselves…"

"Jolly good."

"When should I tell Margaret to expect you?"

"On Monday. We have a prior engagement this weekend."

"Wonderful. I'll let her know. Thank you, both—again—for being so patient with us."

"That's quite all right. I'll update you daily—"

"No need. Just tell me when it's over."

"As you wish. Is there anything else?"

"No, that's all."

"Then do have a pleasant trip."

"We will. Bye for now."

That done, Genie turned to go back inside the fast-food restaurant and walked straight into Phee.

"Oops! Sorry, darling."

"You've been out here forever."

"Yes. Paul called. He's pissed off we're not at home."

"He's got a nerve when he's left you to deal with the poltergeist on your own."

"He doesn't know we have a poltergeist."

"He might by now."

Genie chuckled. "That he might. Are we all booked in?"

"Yep. What are we going to do about clothes? Go back to the house?"

"I thought we could pick up some underwear, maybe a couple of outfits on the way."

"Where? By the time they're done with the car, all the shops will be shut." As Phee spoke, the car cleaners closed the back doors of their van, and the one Genie had spoken to earlier looked around the car park, waving when he spotted them. Genie and Phee started to walk over.

"How about the supermarket?" Genie suggested.

"For clothes or toiletries?"

"Both. It might not be high fashion, but—"

"We'll be wearing bathrobes for the next week," Phee finished.

"Quite." Genie smiled as they met up with the car cleaner.

"All done," he said, beckoning for her to follow him on a tour of their work, and Genie was impressed by how thorough they'd been. The car hadn't been so clean and shiny since she'd bought it.

"Upholstery's still slightly damp in the back." He gestured to the paper cover on the seat. "I'd avoid sitting there until tomorrow if you can. You paid online, didn't you?"

"I did, yes, and I'll be leaving a glowing review. Thank you so much!"

"No problem." He handed over the keys and with a swift smile climbed into his van.

"Are you ready?" Genie asked.

"Yep. Let's do this. Ooh! One sec." Phone in hand, Phee leaned close and pressed her cheek to Genie's. "Smile!" They both made faces half smile, half pout; Phee took the photo, tagged it *#roadtrip with mama* and shared it on her profile.

Genie hadn't even started the car before her phone pinged. Phee's friend Sarah had liked the photo and left a comment: *Gorgeous! Could be sisters! x*

"Is she saying I look young or you look old?" Genie wondered aloud, although with her wrinkles filtered out, it was something of a glimpse into the past.

"You're beautiful, Mother. Get over it."

"As are you, darling girl."

"Hmph. I wish I had your nose. Mine's too…squidgy."

"Squidgy?"

"Boneless. Like Sean's. I'm glad I got his hair, though. No offence."

"Oh, I'm with you on that." Genie's hair was dark too but fine and straight, not thick and wavy like Sean's and Phee's. She studied the photo a moment longer, seeing more of Sean than herself in Phee's features—strong eyebrows, in Phee's case tamed to frame her brown eyes, the slight dimples in her cheeks and that cute bobble chin—as well as a serendipitous opportunity to come clean about their trip. Before she did, however, she put her phone away and got them on the road.

"Can I put on some music?" Phee asked.

"Absolutely." Genie left a beat, then said, casually, "Funnily enough, I had a good natter with Sean this morning."

Phee hummed, confirming she'd heard, but she was—Genie hoped—distracted by finding something they'd both want to listen to and didn't say anything.

"I told him about our poltergeist."

"OK."

Genie waited. Music started coming through the car's speakers, too quietly to make out the song, and Phee made no move to turn it up. Still, Genie waited, and then, at the point where it seemed Phee was expecting her to continue unprompted, Phee asked, "What did he say?"

"About the poltergeist, very little. Mostly, we talked about Jess."

"Sticking with the ghost theme, then."

A chill rushed up Genie's back, and she tightened her grip on the steering wheel to conceal the shiver. The connection hadn't escaped her, despite what she'd told Xander. She'd registered it the moment she'd picked up the score and seen the title 'L'Alouette', an entirely different composition from 'Alouette', yet it had planted the children's song in her head and with it a wisp of something—a feeling rather than a memory—that she hadn't yet placed beyond knowing it was to do with Jess.

"Her funeral was lovely, Sean said."

"Yeah, I've never really got that."

"I suppose he meant it was a celebration of her life rather than a gloomy affair."

"No, I mean…Jess was your bestie, right? And you were all at uni together."

"Hm?"

"Well, did you fall out or something? Because you talked to each other every day, but you didn't go to her funeral and Sean did. Is that weird, or it is me?"

"No, it's not you." Phee's observation hit the same nerve Sean had twanged earlier. Had Genie been the only one to abide by Jess's wishes, or the only one upon whom those wishes had been conferred? She'd spent much of the movie trying to convince herself it was the former. She'd failed, hence this trip. "You must understand, Jess was a very private person. And conscious of her appearance."

"Vain, you mean."

Genie laughed, thinking back over the hours of hair straightening and make-up perfecting and trying on a hundred different combinations of dresses and shoes before every night out. "She could be. She would've hated anyone seeing her so sick, especially towards the end."

"Oh, yeah. Like Sarah's mum." Phee became quiet, and Genie respected her silence, knowing she was thinking about Sarah's mother's battle with cancer. The girls were quite young when she died, and the four-year difference in their ages had been much starker, but they'd always been close, so Phee had witnessed the final stages of the disease, although she'd never talked about it, or not to Genie.

A few minutes passed. Genie was counting the time in miles, so she couldn't be sure how long, but she didn't want to miss her window of opportunity.

"I'd like to invite Sean to join us for dinner one evening. He's only an hour or so from Wharton Hall. Is that all right with you?"

"Sure!" Phee changed the song on the stereo and turned up the volume a notch or two—still too quiet for Genie's old ears. "He must be a good person to have around when you're sick. Like, you know, properly sick, how Sarah's mum and Jess were, not..." She trailed off and turned to look out the passenger window.

"Yes, he must," Genie agreed, glossing over Phee's avoidance and her own sudden tearfulness. How much her daughter had changed these past years. Some of it was natural development taking its course, the emotional roller coaster every adolescent must ride in the face of peer pressure, the stress of making big study decisions, choosing a career, proving they could be a grown-up. Gone were the days when Phee had trusted her mother with even the smallest of confidences—crushes on musicians and social media superstars, her often unpopular opinion of this perfume or that fashion. No more. Phee had become secretive and sullen and nothing like the gorgeous young woman who had pleaded for the most outlandish bedroom makeover not five months ago. Every part of Genie ached with maternal need to protect her daughter, to ease her pain and sadness, but what could she do when Phee, like Jess, was pushing her away?

"This is all I'm going to say, OK?"

"About what?"

"You know what. I just want you to know I support you whatever happens, whatever you decide. That's all."

"Hmm." Phee faced front again and turned up the stereo, making further conversation impossible, but Genie meant it. Unless Phee chose to open up to her, she would not mention it again.

***

Phee awoke, shivering and with the vilest taste in her mouth, but no nausea, which was an amazing feeling. It had been constant for weeks.

"We're here," her mum said.

"How long have I been asleep?"

"A couple of hours."

"Wow." That would be why she was so stiff then. She fished around for the bottle of water they'd bought when they'd stopped off at the supermarket—the last thing she remembered of their journey—and sipped, taking the time to figure out her surroundings. They were parked, along with about ten other cars, in a small car park with old-fashioned streetlamps and a tall hedge. That was about all she could see, even when she followed her mum to the back of the car to retrieve their basic carry-on bags, purchased to hold the small selection of toiletries and underwear, plus a bikini, T-shirt and pair of pyjamas each. Phee wished she'd bought a hoodie; she couldn't stop shivering.

"You'll feel better once you've had something to eat," her mum said as they set off in the direction indicated by an arrow on a stick at the car park's entrance; glowing windows were now also visible between the swaying branches of the big old trees up ahead.

"You weren't going to say anything else," Phee pointed out as they crunched their way along a narrow gravel path surrounded by disturbingly neat flower beds planted with rose bushes that glowed an even sicklier green than Phee did every morning. At least the roses could blame the rock-shaped solar LEDs; Phee's predicament was all her own doing.

"I'm not. We've only eaten popcorn and a cheeseburger all day, and we could both do with a decent meal." Her mum held open the door. "Let's be hoped it's not one of those places that thinks quinoa is a decent meal."

"What's quinoa ever done to you?" Phee stepped inside and immediately resorted to mouth-breathing. There were so many smells of food and coffee and perfumed oils and lotions, the pungent mixture turned her stomach, and she gritted her teeth, telling herself not to be sick, although maybe eating something would help. "Food would be good," she said.

"What d'you fancy?"

"Something quick so I can go to bed."

Her mum's eyes went all soft and sympathetic again. "I'll get us booked in and ask for room service. How about that?"

"Fine. Whatever." Phee flopped into one of the low chairs lined up against the wall and chanced another small sniff. Her mouth instantly filled with saliva, and she shot to her feet, scanning the various doors, all with signs, none of them a toilet. That left her one choice: she bolted outside and as far down the path as she could, then she spewed, somehow missing the rose bushes but catching another whiff of that horrible berries and coffee stink. She spewed again, and again, and thought *screw you, morning sickness* because it was nothing like being normally sick, when you felt better once you'd thrown up. This didn't go away, and she was so done with it when it wasn't even morning, *and* she had an audience. She wiped her mouth and sneaked a look, not surprised to discover her mum helicoptering with their bags dangling from her shoulder and that stupid face on her again.

"Can we go to our rooms yet?" Phee snapped out the question and hated herself for it, but her body and brain felt totally out of her control.

"Yes," her mum replied coolly, no soft mushiness now. "Someone's going to bring us a toaster, bread, butter and preserves."

"That's like hospital food. Did you tell them I'm sick?"

"You're vomiting in their flower bed."

A quick look through the window confirmed Phee was in plain sight of everyone in the reception area. "Well, that's just great."

"The toast will help. Come on. We're in rooms twenty-four and twenty-five—should I lose you along the way." Her mum didn't wait for her, which was fair enough. Phee was being a bitch.

***

The toast worked. For a little while, anyway—long enough to say sorry for being a bitch, take a shower and get into bed, all forgiven. Then she'd zonked out, oblivious, until she'd woken in the same position a minute or so ago, no clue how long she'd slept or what the time was. She felt around under her pillow for her phone and, not finding it, remembered it was still on top of the drawers across the room. But the bed was warm and comfy, and if she stayed absolutely still, she didn't feel sick…

"Darling, are you awake?"

…and she could pretend she was still asleep, except…

Except she didn't want to. She wanted more toast. And she wanted her mum.

"Yeah. What time is it?"

"A quarter past nine." The door between their rooms opened a few inches, and her mum's head poked through the gap. "May I come in?"

"Uh-huh." Phee shuffled up and over, leaving sitting space on the side of the bed. Her mum accepted.

"How did you sleep?"

"Like a log, apparently. Eleven hours?!"

"You did say you were tired."

"I did." Eleven hours was a *long* sleep. Still, she couldn't deny she felt tons better for it. "Did you sleep well?"

"Yes, I did, thank you, although I have been awake a while, enjoying the peace. It's such a relief to be away from all that nonsense at home, don't you think? And it's a gorgeous day out there."

Phee could see that from the yellow light sneaking around the edges of the window blinds. Her mum noticed her looking and got up to open them.

"Have you phoned Sean?" Phee asked.

"Not yet. I doubt he's up."

Phee opened her mouth, then clamped it shut again. She'd already slipped up once, when she'd said Sean would be a good person to have around if you were really ill, and it seemed she'd got away with it. But saying *If he's got Dylan today, he'll have been up for ages* would have been game over. Even not saying it, her mum was suspicious, and Phee hated the awkwardness between them. She wanted so much to tell her and kept trying, but she couldn't make the words come out. She watched her mum fuss with the cords on the blind, then straighten Phee's phone.

"Six percent battery."

"I forgot to plug it in. Have you had breakfast yet?"

"No. I was waiting for you. Do you feel up to it this morning?"

"I want to try." Breakfast and more.

"Where's your charger?"

"In my bag—front pocket. You can get it out, I don't mind."

Her mum opened the zip as if the bag's contents were explosive and fished around inside. "It's not here. Just a piece of paper. You can use mine for now."

"Take it out."

"The paper?"

Phee nodded.

Frowning, her mum extracted the folded square of paper and looked to Phee for instruction.

"Just look at it, Mum, please, because I can't..." She didn't need to say more. Her mum was holding the paper at arm's length and squinting.

"Twelve weeks."

"Thirteen now."

Much like Sean had been, her mum was transfixed, but everything else was so different. Seeing Sophie and Sean with Dylan, listening to Sarah's stories about uni, not being able to drink on a night out, the constant throwing up and tiredness—she'd been so sure that she was keeping this baby. Now, the only thing she was sure of was that she didn't want her mum to become attached to that ultrasound picture.

"I don't know what to do."

"Do you want to talk about it?"

"Maybe, but not yet."

"All right." Her mum folded the picture and returned it to Phee's bag. "So where is your charger?"

"In there somewhere." Phee sprang out of bed, only realising when the nausea caught up with her, and ran into her mum's arms. "I love you."

"I love you too." Her mum squeezed gently and released, while Phee clung on, ready to make up for all the months she'd gone without and *maybe* feeling a little less sick than before.

The story continues in
Alumni: Resolutions

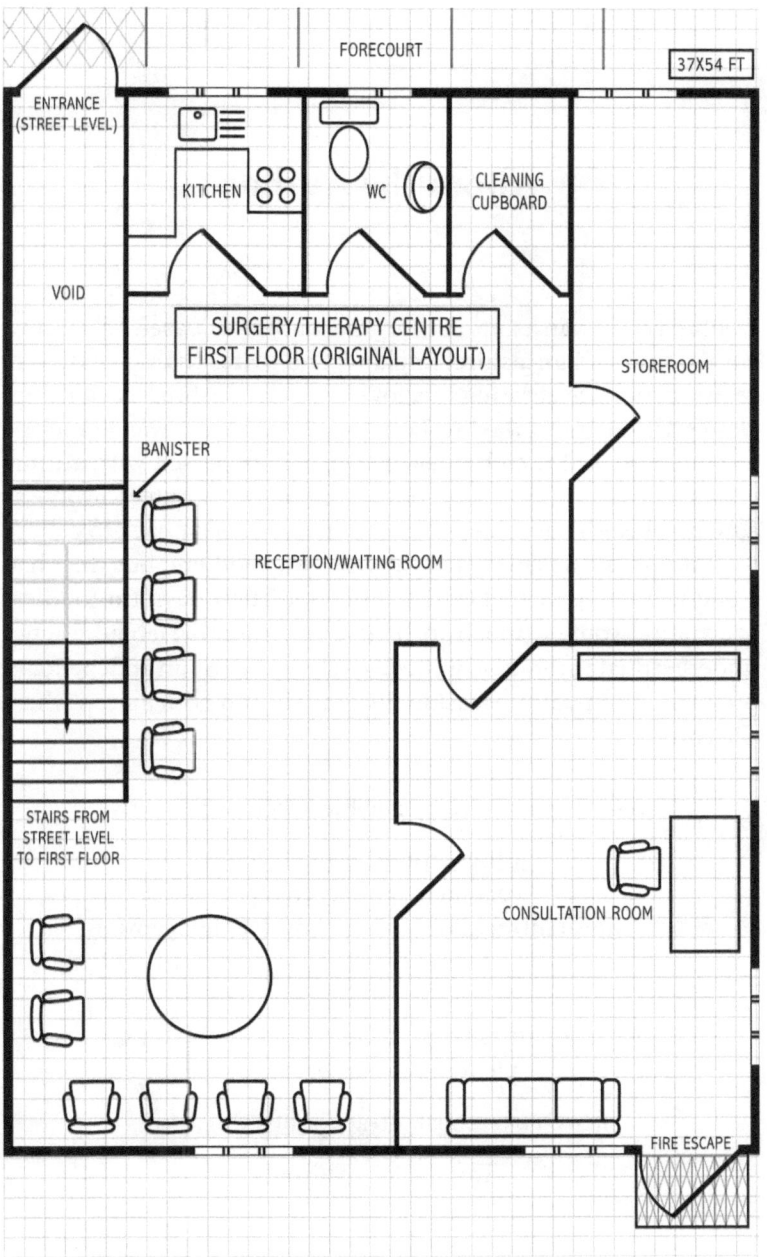

FORECOURT

37X54 FT

ENTRANCE
(STREET LEVEL)

KITCHEN

WC

CLEANING
CUPBOARD

VOID

STOREROOM

SURGERY/THERAPY CENTRE
FIRST FLOOR (ORIGINAL LAYOUT)

BANISTER

RECEPTION/WAITING ROOM

STAIRS FROM
STREET LEVEL
TO FIRST FLOOR

CONSULTATION ROOM

FIRE ESCAPE

About the Author

Debbie McGowan is an author and publisher based in a semi-rural corner of Lancashire, England. She writes character-driven, realist fiction, celebrating life, love and relationships. A working-class girl, she 'ran away' to London at seventeen, was homeless, unemployed and then homeless again, interspersed with animal rights activism (all legal, honest ;)) and volunteer work as a mental health advocate. At twenty-five, she went back to college to study social science—tough with two toddlers, but they had a 'stay at home' dad, so it worked itself out. These days, the toddlers are young women (much to their chagrin) and Debbie teaches undergraduate students, writes novels and runs an independent publishing company, occasionally grabbing an hour's sleep where she can.

For more stories by Debbie McGowan, visit:

hidingbehindthecouch.com
debbiemcgowan.co.uk
www.beatentrackpublishing.com/debbiemcgowan

For more titles from Beaten Track Publishing,
please visit our website:

https://www.beatentrackpublishing.com

Thanks for reading!